OLD FASHIONED

PHANTOM QUEEN BOOK 3 - A TEMPLE VERSE SERIES

SHAYNE SILVERS
CAMERON O'CONNELL

ARGENTO
PUBLISHING

Shayne Silvers & Cameron O'Connell

Old Fashioned

The Phantom Queen Diaries Book 3

A TempleVerse Series

ISBN 13: 978-1-947709-14-0

© 2018, Shayne Silvers / Argento Publishing, LLC

info@shaynesilvers.com

CONTENTS

SHAYNE AND CAMERON

Shayne Silvers, here.

Cameron O'Connell is one helluva writer, and he's worked tirelessly to merge a story into the Temple Verse that would provide a different and unique *voice*, but a complementary *tone* to my other novels. *SOME* people might say I'm hard to work with. But certainly, Cameron would never...

Hey! Pipe down over there, author monkey! Get back to your writing cave and finish the next Phantom Queen Novel!

Ahem. Now, where was I?

This is book 3 in the Phantom Queen Diaries. This series ties into the existing Temple Verse with Nate Temple and Callie Penrose. This series could also be read independently if one so chose. Then again, you, the reader, will get SO much more out of my existing books (and this series) by reading them all in tandem.

But that's not up to us. It's up to you, the reader.

What do you think? Should Quinn MacKenna be allowed to go drinking with Callie? To throw eggs at Chateau Falco while Nate's skipping about in Fae? To let this fiery, foul-mouthed, Boston redhead come play with the monsters from Missouri?

You tell us...

DON'T FORGET!

VIP's get early access to all sorts of book goodies, including signed copies, private giveaways, and advance notice of future projects. AND A FREE NOVELLA! Click the image or join here: www.shaynesilvers.com/l/219800

FOLLOW and LIKE:

Shayne's FACEBOOK PAGE:

www.shaynesilvers.com/l/38602

Cameron's FACEBOOK PAGE:

www.shaynesilvers.com/l/209065

We respond to all messages, so don't hesitate to drop either of us a line. Not interacting with readers is the biggest travesty that most authors can make. Let us fix that.

CHAPTER 1

*T*he vicious pounding of a heavy fist on my apartment door woke me from a bleary-eyed sleep. I groaned, rolled over, and thrust my head under the nearest pillow, begging God to make it stop. But—seeing as how God didn't owe me any favors—the racket continued until I was compelled to plug my ears and swear, for the thousandth time, that I would never, ever, drink again.

Or, you know…drink less, at least.

I clenched my teeth, wondering why on Earth the maids had chosen to ignore the *Do Not Disturb* sign, before I remembered that I was in my own bed and not my Las Vegas hotel room; I'd flown in last night on the red eye after a wild weekend. The wildest weekend, in fact, I'd ever had. And—to put that in perspective—I should mention that my weekends routinely involve life-threatening danger, fucking *magic*, and copious amounts of booze.

But, silver lining, I'd checked a few items off my bucket list I'd never even thought to write down—like mud wrestling dragons, breaking into a Casino vault, fending off a horde of shapeshifting strippers, and dick-punching a celebrity. Fortunately, a great deal of that was fuzzy and half-remembered; I'd rarely found myself doing anything without a drink in hand, courtesy of Sin City's legendary hospitality. Unfortunately, that meant I owed my body 48 cumulative hours' worth of hangover...and the bitch had come to collect.

Basically, I felt like death.

If death had been run over by a trucker, thrown in the back of a tractor trailer transporting diseased animals, and left to rot in a desert until lizards lounged on his sun-bleached bones.

And someone...Wouldn't. Stop. Knocking.

"Fine, alright! I'm fuckin' comin'!" I screamed, my Irish brogue making me sound a lot less grumpy than I rightfully felt—a regrettable side effect of having an accent people dub "sing-songy." To be honest, that's probably why I cussed so much; I got tired of people treating me like a snarling puppy whenever I threw a temper tantrum.

Fun fact: no one calls you cute if you say fuck all the time.

I growled, kicked off my covers, and threw on a long robe; spring had arrived in all its glory a week ago, so I'd begun crashing in a Men's XXL jersey. But at six-feet-tall, and most of that legs, I couldn't afford to answer the door in my nightly attire, no matter how stylish my retro Red Sox jersey was. Not unless I wanted to give someone a show they hadn't paid for.

I shuffled towards the door, but tripped over a small suitcase I'd stolen from my Russian friend, Othello, a world-class hacker and COO of Grimm Tech—a company in Germany that produced, amongst other things, an assortment of toys with magical properties. I cursed and lashed out, kicking it across the room, then froze.

Shit.

I ignored the knocking for a moment and doublechecked to make sure the suitcase was unharmed. Inside was a copper disc that fit in my palm. I only had a rough idea of what it did, because by the time I started quizzing her, all Othello would say was that she was the most brilliant woman alive; she'd had several dozen shots of vodka at that point. Apparently, it was what she called a "galvanizer," whatever that meant. I don't know why I'd taken it, except maybe to poke fun at the most brilliant woman alive for not keeping her shit locked up in a secure vault somewhere.

That's right, just keeping her ego in check, one theft at a time.

Once I knew the case was undamaged, I shoved my hands over my ears to block out the incessant hammering and tried to decide how I would kill whoever was at my door. I had plenty of guns thanks to a special delivery from Death, yes that Death, one of the four Horsemen of the Apocalypse. I could easily whip out a weapon and put a bullet through the door.

Or there was always the good old-fashioned Chuck Norris approach—a windpipe-crushing roundhouse to the throat.

By the time I made it to the door, I was already plotting what I'd do with the body, and what I'd tell the police if I ever got caught. I wasn't sure my "they wouldn't shut the fuck up and leave me alone" defense would be enough to swing the jury. Could having the worst hangover of your life count as an insanity plea? Sadly, once I glanced through the peephole, my meticulously planned murder fell apart.

Because nobody gets off scot-free after killing a *cop*.

I inched open the door, hiding my makeup-less face behind my bangs—a wave of vibrant red that would hopefully distract my visitor from the bags under my red-rimmed eyes. "Jimmy, now's not a great time," I said.

I decidedly avoided mentioning my shenanigan-fueled weekend; I wasn't sure how many laws we'd broken, but—considering the immortal status of some of our attendees—I was willing to bet we'd end up on the far side of 25 to life.

"Get dressed, Quinn. And hurry," Jimmy snapped, his deep baritone rumbling through the crack in my door.

"Excuse ye?" I asked, poking my head out into the hallway, too annoyed by his abrupt tone to care about how wrecked I looked. Detective Jimmy Collins, a former lover and decorated member of the Boston Police Department, loomed over me, his expression cold.

Of course, that probably shouldn't have surprised me; I hadn't seen or spoken to him since an incident a couple of months back in which he'd died in an alternate dimension, only to be brought back to life through the intercession of a god. Since then, he'd definitely given me the cold-shoulder, dodging my phone calls like it was his job. Until, that is, he'd tried reaching out to me last week. Sadly, I'd been a little busy recovering from a coma—the unfortunate result of fighting angels and demons in pursuit of a holy relic that I'd stashed away on a windowsill in my living room.

I know what you're thinking...Vegas probably hadn't been the best convalescence I could have chosen after being officially brain dead for almost a week.

Sue me.

"It's police business," he said, the skin around his eyes tight, his jaw clenched. I ogled the man; I couldn't help it. Jimmy had a face and body fresh from a catalogue—broad shoulders and narrow hips, a strong jawline, and skin so smooth it seemed to emit its own light. He'd grown out his facial hair since I'd seen him last—the beard meticulously faded, offsetting his wide cheekbones.

"Listen," I said, batting my eyes at the not-so-nice detective, "I'll admit t'ings got a wee bit out of hand. But it was all in good fun. We didn't even realize we were stealin' from the mob until after it happened. And, before ye ask, we gave it all back. Even the strippers promised not to press charges, so…" I drifted off as Jimmy's expression shifted from irritation to disapproval. "Um…what sort of police business, did ye say?" I asked, sensing he had no idea what I was talking about.

"I didn't," Jimmy clarified, though I could see the wheels turning in his head.

"Well, ignore all that, then. What can I do for ye?" I asked, sweetly.

"I don't have time for this, Quinn. Get yourself dressed. I'll wait in the hall."

I scowled. "Aren't ye forgettin' somethin'?" I asked. "Like 'hello, Quinn, nice to see ye, sorry for never callin' ye back'?"

"That's not why I'm here," Jimmy said, studying the hallway as though someone might step out at any moment. "Like I said, this is police business. You've been…requested. I tried getting in touch with you for over a week, but you never called me back, so now I'm here to collect you in person."

"Is that why you're actin' like an arse right now?" I asked. "Because I didn't call ye back right away? I was out of town and me phone broke. I planned to call ye back soon."

"Before or after you stole from the mob? And…" Jimmy leaned in, sniffed, and recoiled. "Drank your weight in *Clontarf?*"

I glared at him, then surreptitiously sniffed myself, wondering how Jimmy had picked up on the exact brand of whiskey I'd been drinking all weekend long. I certainly couldn't smell anything, although I wouldn't have expected to; I'd showered and brushed my teeth before going to bed just a few short hours ago. I scowled, trying my best not to think about the fact that he smelt pretty good by comparison, his cologne clean and sweet, like honeysuckle, although there was something else there—the faintest aroma of stale smoke. "I'm a grown woman, Jimmy Collins. If I want to get into trouble and drink with me friends, then that's what I'll do."

Jimmy rolled his eyes. "I don't care what you do or don't do, Quinn. If I had it my way, I wouldn't even be here. But right now, my orders are to take you to a crime scene. So, let's dispense with the pleasantries and move it along."

I ran my tongue across my teeth, trying to contain the mixed emotions I felt welling up inside: anger, frustration, disappointment. "Alright, then," I said, finally. "Ye stay the fuck outside. I'll be out in a minute." I slammed the door in his face, seething and—if I was being honest with myself—more than a little heartbroken. It wasn't like I had crazy high expectations or anything. I mean the man had gone out of his way to avoid me.

But I'd never dreamed our reunion would play out this poorly.

"Did you know that, in America, a divorce occurs every 36 seconds?" a voice, slight and feminine, rang out from my living room.

I sighed.

"No, Eve, I didn't know that," I replied. "But I'm not surprised."

Eve, my spoil of war and budding Tree of Knowledge, liked to impress me with her freakish knowledge of statistics—although I was beginning to suspect that her knowledge bombs came at a price; she often spouted out whatever information she thought was most applicable at the time, regardless of the social consequences.

"Did you know individuals between the ages of 18 and 29 generally have sex 112 times a year? That equals a little more than twice a week. What happens if you go longer than the average span, do you think? Are you feeling ill? Anxious, maybe?"

I turned on the shower and fetched a towel from my room, ignoring the pernicious houseplant.

"Did you know—"

"Did ye know that baby trees make the best firewood?" I fired back, before she could finish.

Eve was silent, and, for a moment, I thought my not-so-veiled threat might have finally shut her up. I stepped into the shower.

"I don't think your source is credible!" she called out.

I groaned.

CHAPTER 2

I shut the door, locked it, and found Jimmy leaning against the wall, practically dozing off. I fought the urge to tip him over as I cruised past, the clip of my boots like gunshots on the hardwood. Jimmy fell into step behind me. I hoped—spitefully—that he appreciated the view. I'd put in a little extra work getting ready, donning my tightest, most hip-hugging jeans. I'd even gone through the trouble of putting on makeup, though less than I would have normally if I were trying to show off; there's nothing classy about showing up to a crime scene looking like you're going to a ball.

I'd decided to leave the disc in Othello's suitcase, at least for now. Until I knew exactly what the device was capable of, it seemed wise not to play with it, especially under police supervision; the last one I'd played with had torn a hole between our dimension and one of the various planes of Hell.

She really did have the best toys.

"Who were you talking to in there?" Jimmy asked as we descended the stairs and headed out the door.

I glanced back at him, eyebrow raised. Had he heard Eve and me talking? Through the door, with my shower running? How much had he heard? "I got a plant. I read it's therapeutic to yell at inanimate objects when you're pissed off."

Jimmy grunted but said nothing.

Which was fine by me.

*T*he drive to the crime scene was, as you can imagine, mind-numbingly awkward; I stared out the window while Jimmy did his best to keep his bulky body on his side of the car. He'd apparently made it his mission to answer my questions in ten words or less, which proved especially convenient when I asked close-ended ones like "are we goin' there directly" or "do we have time to stop for breakfast."

In case you were wondering, we were, and, no, we didn't.

"Oy," I said, swinging around to look at Jimmy, "Where's Maria?"

Detective Maria Machado was Jimmy's partner and, although she and I had never really seen eye-to-eye, literally or figuratively, I hoped I could rely on her to put aside her personal feelings long enough to give me some straight answers. Like, for example, what had been shoved up Jimmy's ass since I'd last seen him. I was betting on a pineapple. Or a porcupine. Something large and prickly.

"She's already there," Jimmy replied.

"At the crime scene?" I asked.

Jimmy nodded.

"And why d'ye two want me at a crime scene, again?" I asked.

"We don't. My Captain was against it even. But the FBI requested I bring you in, and we're trying to play nice, so here we are."

My mouth may or may not have hung open long enough for drool to spill out. I snapped it shut once I realized Jimmy wasn't going to elaborate. The Federal Bureau of Investigation had requested *me* at a crime scene? But why, what had I done? Granted, as a black magic arms dealer, I regularly played fast and loose with the law, but I purposefully avoided doing anything that would draw Federal attention, even if I didn't technically answer to Regular law enforcement.

Well, not *only* Regular law enforcement.

In general, those of us who considered ourselves Freaks—you may know us better by our household names: werewolves, vampires, wizards, monsters, and so on—were held in check by our own ruthless organizations. Institutions like the Sanguine Council—a conclave of vampire over-lords—or the Academy—a wizarding school that fielded agents who cracked down on supernatural crime when it threatened to expose us to the unsuspecting world. In Boston, on the other hand, the law was upheld by a mysterious group known as the Faerie Chancery, comprised mainly of Fae exiles.

Sadly, I was on everyone's radar, at this point, including, it seemed, the FBI.

"What would the FBI want with me?" I asked, returning to the issue at hand.

Jimmy pursed his lips. "I'll let the Special Agent in Charge explain that to you."

I folded my arms across my chest, and we rode the rest of the way in silence, headed southwest. I watched with growing trepidation as Dorchester's cozy shops, townhomes, and apartments gave way to West Roxbury's residential neighborhoods. I knew better than most that West Roxbury—with its churches and its gentrified, upper-middle class population—was well outside Jimmy's jurisdiction, which didn't bode well; for Jimmy and Maria to have been assigned to the case, a crime had to have been committed in their district—but we'd left that part of town behind ten minutes ago.

Which meant we were heading to a separate—and therefore additional—crime scene. Factoring in the FBI's presence, and the fact that the Bureau rarely got involved unless a crime crossed state lines, I figured there were at least three crime scenes in total.

This had to be karma, I decided.

But I hadn't even meant to dick-punch that kid in Vegas…

CHAPTER 3

There were eight houses on Elven Road, and a police cruiser in every driveway. We parked across the street at a 7-Eleven and walked over, ducking under caution tape after Jimmy flashed his credentials at the uniformed officer guarding the area. The beat cop looked me up and down, clearly wondering what I was doing there. I marched past, ignoring him—I knew about as much as he did, after all, and didn't appreciate being stared at.

Jimmy passed me a visitor's badge attached to a lanyard, "Put this on." I did so, adjusting my hair as I studied the area. I'd assumed the crime scene would be swarming with cops and forensics teams, but it wasn't. In fact, if it weren't for the patrol cars and caution tape, I'd have written this street off as your basic, residential street in a quiet, suburban area—the sort of place where people wave to each other as they step outside to watch their kids get on the bus to school.

The illusion of safety on streets like this always fascinated me; the people who assumed nothing could go wrong on such a dull, ordinary stretch of road. It was that illusion which so often drew families away from the urban sprawl—the assumption that their kids were somehow safer here than there. On the other hand, as a pure-blooded city girl, these neighborhoods gave me the creeps.

Thanks, *Stepford Wives*.

As I followed Jimmy down the sidewalk, however, I realized Elven Road wasn't your typical suburban avenue. In fact, it was pitifully short and out of the way, running perpendicular to trafficked streets on either side; drivers rubbernecked as they passed, but otherwise the police enclosure had no impact on the morning commute.

I hit a crack in the sidewalk and stumbled before deciding to concentrate on walking, and worry less about where we were. At least the crisp morning light was less nauseating than I'd expected, especially now that I had coffee—Jimmy couldn't stop me from ducking in under the pretense of using the bathroom, and even 7-Eleven's crummy brew offered salvation with enough cream and sugar. As we got closer to the other side of the street, I realized that every house had been cordoned off individually, which struck me as especially odd. Some sort of chemical attack, maybe? Multiple break-ins? What else would turn eight houses into crime scenes?

I decided not to dwell on it; I'd find out soon enough, I figured.

We met Maria near the last house on the block. She sat on the hood of a police cruiser, sipping coffee judiciously, her cup stained with matte red lipstick—strange, since she wasn't really the lipstick type. Definitely more of a tinted lip balm kind of gal. When she saw me, her eyes hardened. I waved with enthusiasm, just to be obnoxious, wondering why no one was on Team Quinn, today. Maria and I had never been on great terms, but when last we'd spoken she'd at least made an effort to be civil.

"So, you found her, after all," Maria said. "Too bad."

Well, so much for civility.

"What the fuck is the matter with ye two?" I asked, giving voice to a morning's worth of pent-up frustration. "It's not like I asked to be here, ye know. In fact, I t'ink ye can handle this on your own." I plucked the lanyard from where it hung at my chest and tugged, popping the clasp. I tossed it at Jimmy. "I'll find me own ride back, t'anks."

"Detectives," a male voice called from the nearby doorway, spinning us all around. "Is that the woman I asked you about?" The man had a navy-blue suit jacket slung casually over one shoulder, the sleeves of his wrinkled white shirt rolled up over his heavily-tattooed forearms. There was something swarthy about him I picked up on right away—between his deep boater's tan and quick smile I could sense an easy-going nature. His accent was vaguely Hispanic, like you might find in New Mexico or Arizona. He pulled the door closed behind him, descended the steps, and approached. I noticed Maria giving the man a lot of attention, which explained the lipstick.

"I'm glad you could make it, Miss MacKenna," he said, holding out a hand for me to shake. "I'm Special Agent Jeffries. Or Leo, if you'd prefer."

"It wasn't exactly me choice," I replied, but shook his hand anyway. "And ye can call me Quinn. Every time someone calls me Miss MacKenna I get flashbacks to Catholic school and end up jerkin' me hands back to avoid the ruler."

Jeffries laughed. "Well, I'd hate to trigger you. Quinn, it is." He turned to Jimmy and held out his hand. "I'll take over from here," he said, eyeing the lanyard I'd unceremoniously thrown at the increasingly dickish detective. "I appreciate it."

Jimmy handed the lanyard over and jerked his head at Maria, a nonverbal "let's get the fuck out of here," if I'd ever seen one. Together they headed back down the street without so much as looking back. I frowned as I noticed Jimmy hunting through his pockets, only to pull out a pack of cigarettes. "Since when does Jimmy smoke?" I asked, mostly to myself.

"This case has a lot of people on edge," Jeffries said. "But frankly, I think there's something else bothering Detective Collins. Something he doesn't want to talk about." The Special Agent shrugged, clearly deciding not to elaborate, and waved me to follow before I could ask him what he meant. "Come on. Work awaits."

"How about ye tell me what I'm doin' here, first?" I asked, planting my hands on my hips for good measure. "Jimmy wasn't exactly full of information."

"We can talk more inside. Besides, I'd like you to meet a few more members of my team."

"Your team?"

Jeffries took the steps two at a time—guess he was one of those guys— and opened the door. "Yes. Officially, we're part of the Bureau's Special Inquiries Cold Case Office. Bit of a mouthful. Of course, the local branches have another name for us." He ushered me inside.

"Like what?" I asked as I passed by into the foyer.

"They call us Sickos," a woman said, from within the house. "Get it? S. I. C. C. O. It's actually pretty clever, all things considered." The woman— easily one of the most well-proportioned, muscular women I'd ever seen—

approached, extending a hand. "I'm Special Agent Sigrid." Her handshake was as firm as she was stunning, her features fair and Nordic.

"Quinn MacKenna," I replied.

"Hilde here is the Assistant Special Agent in Charge," Jeffries said. "I keep trying to get demoted, hoping they'll give her my job, but so far she's managed to weasel her way out of it."

Hilde rolled her eyes. "The only reason I stick around is because you're steering the ship, Leo. And that's especially true for the boys. I'm pretty sure Lakota would have a meltdown if you ever even joked about retirement."

Jeffries blushed and ran a hand through his mane of thick, dark hair. I realized there were flecks of gray in it, poking out here and there. "You're probably right."

"So," Hilde said, "should I give her the grand tour?"

"Actually, I think Quinn and I should talk first," Jeffries said. "Could you go make sure Warren's finished? You know how he gets around new people."

"Sure," Hilde said, turning to head up the stairs.

Jeffries invited me to join him at the dining room table, pulling a chair out for me before taking his own. I hesitated, gazing around the room, wondering why—if we were technically in a crime scene—we weren't wearing gloves or plastic booties. Jeffries seemed to sense my hesitation and the reason for it. "Don't worry, forensics has been through here already. A few times. There's nothing worthwhile down here, anyway. Everything happened upstairs."

Everything like what? I sighed and took a seat, determined to get some straight answers before I went anywhere else. "Alright, so I'm here, and I'm listenin'," I said. "I t'ink it's about time ye tell me why ye had me brought here in the wee hours of the mornin'."

Jeffries grinned and steepled his fingers. "I'll tell you everything you'd like to know. But first, I'd like you to tell me everything *you* know about Freaks."

It was official; I should've stayed in Vegas.

CHAPTER 4

*M*y eyes widened momentarily, but I managed to mask my surprise by taking a sip of my coffee and tucking a strand of hair behind one ear while I considered how to respond. I had no idea what kind of game Jeffries was playing, but I wasn't about to confess to knowing what a "Freak" was—not in front of a Federal agent. "I'm sorry, did ye say freaks?" I asked. "Like, what, kinky people with fetishes? Is that what ye mean? Toe-suckers and shoe-humpers?"

Jeffries chuckled, but I noticed he was watching me like a hawk, gauging my reaction—the way Dez used to when trying to catch me in a lie. All-in-all, I was quickly beginning to realize how terrible a decision I had made in answering my fucking door this morning.

"No," Leo said, eyes twinkling, "we have a different unit assigned to people like that. I'm talking about people—and, in many cases, creatures— who have extraordinary abilities and who live among us."

I raised an eyebrow. "Like superheroes? Aren't ye a wee bit old to be playin' make believe, Agent Jeffries?" I asked, keeping my face calm, trying to get a read on him and find out how much he really knew.

Jeffries studied me, his head tilted as if listening to a frequency I couldn't hear. He frowned, then pointed to his suit jacket, which he'd folded over the back of his chair. "What color is this?"

I blinked owlishly, suspecting Agent Jeffries might be clinically insane.

13

The sad part was that it would make sense; in my experience, most Regulars who saw Freaks for what we were had a stilted, warped understanding of reality. Typically, you'd find them on the fringes of society, disregarded. Like the preacher heckling sinners from the street corner, or the woman on the subway, twitching every time the lights flickered. Most people dismissed their behavior—crazy is as crazy does. But what if that preacher could see demonic influence, trailing behind you like a shadow? Or what if that woman knew what lived in those dim subway tunnels—beings without eyes, without faces? The truth—that Freak encounters have been responsible for quite a few psychotic breaks—was out there, Scully.

"It's blue," I said finally, shrugging. If the deranged Special Agent wanted to play "I Spy" in the middle of an investigation, sitting at a dining room table which doubled as a crime scene, I wasn't going to argue. Or move, even.

The crazies hate sudden movements.

He nodded. "Now tell me it's red."

"Seriously? I—"

"Please, it'll only take a moment," Jeffries said. He seemed quite serious—and surprisingly sane.

"Fine. Your suit is red."

Jeffries blinked. Once. Twice. Then he settled back in his chair. "Remarkable," he murmured, staring at me so hard it felt like he was looking through me.

"What is?" Hilde asked as she entered, pulling up a chair alongside her boss.

Jeffries never took his eyes off me. "I can't tell if she's lying or telling the truth," he muttered in response, sounding very, very troubled.

I frowned. "What the hell is that supposed to mean?" I asked. Of course, I had lied to him about the color of his jacket—he'd asked me to. Unless he meant I'd been lying about something else…

I glanced over at Hilde to gauge her reaction but was shocked to find her sizing me up like I would an opponent—someone I might have to break if things got ugly. I scooted back from the table out of habit; swinging my knees around, prepared to stand. Hilde's eyes narrowed. I wasn't sure why, but it felt like the temperature in the room had suddenly fallen a few degrees; goosebumps prickled the skin on my arms.

What the hell was going on here?

Jeffries shivered, seeming to come back to himself. "Hilde, that's enough. She hasn't done anything wrong. In fact, I don't think she's even doing it on purpose."

"Doin' *what?*" I asked again, still staring at Hilde. Or, more specifically, her hips. Plenty of people argue about what to look for in a fight—an opponent's eyes, the twist of their shoulders, the swivel of their feet. But, in my experience, every fighter I'd ever met depended on their hips to start the party. If she rose, even the slightest bit, I'd have a couple seconds to react.

If that.

"You're blocking my ability," Jeffries said.

My eyes shot to the Special Agent, dismissing Hilde altogether. I couldn't help it; his answer had surprised me that much. "Your what?"

Jeffries smiled. "My ability. Call it a gift," he said, shrugging. "A curse, too, at times. You'd be surprised how often people rely on lies. Excuses, exaggeration, even the lies they tell themselves."

"Wait," I said, "so ye can tell when people are lyin'?"

Hilde snorted. "He can tell when you're lying, when you're being hyperbolic, when you're trying to be nice..." She glanced over at her boss with a wry smile, and I realized the temperature in the room had gone back to normal. "Any idea how hard it is to work for a guy like that?"

I grunted, thinking about all the odd jobs I'd had over the years before I'd begun peddling magical artifacts for money. Hilde was right. If even half my bosses had known what I really thought about them and their crummy job, I'd never have made it past my first interview.

But, wait a second...that made Agent Jeffries a Freak.

"She's got it now," Hilde said, watching my face with a smug grin.

"But how?" I asked. "Why?"

Jeffries held up a hand. "I know, you're probably asking yourself a lot of questions right now. But before I answer them, I need you to tell me one thing. Are you one of us?" he asked. I realized he was gesturing to himself and Hilde. "Usually I'd be able to probe a bit and find out for myself, but you're immune. Which makes me strongly suspect you *are* one of us. Of course, I've been wrong before."

I stared at Hilde. "I'll answer ye, if she tells me what she is," I said. Truth be told, I was curious. But, more than anything, I wanted to see how far Jeffries was willing to go to prove he could be trusted.

Hilde grinned wolfishly. "And what do you think I am?"

I frowned and then studied her, taking her question seriously. "Somethin' do with the cold, I t'ink, after that little dip in temperature. Not an elemental. They don't keep physical forms for longer than a few minutes. Hurts 'em. Ye aren't one of the Fae—ye look too human and none of that's glamour. Probably not a goddess or you'd be so far up your own arse I'd never get a word in. A fighter, from what your body language said a moment ago. Trained. Ye lead with your arms up, though, so not a shooter. Beyond that, I'm not sure."

The two FBI agents exchanged very pointed glances.

"Looks like the detective was right," Jeffries said.

Hilde nodded, then turned to me. "Valkyrie," she said.

My brow furrowed. "Say what now?"

"That's what I am. Or was. A Valkyrie. I've been...loaned out, after a fashion. Leo can fill you in on the details of how that came about better than I can."

I fiddled with my coffee cup. A Valkyrie. One of the legendary warriors who served Odin, the Norse God who literally had a day named after him. That's right, people: Hump Day was all his. I probably should have been more surprised to meet one of the mythical shield-maidens, but after running into, not *one*, but *three* goddesses a couple of weeks ago, I had a really high tolerance for surprises. Still, that left me with plenty of questions. Like what was a Valkyrie doing working for the FBI? Were there other mythological legends on his team?

Was Odin the director of the FBI?

And, for Christ's sake, who killed JFK?

Jeffries hunched forward, elbows resting on the table. "Let me start from the beginning, and then you're more than welcome to ask the horde of questions that are written all over your face. Sound good?"

I nodded, smirking.

"A few years back," Jeffries began, "a colleague of mine had an idea to establish a unit within the FBI that could respond to the growing supernatural threats we were encountering. We didn't call them that, of course, because our fellow agents would have assumed we were crazy. Instead, we handled the investigations in-house, juggling what we knew and what we could prove—and, more importantly, *explain* in a manner our superiors would buy."

Jeffries sighed, his expression wistful. "My colleague was later discredited and kicked out of the Bureau, but not before he'd laid the foundation for S.I.C.C.O. On paper, we're the mop-up crew. They call us in when the cases prove to be unsolvable for one reason or another. We collect the data, the samples, and anything else they feel like passing along. Of course, what they don't know is that we have Freaks on the payroll. Our unique talents give us a leg up tracking down leads, and we survive budget cuts by closing a few cases a year."

Jeffries rose and moved towards the windows, admiring the view outside. "At first, we met a lot of dead ends. Once in charge, I tried to pick competent people within the Bureau, but quickly realized that, the better they were at their jobs, the sooner they realized we weren't dealing with normal human beings—with Regulars. Most couldn't handle that, so the turnover was pretty high. I decided that what I needed, if I wanted to do this job right, was to enlist some of the very Freaks we were hunting. So, I started recruiting. That was a couple years ago."

"Leo found me," Hilde interjected, perhaps sensing her boss' trip down memory lane was bound to be unpleasant, "through a mutual friend. He had a few good people working for him, brilliant people, with excellent deductive skills. But he needed muscle. And experience."

"I think you can guess," Jeffries said, turning to me, "why I had to bring in someone like Hilde. Or, to say it another way, I think you can understand the real reason why we operate independently from the FBI, most of the time."

I paused to consider everything they'd said, fascinated by the idea that there was an organization working within Regular law enforcement which was responsible for handling supernatural crimes—even if the top brass had no idea. But Jeffries was right, I could see one huge flaw in their approach. In fact, I could point directly to the Constitution to expose it. "Because," I said, "ye can't give a Freak a fair trial."

I could read the conflict on Jeffries' face, but his nod was firm and resolute. After going head-to-head with my fair share of monsters, I could empathize. Of course, as a law enforcement officer, Jeffries had a duty to uphold an individual's right to due process—but how would you hold a trial for a vampire who'd gone on a rampage? Assuming you could capture one, what would a jury of its peers even look like? When you got right down to it, that's why organizations like the Sanguine Council existed—to keep its members in check. But there were other creatures running around unsupervised, creatures who weren't bound by any laws, creatures who couldn't be caged or caught.

Only killed.

"Where are ye lot from? Not Boston, I'm guessin'," I added, judging by their accents. I just hoped none of them had ties to Vegas or New York City.

Or else I'd have a few very awkward conversations in my very near future.

Jeffries nodded to my comment. "All over, but not Boston. We don't technically have an official office. We just chase cases," he admitted with a shrug.

"What about the Academy?" I asked. "Have ye thought about bringin' them in to help?" While the Academy and I hadn't exactly gotten along during their last visit, I knew they were capable of apprehending the monsters—though to be honest I had no idea what the Academy did with them beyond that point.

And I probably didn't want to know.

Hilde scoffed. "The Academy Justices only step in when a Freak makes a splash big enough for the Regulars to notice, to ask questions. Extortion? Theft? Murder? Happens every day. No headlines there."

"We take on the smaller scale stuff that isn't on their radar," Jeffries explained. "The less obvious crimes. But, even then, we miss a lot of them. Most Freaks have gotten really good at covering their tracks. Sometimes it takes us months before we have enough thread to pull on."

I suppressed a shiver as I thought about what that meant. "So, what about this one?" I asked. "What are ye chasin' now?"

Hilde glanced at Jeffries. "Do you want to tell her?"

He shook his head. "Best to show her, first. Let her come up with her own conclusions."

Hilde—a mythical being who'd made a career out of snatching the souls of dead men off battlefields—sighed and nodded, gazing at me like I was an animal that's about to be put down. "Good luck up there," she said.

So yeah.

Basically, this was going to get suckier.

CHAPTER 5

*J*effries led the way, guiding me to the first door on the left at the top of the stairs. The other man he'd mentioned, Warren, was nowhere to be found. Before opening the door, Jeffries held up a finger. "There's a trashcan right inside the door, if you feel like you need it."

I briefly considered why I'd even agreed to do this, but realized that—on some level—I felt it was my responsibility. Boston was my town, and if there was someone or something terrorizing it, I wanted to know.

So, I could put an end to it, one way or the other.

"Ready?" Jeffries asked.

I took a deep breath, then opened the door and ducked inside before I could second guess myself—like diving headfirst into frigid water. I realized I'd shut my eyes and forced myself to open them. "Don't be a baby," I muttered under my breath, taking a look around the room.

It was a bedroom. A child's bedroom. The crib tucked against the far wall was one of those gender-neutral shades of yellow. The bed on the other side was covered in blankets and pillows, though too small for anything bigger than a kindergartner. I stepped forward, the plastic booties Hilde had given me sliding smoothly across the plush carpet. Jeffries trailed me, tracking where my eyes went.

I studied the various placards resting on the ground, on the bed, and against the crib, wondering—and dreading—what each stood for. Jeffries handed me a stack of Manilla folders, each labeled and tabbed to correspond with the placards. But before I could peruse them, he nudged me and pointed to the wall behind us. Above the doorway, in blockish, dark brown letters:

They are coming.

"Who's comin'?" I asked out loud.

Jeffries shrugged. "Every house has a message written on one of the walls. Most, like this one, are straightforward, but vague. *They are coming. No one is safe. Kill or be killed.*"

"Most?" I asked, picking up on Jeffries' use of the conditional.

He nodded and indicated the folders. "It's all in there. Start with this room, though, and tell me what you think."

I sighed, realizing Jeffries wasn't going to feed me information; he wanted a fresh set of eyes, and mine were more or less virginal. I flipped open the folder labeled A1. Inside were a series of photographs pinned together with a paperclip, a set of test results tucked behind. Not having the faintest clue how to read the lab results, I left them alone, handing the stack of folders back to Jeffries as I retrieved the photographs and shuffled through them. I frowned, trying to understand what I was looking at, to put the puzzle pieces together.

Once I finally did, I realized why Jeffries had insisted on the trashcan. I closed my eyes and took a series of deep breaths, glad that all I had in front of me were a bunch of Polaroids, and not the real thing—the mutilated body of a young woman who'd been gruesomely attacked and murdered. Part of me wanted to stop there, content to leave it at that—but another part of me knew that I wouldn't be able to tell Jeffries anything unless I took a closer look. I opened my eyes and went back through the images, one at a time.

"What's in the other folders?" I asked, praying they didn't contain more pictures of corpses.

"The rest from this set are blood pattern related, mostly. Some suspicious fibers. Rumpled areas where the killer might have sat or put his hands."

"His?"

Jeffries shrugged a second time. "Statistics support that conclusion."

I frowned. "Do your statistics take Freaks into consideration?"

"No. We don't have enough data for that sort of analysis, and our lab techs wouldn't know what to do with half the shit we find at crime scenes."

I nodded. From a forensics perspective, tracking a Freak would be a nightmare. But deep down, I worried about the lack of data collection; it wasn't that I thought Jeffries was wrong to assume the killer was male so much as I worried about the gap between the FBI's profiling techniques and the crimes Freaks commit. Highly-trained Regulars analyzing and predicting human behavior made sense, but what about inhuman behavior? Could Jeffries and his team even rely on predictors?

"So," Jeffries said, interrupting my muddled thoughts, "what do you think?"

"Did ye say there was more than one set of these?" I asked, waving the folder in my hand for emphasis, too distracted by the Special Agent's previous statement to answer his immediate question.

"I did."

"So, there's another stack of folders? An A2?" I asked.

Jeffries cocked an eyebrow. "There is. We have a stack of those...for every house on the block."

I felt my stomach lurch and edged toward the trashcan, praying I wouldn't be sick. Eight houses. Which meant eight victims. All on this street. "Are they all like this?" I asked.

Jeffries nodded. "They were all killed in similar ways, yes. Faces and genitals mutilated, entrails removed..." Jeffries drifted off, perhaps sensing my discomfort.

"Well, if ye want to know what I t'ink, I'd say you're lookin' for one sick bastard..." I said, pausing for a moment to let my stomach settle; between Jeffries' show-and-tell and my hangover, I had a feeling it was only a matter of time before I upchucked my coffee—cream and all.

"But you're wondering what got him on our radar?"

I nodded, grateful that he'd anticipated my unasked question.

"Here's what we know so far. If anything jumps out at you, let me know. Fact number one, three days ago all eight families on this block planned a week-long vacation. They all left within hours of one another. Those we've been able to reach told us they didn't even think to contact their jobs or their extended families to let them know they were planning to leave. None plan to return until their vacation is complete. They don't even seem to care that someone found bodies in their houses."

I crossed my arms, frowning. That was odd. "A vampire gaze, maybe?" I guessed.

Jeffries nodded. "We considered that."

"T'ing is," I said, thinking out loud, "the Sanguine Council doesn't have a branch here, and even rogue vamps know better than to stir up trouble in Boston."

"Yeah, we've noticed there's a downtick in supernatural groups here. Why is that?" Jeffries said, making notations in a small notebook.

I shook my head. I liked Jeffries, but I wasn't about to go blabbing about the Chancery to an outsider. "You'll have to take me word on it."

Jeffries' pen stopped scratching and he peered up at me suspiciously. Thankfully, he didn't press. "Well, moving on, then. Fact number two, each of the victims recently gave birth. Within the last month or so, according to the medical examiner."

Okay, I was definitely going to throw up. I shuffled a step closer to the open maw of the plastic receptacle, taking deep, soothing breaths. "Somethin' ritualistic, maybe?" I managed, a moment later.

"One of my people looked into that," Jeffries replied, "I doubt it's coincidence, but we aren't sure either way. Fact number three, each of the victims were found in different parts of the house, accompanied by blood spatter in the room in which they were found. However, no trail could be found leading to the rooms themselves. The rest of the house, the doors, windows, floors, and what have you, were untouched. It's like the women's corpses dropped out of thin air."

I considered that for a moment. "And have ye looked into Gateways?" I asked.

Jeffries frowned. "Into what?"

"Gateways. It's a wizard t'ing. They're like doorways between one place and another."

Jeffries eyes widened. "You mean wizards can create rifts in space between two places whenever they want?"

"Well, sure. Only the powerful ones, though, from what I understand."

"That's...disconcerting," Jeffries said, eyeing me as if I were pulling his leg. I realized it must be hard for the human lie detector to take me at my word—spoiled much? "So, what's to stop a wizard from robbing a bank? Or assassinating a world leader?" Jeffries asked.

I judiciously refrained from mentioning my recent, accidental foray in the vaults of a Vegas Casino courtesy of a Gateway created by Callie Penrose—an acquaintance from Kansas City I'd made over the weekend – a friend of Othello's.

No felonies to see here, folks.

"I wouldn't worry about it," I said, trying to ease the Special Agent's mind. "The really powerful wizards out there wouldn't have a whole lot to gain from that sort of t'ing. Besides, that's what the Justices are around for, don't ye t'ink?"

"I guess so," Jeffries said, sighing. "Still, that's an angle I hadn't considered. Not sure what a wizard could hope to achieve from all this, but I can look into it. Maybe it has something to do with the messages he left in these houses."

"Ye said there were a few which stood out to ye?" I asked, curious to see the others, so long as I didn't have to look at any more photographs of dead women in the process.

"Just one. I don't know what it means, but I have one of my people looking into it." Jeffries sorted through the stack of folders until he saw the one he wanted. "Here. Check it out."

I opened the folder. Inside were the various messages, painted in the same manner on walls, desks, and mirrors. For the most part, Jeffries was right. Along with those he'd mentioned, I saw other apocryphal phrases like "the end is nigh," "you will all burn," and so on. One, however, differed significantly from the rest. I pulled it out and showed it to Jeffries, who flashed me a thumbs up. I glanced at the picture once more, trying to make sense of the words.

"Beware the Fomorians," Jeffries intoned, as if saying the words out loud would solve the mystery they represented. "Any clue what it means?"

I shook my head, but in the back of my mind, where my half-remembered dreams were kept locked away, I felt something stir. The ghost of a memory, calling out...

"Leo! Pizza's here!" Hilde shouted from below.

Oh, sweet Jesus. Pizza.

Maybe God didn't hate me after all.

CHAPTER 6

*H*ilde passed me a paper plate with three slices on it while I tried
to ignore the eerie, empty street; now that I knew why it was
abandoned, the stillness had a grating quality to it—like when you're thirty
thousand feet up and can't get your ears to pop.

"You alright?" Hilde asked.

"Aye," I replied, not wanting to talk about what Jeffries had shown me,
especially while I was eating. Hilde accepted that without comment, which I
appreciated; most women would have felt the need to talk it out, maybe
compare notes and make each other feel better. But I'd never been one of
those women; I kept my pain inside, where it could only hurt *me*.

We ate outside next to the patrol car. Apparently chatting at the dining
room table was fine but eating at it would have been crossing the line.
"Wouldn't want to be rude," Jeffries had said. "Bad enough they'll have to
come home to find a murder scene in their house without finding crumbs
everywhere."

Two others had joined us initially, emerging from one of the other
houses. The first, Warren, was a thin, effeminate man dressed in a tweed
suit that was definitely not standard issue. I noticed he seemed inexplicably
happy to see me, especially considering what Jeffries had implied earlier
about his aversion to strangers. Hilde watched our brief interaction in

complete and undisguised shock, her mouth hanging open long enough to let bugs in.

The second was the young man Hilde had mentioned earlier, Lakota, a Native American kid with a round face and long, luxurious hair pulled back in a braid. He'd taken his pizza and left without a word, which hadn't seemed to bother Hilde much, though I saw her follow the kid with her eyes as he departed, something motherly and sad lurking there.

"So, what'd Jimmy say about me, exactly?" I asked, after practically inhaling the first slice. I'd been curious ever since Jeffries mentioned Jimmy's involvement and figured now was as good a time as any to bring it up.

"From what Leo said," Hilde replied, "I don't think Detective Collins meant to say anything at all. When we first got here we poked around a little, trying to figure out if anyone in Boston PD had worked with Freaks before. You find them here and there. Cops with sensitivities. Criminal informants with ties to the supernatural community. Whenever we go somewhere new and we need to get the lay of the land as quick as we can, we try to find someone who can feed us reliable and up-to-date info."

Hilde leaned back against a patrol car much the way Maria had earlier— if Maria were a fitness model who slayed monsters for a living. "Detective Collins was cagey," she said. "Leo picked up on it right away and pressed until Collins admitted knowing someone who could give us a rundown on how Boston worked. We urged him to reach out to you, though getting the request through his superiors took some convincing."

I nodded, then frowned as I processed her timetable. "Wait, Agent Jeffries said these people left three days ago..." I said, struck by the fact that I hadn't connected the dots until now. "But Jimmy's been blowin' up me phone for two weeks now."

"She doesn't know about the other ones?" Warren asked, his mouth full; the words came out garbled.

"Other ones?" I asked, remembering too late that there were probably at least two other crime scenes out there. Of course, I might have simply repressed it; it's not like I *wanted* there to be more scenes like the ones Jeffries had shown me. Or, maybe it was the lingering effects of my hangover, clouding things.

"Sorry," Jeffries said, strolling up to us, catching the tail end of the conversation. "I figured I could wait to fill you in after lunch."

I hurriedly scarfed down my third slice and presented my empty plate as evidence that lunch was officially over. I wasn't eager to hear the details from the other crime scenes, but the more I knew, the better my odds of helping them put down the son-of-a-bitch.

Jeffries chuckled. "Alright," he said, "for starters, we've been chasing this guy since December."

My eyes widened.

"Exactly. And, since then, he's left us a pile of bodies, every month, in a different city. He started in Los Angeles. Then Albuquerque, Chicago, and now here."

I did the math, counting out the months one finger at a time, and frowned as that left one month unaccounted for. "But it's April, now…"

"Indeed. The unknown subject has struck twice in Boston, which is significant deviation from his established pattern," Warren explained, sounding much more professional without the pizza in his mouth. "However, everything else about the *modus operandi* is the same. Or as similar as can be expected, given the subject's predilections."

"He's been killin' women all over the country? Why haven't I heard anythin' about it?" I asked.

"Oh no, not only women. The subject is ascribing to a very particular methodology which ties directly to—"

Jeffries held up a hand to interrupt what I imagined was about to be a very long-winded explanation on Warren's part. "As far as we can tell, he's mimicking another serial killer, at least in terms of the way he tortures and murders his victims. But everything else points to an obsession with a popular Christmas carol. We didn't figure that out until Chicago, but now that we know what to look for, it's fairly obvious."

"A Christmas carol?" I asked.

"In Los Angeles, we found twelve members of a percussion band murdered and left on display in the middle of a college football stadium," Hilde said, her tone cold. "In Albuquerque, eleven Navajo men in a hogan, with tobacco pipes in their mouths. In Chicago, ten members of the Vice Lords gang in a trampoline park. And here, in Boston, nine debutantes in a dance studio."

I could barely comprehend what Hilde was saying. So many people dead, and in such horrific ways. I had to lean on the hood of the patrol car when the significance of the diverse victims and their circumstances finally hit me. Twelve drummers drumming, eleven pipers piping, ten Lords a' leaping, and nine Ladies dancing.

"And, of course," Warren supplied, "we have our eight mothers. Maids-a-milking, as it were."

I made it to the grass before puking, the pizza tasting much worse coming back up than it had going down.

Because even if God didn't hate me, the Devil clearly did.

CHAPTER 7

*H*ilde passed me a handy wipe and a tin of breath mints she'd fetched from her purse. I used the former to dab at my mouth and the latter to obscure the bilious aftertaste, then I returned to the driveway feeling marginally better. Judging from Warren's piteous expression, I was willing to bet Jeffries had chastised him for his lack of tact.

"Rough weekend, still recovering," I said, playing the whole thing off. In my experience, that was the simplest solution to an embarrassing situation; pretend it doesn't bother you and people move on pretty quickly...unless someone puts it on YouTube. Then you're fucked. "Ye said our guy was mimickin' another serial killer?" I asked, in a bid to change the subject to something lighter.

You know, like graphic murder sprees.

Jeffries encouraged Warren—who was practically shaking like a poodle in his eagerness to share—to fill me in, "Go ahead."

"Our unknown subject is modeling his kills after Jack the Ripper," Warren explained. "Well, after the killings committed in the 1800s which have been ascribed to Jack the Ripper, at any rate."

I shot a look at Jeffries. "*The* Jack the Ripper? Why him?"

Jeffries shrugged. "No clue. At the moment, all we have are questions like that. Why Jack the Ripper? Why the Twelve Days of Christmas? What prompted the move from city to city? Why hit Boston twice?"

"I've got one," I said, "how come this is the first I've heard of these murders? Shouldn't the press be all over somethin' like this?"

Hilde and Jeffries exchanged a look.

Eventually, Jeffries filled the silence. "Because the crimes have been so widely spread, thus far, we've managed to avoid media attention. Chicago was chalked up to intergang violence. The Navajo were on tribal land, where crimes rarely receive media attention." Jeffries shook his head. "That, and none of the loved ones seem to want to step forward. It's like they don't even realize they've lost someone. It's...disconcerting, at best."

I frowned, realizing the Special Agent had just admitted to keeping these murders secret from the public at large. Not that I was a fan of panic in the streets, but still, wouldn't it help to warn people?

"I have a theory as to the latter," Warren interjected, before I could follow-up. He thrust a finger in the air and continued as though we'd begged him to, "I believe the unknown subject is, somehow, removing the psychic energy that surrounds his victims. Essentially cutting them off at an atomic level from the rest of us."

"Warren is a psychic," Jeffries explained. "Normally he'd take one look at a crime scene like this and be able to tell us all sorts of things about the victims, about their last moments, about the killer. It's handy, but hard on him, as you can imagine."

Warren glanced over at his boss in gratitude. "Residual psychic energy," Warren said, turning to me. "I can contextualize it. It's easier with dead people. The living give off too many signals...it's like trying to read a book with words swimming all over the page. That's why I'm usually so awkward around people I don't know. Looking at them makes me nauseous."

"Ye seemed fine when we met," I said, tilting my head a fraction.

Hilde perked up at that, recalling her surprise from earlier, perhaps. Warren nodded, grinning. "Oh, absolutely. I'm not sure how you're doing it, but you're giving off exactly zero residual psychic energy. I've never seen anything like it. Not in a living person, anyway." Warren frowned as if he'd just thought of something unpleasant.

"What's that supposed to mean?" I asked, more than a little disturbed by that implication; I preferred to have as little in common with corpses as possible.

"Well," Warren said, "the only other time I've come across something like this is when we were put on this case. With these victims."

Three sets of eyes swiveled towards me.

I held up my hands and chuckled. "I'm not the killer, I swear. Hell, I was in Vegas all weekend," I said in my defense, then cringed. Shit. I really hoped Jeffries didn't look into that alibi. The FBI poking around into what I'd been up to in Vegas could land me in a whole different pot of hot water.

"But you already admitted that a powerful wizard could simply create a Gateway from one place to another," Jeffries said, using my own words against me.

I sighed in exasperation. "Aye, but I'm not a wizard."

"Then what are you?" Hilde asked, shifting her weight forward onto the balls of her feet. "You never did say."

"I don't t'ink ye have a term for what I am," I replied, reading Hilde's body language and recognizing it for the threat that it was. "But I suggest ye t'ink twice before ye do somethin' you'll regret, Agent Sigrid. I'd hate to hurt someone who gave me a breath mint."

Hilde scoffed.

Jeffries held up a hand as if to calm us all down, but I noticed the other inching towards his weapon. "I think we should all relax. Talk this out."

Down the street, a trashcan fell over.

The din of it crashing against the ground startled all of us: Jeffries whirled, gun in hand, sighting down the barrel; Hilde dropped to a crouch, brandishing—I shit you not—a sword and shield, her hair magically tied back in a loose braid, her black suit and tie now a suit of black, bloodstained armor of the *Heavy Metal* variety.

Warren, on the other hand, squealed and hid behind a patrol car.

I raised both hands defensively and daydreamed about taking a real vacation. Somewhere isolated, tropical...

Like a deserted island.

"She's not your killer," Lakota said, one foot propped up against the trashcan he'd purposely kicked over. He finished the last bite of his pizza and sucked the grease off his fingers as he strolled towards us. Jeffries cursed and holstered his weapon. Hilde, however, seemed content to leave hers out.

I appraised her new look. "That's a cool trick. Do ye keep all that in your purse or does it appear out of thin air?"

Hilde grunted and released her hold on the sword and shield, both winking out of existence an instant before they hit the ground. Her armor flickered before my eyes, transforming into cloth, and her hair cascaded down to her shoulders in slow motion, like a scene from *Baywatch*.

Not gonna lie, it was hot—in a devil-may-care sort of way. But honestly, all I wanted to know was where she'd gotten her outfit. Because, in my experience, every girl needs a getup that turned her into friggin' Joan of Amazonia. Saxon Fifth Avenue, maybe? Bloomingdanes? TJ Axxed?

Totally going to find out.

Over drinks…if she felt like sharing.

Because nobody in their right mind picks a fight with Valhalla Barbie.

"Don't do that again, Lakota," Jeffries admonished. "I could have shot you."

Lakota rolled his eyes. "You wouldn't have shot me."

Jeffries grumbled something under his breath about respecting one's elders and how his boss would have shot him on the spot.

"Lakota, why isn't she a suspect?" Hilde asked, cutting through their exchange before it devolved any further.

"Well, she's definitely a killer," Lakota replied, giving me the full weight of his attention—the authority in his gaze surprisingly hefty despite our age difference. "But she's not *our* killer."

So, I'd gone from suspect to murderer.

And, once again, I was the center of attention.

Talk about out of the frying pan and into the fire.

CHAPTER 8

*L*akota grunted. "She's tainted, but no more than any of us." He squinted at me, then turned to his boss. "No innocents, as far as I can tell. She's remarkably at peace, especially compared to you and Warren. Her energy is much closer to Hilde's, actually. Violent. Practical. Still finding her center."

"Is he psychic, too?" I asked Warren, who'd poked his head up from behind the car long enough to hear Lakota's spiel. He shook his head vehemently.

"No, Lakota is something else," Jeffries replied. "He—"

"Leo," Hilde interrupted.

"It's fine," Lakota said, his eyes dancing with malice. "Tell her." When Jeffries didn't respond, Lakota plucked a stray hair off his suit and answered my question himself, "They don't know what I am. I was raised in the foster system and arbitrarily named after a tribe by my first set of racially insensitive white adoptive parents. No idea where I came from. Eventually, Leo found me. He was the one who realized I was a Freak. That I could see things other people couldn't."

"Like what?" I asked.

"Like souls. Or whatever you want to call them," Lakota said, his anger fading away as he spoke. "I can see the stains on them. I can sense their intentions, good or bad. Doesn't matter who or what they are, Regular or Freak. Every one of them has a soul."

I had a flash of insight as I studied Lakota's face, recognizing his expression for what it was: guilt. "So that's it," I said, turning to Jeffries. "That's how ye know which monsters to kill? He's, what, your judge and jury?"

Jeffries winced, but nodded.

I shook my head. Lakota was an FBI agent, sure, but also young, and Jeffries used him to decide the fate of the creatures they went up against, to more or less sign their death warrants. His gift aside, it would be impossible not to doubt yourself, to fret over whether or not you'd made the right choice.

No wonder he wasn't exactly a people person.

We stood there, the beautiful sky overhead, trapped in our ugly thoughts. I glanced at their faces and realized Jeffries and his team were waiting for me to pass judgment on them. To tell them what they were doing was wrong, or to demand they find a better way. I knew they'd heard it all before.

"Can I ask ye a question?" I said to Jeffries, who wouldn't meet my eye.

"Sure."

I pointed at Lakota and Warren. "Do ye ever let these two go on vacation? Because I t'ink we could make the MIT kids who scammed Vegas look like idgits in comparison."

Jeffries snorted, but the two younger agents looked at each other in surprise, as if suddenly realizing the fiscal potential of their combined gifts. Hilde swatted Warren's arm, lightly. "Don't even think about it," she warned. "You either." She pointed at Lakota, who raised his hands in surrender, grinning.

Jeffries shot me a grateful look.

I nodded in reassurance.

The truth is, I knew better than most that sometimes working with the monsters made you feel like one, and that taking them out came at a price. I'd spent years trying to decide if doing my job made me a bad person, struggling with the moral ambiguity of knowing the goods I sold had the potential to hurt people.

I still struggled with it, some days.

But that's why God made whiskey.

Lakota was right; I'd killed both in cold blood and in self-defense. And I was sure there were people out there who'd been killed with weapons I'd sold, strangers whose names I would never even know. And that *did* bother me. But the world was a cruel place full of cruel people, and I didn't have the time or energy to make it better.

The Sickos, on the other hand, were working day in and day out to do just that; if I could offer them a little peace of mind by reserving judgment, I would.

They'd earned it.

Of course, it wouldn't hurt if they returned the favor by reserving their judgment of *me*.

CHAPTER 9

I left after assuring Jeffries that I would look into things on my end. He offered to give me a ride, but I declined. I needed time to process on my own. I called an Uber—my go-to method of transportation after having totaled my car a while back in an unfortunate run-in with a bridge troll whom I occasionally played poker with—and tried to order my thoughts.

Jeffries and his team were the easiest to sort out. At first, I hadn't been sure if I should even get involved; I'd been asked to participate in an ongoing investigation by Jimmy once before, over a year ago, and it hadn't gone well. At the time, I figured it was one of those experiences you can't say no to, especially if someone offers you a free ticket—like skydiving.

Except I doubted skydiving gave you such horrific nightmares.

The truth was—nightmares aside—I couldn't help but be impressed with the Sickos and their mission statement. I mean, sure, being an arms dealer probably wouldn't earn me any brownie points from the Special Agent in Charge or his band of merry misfits, but knowing there was a sanctioned organization out there trying to make the world a safer place by taking out those Freaks who preyed on others was reassuring. Hell, helping the Sickos might even balance the scales, karmically speaking.

I'd end up saying Our Fathers until Judgment Day, otherwise.

Sadly, I wasn't sure how much I could really do. The fact that there was a

Freak out there torturing and killing people to the tune of a Christmas carol made my poor stomach churn. But I wasn't a cop, or a private detective, with eyes and ears all over the city. At best, I had a few favors I could call in and—maybe—pool together some information. But if the Sickos hadn't gotten a bead on their killer yet, I doubted I'd have better luck.

Unless I was thinking about this all wrong. Whoever the killer was, he was probably new in town; he'd kicked this whole thing off in Los Angeles, after all. In any other city, that wouldn't have made any difference, but this was Boston. And—if I knew anything about Boston's Freaky underground—it's that outsiders weren't welcome. In fact, any Freaks moving into the area were typically subject to registry...by the Faerie Chancery.

I sighed.

I'd kept the Chancery's existence from the Sickos for a reason. From what I'd seen over the last several years, the Chancery may as well have been the mob: they had a monopoly on all things Freak, imposing their own rules and applying their own punishments to those who broke them.

I'd managed to avoid tangling with them up until now, but I had a feeling my days were numbered; I'd caused a bit of a stir recently while fighting a millennia-old monster on live television courtesy of Dorian Gray, who'd broadcasted the whole thing as a ploy to distract the rest of the supernatural community from an apocalyptic event taking place in New York City. After winning that fight—mostly through luck—I'd earned a little notoriety, though I wasn't thrilled about it; my job was a lot easier to do from the shadows, well out of the spotlight.

That, and I preferred not having to answer to anyone, the Chancery included. Thus far I'd managed to stay out of their crosshairs by selling to them, indirectly, as freely as I sold to anyone else—supply and demand.

But that could all be about to change.

After I'd gotten back from New York City, the Chancery had sent me a summons which mirrored a letter I'd received from them a few months before—for some other crazy shit that had gone down that wasn't even my fault. Well, mostly not my fault. My point is, at the moment, it felt like I had Faeling debt collectors crawling up my ass.

I'd decided last week to ignore both and let the chips fall where they may. But now I realized that, if I met with them, the Chancery might be able to tell me who was in town murdering Regulars. Or—barring that—tell me who'd come into town in the last couple weeks; the Sickos could take it from there.

I cursed silently.

Guess I was meeting up with those Faeling bastards after all.

But first, I needed a nap.

J got home, fully prepared to pass out for at least a solid hour, only to find my door unlocked. I tested the knob and dropped immediately, sliding to my left with my back pressed against the wall, ducking low in case someone planned to gun me down. It may seem silly, but these are the things you get used to in my profession; an unlocked door could as easily mean a hitman as it could a landlord letting in a maintenance guy without your permission. After a minute of waiting, I nudged the door open.

"Hello, my lady," Dobby said, sitting in a chair on the far side of my living room. "Is everything alright?"

I cursed, feeling a little silly, and rose from my very uncomfortable squatted position. "What are ye doin' here, Dobby?" I hissed. "And how did ye even get in?"

Dobby, a spriggan I'd been charged with keeping an eye on, raised an eyebrow, which looked somewhat ridiculous given how comically large his eyeballs were; I'd jokingly nicknamed him after J.K. Rowling's creation, given their startlingly similar appearance, but he'd accepted the moniker before I could change his mind. Interestingly, he seemed to have grown a little since then—now perhaps the size of a prepubescent teenager, as opposed to a second grader. I wasn't sure what that meant, but part of me worried about what it might mean for his other half—the giant shadow monster he became when the lights went out.

Because, of course, spriggans could do that.

"Locked doors rarely pose a challenge to my kind. I recommend installing wards, if home security is especially important to you. To answer your original question, however, I have come seeking your advice," Dobby said, sounding even more rational and intelligent than when I'd last seen him—when he'd run and hid from me rather than tell me what he knew about my abilities.

"Does that mean ye plan to tell me what ye know, then? About what I am?" I asked, choosing to finish what we'd begun weeks ago before offering any advice.

The thing is, my mother, who might have had the answers I sought, died giving birth to me. And my father had never been in the picture to begin with. Lately, I'd begun to strongly suspect that my dad might be a Faeling, and that I was a half-breed of some sort, a hybrid—something which wasn't supposed to exist. But the last time Dobby and I had spoken, he'd intimated that he knew more than that...before promptly using a magical ring I'd given him to disappear and flee.

Dobby had the grace to look a little ashamed. "I am sorry I ran from you, my lady. I know you want answers, but it is too soon for you to know the truth."

"It's what?" I spluttered.

Dobby shook his head, and I could see he was genuinely sorry. "I am not keeping things from you to be spiteful, or coy. You must discover your origins on your own, or not at all. That is the covenant which you have made, though you had no hand in its design."

I tossed my phone on the kitchen counter in frustration and fetched a glass from the cupboard. After gulping down some water, I turned to face the diminutive creature. Getting pissed off at a Faeling as old and powerful as Dobby would be as ineffective as throwing a tantrum; no matter how badly I wanted to wring the truth out of him, he'd stick to his party line. That didn't mean I had to like it, though. "Well, is there anythin' ye *can* tell me?" I asked, trying to keep the anger out of my voice.

Dobby smiled, but it was a sad, slightly downturned thing. "Perhaps. But first, you must tell me what you know so far."

I filled Dobby in on what I knew about my power. Years ago, I'd discovered that I could nullify magic in various ways. If a wizard tried to cast a spell on me, for example, it would crash against some invisible force and simply fizzle out—a magical malfunction that left most spellcasters feeling emasculated at best. For those Freaks whose very essence was tied to magic of one sort or another—vampires, werewolves, and the like—this nullification manifested itself in a remarkable decrease in their speed, strength, and stamina. They became as weak, or as strong, as their human bodies would normally be, stripped of their supernatural mojo, essentially.

Lately, however, I'd realized that this ability was tied to a field which clung to me like a second skin. That field could be manipulated, even expanded; I'd done so a few times now, mostly on instinct. But recently, that field had been going haywire. A friend named Hemingway—also known as Death, one of the four Horsemen of the Apocalypse—had tested my field and walked away shaken. Then, a few days later, Johnny Appleseed had used me like a generator to plant a forest on the Brooklyn Bridge.

Talk about green energy.

And then, of course, there were the angels and demons I'd gone up against. "They couldn't touch me," I explained. "And I couldn't touch them. I didn't cancel out their power as much as repel it. Like oil and water," I said, stealing the phrase from an old acquaintance who'd seen me take one on.

Dobby nodded as if everything I said made perfect sense to him, which earned him a glare. He held up a hand. "I can't tell you much you haven't already learned on your own, my lady, except to say that nothing you have experienced is unexpected or presents a significant danger to you." He frowned, then. "Although perhaps it would be best if you refrained from testing the limits of this field you describe."

"Why?" I asked.

Dobby hesitated, considering his response. I fought off another brief flash of irritation and waited for him to explain. He sighed. "The one who tested your power, and the one who used it...I suspect you could inadvertently cause such extreme reactions in others with similar affinities, if you are not careful."

"Affinities?"

Dobby smirked, as if answering that question would give the game away. "You'll understand one day, if you are meant to. In the meantime, I would be wary of those you feel strongly attracted to, or repulsed by."

I massaged my temples. Dobby's riddles threatened to bring back the pounding headache I'd woken up with, but at least I knew that nothing was technically wrong with me—that my power wasn't on the fritz, which had been bothering me for a while now. It also explained, at least a little, my animal attraction to Appleseed, and my instinctual revulsion to Hemingway. I flopped on the couch and threw my arm over my face dramatically. "Why can't ye be a half-giant groundskeeper tellin' me that I'm meant to be a wizard?" I asked, with a sigh.

"Because my name's Dobby, not Hagrid," Dobby said, chidingly.

I winced, realizing Dobby had discovered the origins of his name. "Since when d'ye start readin' Harry Potter?" I asked.

39

"Your newest addition filled me in," Dobby said, sounding amused.

I shot him a questioning look, then tracked his stare to the houseplant on my windowsill. "Eve!" I yelled, exasperated.

"Did you know that J.K. Rowling's parents met at King's Cross Station?"

I ignored the plant, rolling my eyes, then turned my attention back to the spriggan. "T'wasn't supposed to be permanent," I said. "A joke, that's all."

"I do not mind," Dobby said. "I do serve you, my lady, as faithfully as my name suggests. So long as you know that I won't be cleaning up after you and would prefer to wear my own socks."

I grunted. "I don't t'ink I have any in your size, anyway. Speakin' of, how come you're gettin' bigger?"

Dobby studied his hand, turning it this way and that. "I am not...certain. It concerns me that I cannot recall ever having grown before. Although memories of my past are still...hazy." He glanced up at me, shrugged, and smiled. "At least I don't have to climb on things as often."

I snorted. "So, why d'ye break into me apartment and nearly give me a heart attack?"

The smile on Dobby's face fell. "I have an uneasy feeling," he explained, "and was compelled to come. I believe something has happened to Christoff. He has not visited since you left for New York City, and it seems the bar has been shut down for several days. I wondered if you could tell me if I was simply being paranoid, or if I have legitimate cause to be concerned."

"I'm not sure," I said, honestly, a sick feeling suddenly punching into my stomach and twisting. I didn't remember Christoff saying anything about taking a vacation before I'd left, and I hadn't spoken to him since returning. Honestly, I couldn't remember Christoff ever having gone on vacation; the man practically lived at the bar when he wasn't at home spending time with his wife and kids...or hunting deer in one of the state forests outside Boston.

Because—when he wasn't busy running one of the most popular bars in the city or being a dad—Christoff was a full blown werebear. A Kamchatka brown bear, to be precise. I'd only seen him shift once, to protect his friend and former bar manager, Ryan O'Rye, from the bridge troll I mentioned earlier. That's how we'd met, actually, and Christoff and I had been on friendly terms ever since. If anything, I thought of him as a kindly, Russian uncle...who could probably fit my whole head in his mouth if he ever felt so inclined.

"Does the bar usually close without warning?" Dobby asked.

I shook my head. "I don't t'ink it's ever closed, except when they're changin' the décor...but Christoff would never go on vacation while that was happenin'. And he'd tell you. He'd have told both of us." I swung my legs around and sat up. "Let's go to the bar and check in," I suggested, though I had a feeling I wasn't going to like what we found. Of course, that could have been the fact that all I'd had to eat so far today was pizza, and it hadn't stayed inside me for very long. "But first," I said, "let's snag some food."

CHAPTER 10

$\mathcal{I}$ peered through the darkened glass of Christoff's bar, hands cupped on either side of my face to block out the glare. The interior had been gutted, no longer cluttered by the myriad shades of green from the bar's previous model—a glorified celebration of all things St. Paddy's Day. I'd witnessed the transition several times over the years and recognized the bar's bare bones as a staging point, ripe with possibilities. Still, if that were the case, Christoff would definitely be nearby overseeing the change in decoration. The Russian businessman took micromanaging to a whole new level.

"What do you think, my lady?" Dobby asked.

"I t'ink I'm glad ye came by," I admitted, careful to make sure no one was around to hear me talking to my imaginary friend; Dobby had slipped on the Ring of Gyges and disappeared the minute we'd left my apartment. I'd tried calling Christoff on the way, hoping he'd answer and clear the whole thing up, but no such luck. I leaned back, studying my reflection in the glass. Beneath the thin veneer of makeup, I looked tired and strung out, my eyes bloodshot. I sighed, knowing I wouldn't be getting a nap anytime soon; since I hadn't found answers here, I could only think of one other option.

Christoff's house.

Christoff lived in Admirals Hill, a residential district in Chelsea which sat right up against the Mystic River. Chelsea, dubbed Chelsalvador by the less tactful Boston residents, was one of those unique cities which—after weathering catastrophes, rampant industrialization, racial tensions, and corrupt politicians—had emerged whole and healthy. Christoff and his wife had moved there not long after getting married, buying their house for a steal after Chelsea's stock plummeted in the early 90s. The neighborhood had seen a few shakeups since then, and their property had tripled in value. Christoff claimed their contacts in the area—the Russian Jews who'd settled there around the beginning of the 20th century and never left—were responsible for his success in America. Apparently, they'd fronted him the money to buy both his house and his bar, and he always spoke about his benefactors with great reverence.

I tried the doorbell first, then knocked. No answer. No cars in the driveway. I glanced at my phone and realized it was only a little after noon. Christoff's kids would probably be in daycare still, or maybe his wife had taken them out while she ran errands. No reason to be concerned. I walked around the side of the house and tried to peer through a window, but the blinds were closed. When I returned, I found the door standing wide open.

I stared, then bolted for the open doorway. "Christoff?!" I yelled.

"He's not here," Dobby said, startling me.

"But the door…wait, was that ye?" I asked, fuming.

"Wards," Dobby said, his voice retreating as he inspected the house. "You all need wards," he repeated drily.

I shut the door and wandered through Christoff's house. I'd been here before, around Christmas a few years back, at his invitation. I'd doubt Christoff was in the habit of bringing home all the strays that came to his bar, but I think he'd sensed something in me—my desire to be around people, but not among them, maybe—and offered, citing Russian hospitality as his excuse.

Ordinarily, I spent the holiday season with my aunt, Desdemona—who wasn't really my aunt but my mother's best friend and the woman who'd raised me after my mother passed.

But, since she and my mother had fled Ireland as young women during the Troubles, and we didn't have any extended family to speak of, Dez had found comfort in spending time with the matronly women in our congregation, a horde of pious gossipers if I'd ever seen one. Which meant, aside from the day before and the day after Christmas, I always ended up with a lot of free time on my hands. Maybe that's why I didn't turn Christoff down; drinking alone loses its appeal pretty fast when even your bartender has better things to do.

Back then, Christoff's house had been a rowdy place, obnoxiously full of light and laughter. His wife had hung Christmas lights on every available surface—winding down the bannister, across the mantle, and along the crown molding. Together, she and Christoff told their children stories of Grandfather Frost and the Snowmaiden at the dinner table, plying me with dishes I'd never seen before, eventually tasking me with painting an ornament to adorn their tree. Basically, the whole experience would have made a great Norman Rockwell painting.

But what I saw now was more like a Jackson Pollock.

The wallpaper and upholstery was torn and gouged, shredded—bits of drywall and leather-like confetti littered the ground. Blood spatter had dried in swathes along lampshades and paintings. The carpet muffled the sound of the broken glass I stepped on. I found myself wishing, irrationally, that I could take off my shoes; Christoff and his wife had been very adamant about not walking around the house in the shoes you wore outside, and I knew they'd be pissed.

If they were still alive.

While trying my best to watch my step, I nearly turned my ankle on a plastic children's toy, painted in blood. I hissed and hopped away, feeling momentarily overwhelmed. My heartbeat raced, and I realized I was on the verge of hyperventilating. What would I find here? Fear hit me like a physical blow to the chest; not fear for myself—I'd regifted that shit a long time ago—but fear for Christoff, for his family. I ground my teeth and forced myself to take a few deep, calming breaths.

In moments, I returned my attention to my more familiar, clinical calculations.

Bullet holes.

Blood spatter.

Claw marks.

All that signified that Christoff hadn't gone down without a fight, and may still be alive, on the run.

Or…upstairs. Dead.

My vision momentarily flashed red at that, but I squashed it down with a very literal gulp. What I needed now was answers, not conjecture, but there was too much chaos to sort through, and I wasn't Sherlock fucking Holmes. Unlike the crime scene I'd been to earlier, this one had been heavily trafficked. Lots of people. Lots of violence. There were bullet holes peppering one wall. Shockingly, none had shattered the windows or caused a stir in the neighborhood. I shook my head in frustration and drew my own pistol from the compression holster that rode my waistline, just to be safe. It didn't make any sense; the claw marks and blood spatter I could understand—Christoff was a werebear after all—but the bullet holes meant guns were involved...and not just any guns.

Contrary to popular belief, trying to gauge the caliber of the bullets from the bullet holes was a waste of time; most entrance wounds were indistinguishable from one another. But, based on the pattern, I could guess the gun was semi-automatic—the trajectory of the holes had an arc to it that comes with firing while moving. Which meant someone had come into Christoff's home with a gun designed to mow people down. Who would do that? And why? And, most importantly, what had happened to the people whose blood decorated the walls?

"Dobby?" I called, dreading what he might have found upstairs.

A crash from above made me jump. "Dobby!" I yelled, breaking for the stairs.

I ignored the shattered bannister and took the steps two at a time, raising my gun slightly; not sighting, but prepared to fire if I saw something worth shooting at. I headed for the sound of the crash, turned the corner, and was immediately pinned to the floor by the weight of a very large man, my gun skidding across the hardwood to end up beneath Christoff's bed.

I realized the fucker must have been hiding behind the doorframe, out of sight, waiting for me to come barreling in, and had used my momentum against me. I cursed myself for being reckless and not clearing the room like I'd been trained. Rookie mistake. The man ground his knee into my spine, yanked my arm behind my back, and pressed the muzzle of a gun against the back of my head. I stopped struggling but hissed out a painful breath. He sure was a heavy bastard.

"Who are you?" he demanded.

"Me and mine are goin' to murder everyone you've ever loved," I ground out, my every breath a struggle with him on top of me.

He grunted. "How'd you get in here?"

"Magic," I snarled.

He pressed the barrel into my scalp hard enough to squeeze my face against the floor. I was suddenly very appreciative of Christoff's no shoe rule. "Are you a witch, then? Or a wizard?"

"Neither. The door was open, ye moron."

He yanked on my arm again, harder this time. "What are you doing in this house?"

I tried to wriggle away, but his grip was locked firmly around my wrist. "Playin' hide-and-go-seek," I sneered, my eyes tearing up.

He dug his knee harder into my lower back.

"I'm lookin' for me friend, ye miserable bastard!" I admitted, the pain too much to ignore, and realizing I was in no position to threaten him.

The pressure eased somewhat, followed by a brittle silence. "What's your friend's name?"

I considered lying, or simply being obnoxious, but realized there was little point; he had me where he wanted me, and I wasn't going to improve my situation by pissing him off—I'd hoped he'd rise to the bait and give me an opening, but he'd proven too professional. Also, he wasn't sounding much like a murderer. "Christoff," I said. "His name's Christoff."

"Who is he to you?" the man pressed.

I grunted. "My bartender."

At that precise moment, I heard a loud *crack* and felt the man slump over onto my right side, collapsing to the hardwood in a heap. I hefted myself up, rolling him off me, and rose, wobbling, to my feet, prepared to fight. But the room, aside from the man who'd attacked me, was empty. I couldn't see the man's face; he wore a red baseball cap and a bulky dark blue jacket, both of which obscured his features in different ways. A baseball bat lay near the doorway.

"Sorry for taking so long," Dobby said, appearing out of thin air as he removed his ring. I'll admit, I almost peed myself. Almost.

"I'm gettin' ye a bell!" I hissed through gritted teeth, before fetching the assailant's gun. I could find mine later, right now I was worried about making sure he wasn't armed.

"If I had a bell, my lady, I doubt I'd have been able to sneak up on this..." Dobby looked down at the man and frowned, then promptly put the ring back on.

46

"Dobby? Dobby!" I groaned, then cursed. I didn't care if he had ended up saving my life with his invisibility trick, I was still going to get the spriggan a damn bell to wear around his neck; I was tired of him pulling a Houdini on me whenever he felt like it.

The man at my feet groaned. I took two steps back and pointed the gun at him. "No sudden movements, or I'll kill ye. Understood?"

"Feels like I got clocked with a hammer," the man said, his accent rough and Bostonian in a way I hadn't picked up on before, like he'd been hiding it. He rose to his knees and spotted the baseball bat. "Or a Louisville slugger."

"Now it's your turn," I said, waving his gun at him for good measure. "What are ye doin' here?"

"Well, Quinn MacKenna," the man said, casually dropping my name as if I'd given it to him, "I'd say I'm here for the same reason you are. Although Christoff isn't my bartender. He's my boss." He raised his hands and fiddled with his ball cap, the Red Sox emblem emblazoned across the front. He drew it back to reveal the face of the man beneath. He had one of those big, scraggly beards that made it impossible to tell how old he was, with otherwise unremarkable features, excluding his light blue eyes.

I didn't like strange hairy men with pretty blue eyes knowing my name. Usually. "Explain."

He grinned at my tone, clearly amused. "Sorry about putting the gun to your head. But you can never be too careful. The name's Robin. I'm Christoff's bar manager. Nice to finally meet you. Although I wish it could have been under better circumstances."

"Be careful, my lady," Dobby said, from beside me, causing me to jump. "He is not what he appears to be."

Robin's bushy eyebrows merged into one as he studied the empty air to my left, before eventually grunting. "So, that's what happened. For a second there, I thought you might be telekinetic or something. Christoff told me you were one of us, but never mentioned what you could do."

"She is not one of you, Redcap," Dobby hissed, sounding more animated than I'd ever heard him. It sounded almost like he was offended on my behalf, somehow.

Robin's eyes went wide, then narrowed to slits. He began to get to his feet, but I deterred him by waving the pistol.

"Nuh uh," I said. "Ye stay right where ye are and tell me why ye got so flustered when me friend here called ye that."

"It's his name," Dobby clarified. "Robin Redcap."

I frowned, a half-forgotten fairy tale springing to mind. Redcap. I stared at the ball cap on Robin's head, every exposed inch of it a deep, vibrant shade—the color of arterial blood. My own eyes widened. That was it. Redcap. Robin Redcap, one of the infamous goblins who dipped their caps in the blood of their murder victims, drawing power from it. In fact, according to legend, Robin was probably *the* most famous of his kind; he was the only redcap who'd ever been given a name.

Robin sighed and fussed with his hat again, bending the bill of it, a habitual gesture that would have been cute if it weren't for the fact that I suspected he'd used the very same cap as a bloody dishrag. "Your invisible buddy over there is right," he admitted. "I mean I don't usually go around telling people who or what I am, not that they'd believe me, anyway. But yeah, Robin Redcap."

"And ye say Christoff hired ye?" I asked. "Why should I believe ye?"

Robin shrugged. "Because it's true? He pulled me in on Ryan's recommendation a while back."

Robin's mention of Ryan O'Rye, an old friend and Christoff's former bar manager, made me hesitate. "But why would Christoff hire a redcap to run his bar?" I asked.

"The Redcap," he corrected, sounding mildly offended. "Well, he had to hire somebody from the Chancery to work for him, and I'd like to think I'm the lesser of several evils. Plus, I know my Scotch."

"The Chancery? Ye work for the Chancery?" I asked, raising the gun once more.

"Whoa! Of course, I do." He studied me, then cursed. "Right. I forgot they've got their eye on you. Look, I'm a rank and file guy. Whatever your beef with them is, it's way above my pay grade."

"What did ye mean when ye said Christoff had to hire someone from the Chancery?" I asked, choosing to ignore his comment, for now.

Robin gave me an incredulous look. "Standard policy. If a Freak in this town wants to run a business, no matter what it is, even if it's legal, they have to clear it with the Chancery, first. Then they get shackled with a partner, someone the Chancery trusts to report back." Robin shook his head at my expression. "It's really not as bad as it sounds. Sure, the Chancery gets to put its thumb in all the pies, but it also offers protection. Keeps the Freaks in line."

I considered that and nodded. It made a certain amount of sense, although it also begged the question: how had I been able to do my job for so long outside Chancery supervision? Or had they had their eye on me all along? I sighed, realizing I'd have to find out some other time. Right now, I had more important business to attend to.

I slid my finger over the trigger of Robin's gun. "Alright, so how about ye tell me why the Chancery didn't protect me friend?"

Robin gestured to his legs. "Mind if I stand up? This is murder on my knees."

Part of me felt like making the infamous redcap stay kneeling until his bones eroded; my shoulder and lower back still throbbed after his little stunt with the gun. But the other part of me appreciated his professionalism, even if it had been at my expense. The least I could do was return the favor. I gave him the go ahead, waggling the gun.

"Thanks," Robin said, as he lumbered to his feet. I realized he was a pretty big guy—a lot taller and broader than what I thought a goblin should be. Less ugly. And a lot less green. Honestly, between the Red Sox gear he wore, his size, and his epic beard, he looked like a Mike Napoli knock-off. "So," he said, after stretching his hamstrings, "I guess I should start with the good news, first. Christoff is safe. He showed up at the bar and I got him and his kids to one of our hideouts. Wards are up. Guards are posted."

A wave of relief hit me, and I almost dropped the gun, but years of experience prevailed, and I caught myself before it barely dipped an inch. Finding Christoff's bedroom corpse-free had given me hope, but there were several other rooms in the house, and deep down I'd dreaded stumbling on the rest of Christoff's clan. "Alright, good. So, what's the bad news?" I asked, bracing myself.

"The bad news is that whoever did this took his wife. And Christoff isn't talking." Robin sighed. "And, worst of all, while the Chancery definitely owes him protection, that protection won't stretch very far if he won't cooperate. I've tried to talk to him, but he's past reasoning with. I've never seen him like this. I know he wants to go after his wife, but he doesn't trust the Chancery to keep his kids safe. To be fair, we have a few members who think children make excellent appetizers," Robin admitted, shrugging. "So, he's stuck where he is, for now."

"For now?" I asked. "What happens if he doesn't start cooperatin'?"

"Depends," Robin folded his arms over his chest, obscuring the big Boston logo stitched across the front. "If they were smart, they'd use him and his kids as bait. Send them out, put a tail on them, and wait for whoever it is to come back and finish what they started. Fact is, they're trespassers causing a ruckus in the city—and they failed to announce themselves beforehand. From the Chancery's perspective, they're the priority. I think Christoff knows that."

Of course, he did. Which meant, situationally, he had no choice but to withhold information. Anything he fed to the Chancery would lead them to his attackers, but their goal would be to shut the bastards down, not save Christoff's wife. I had no idea how the Chancery operated, but I was willing to bet collateral damage meant less to them than imposing their will. It was also entirely possible that Christoff knew who had attacked him and why. Maybe they'd taken his wife for a reason. In the end, none of that mattered. I needed to see him for myself if I wanted answers. "Take me to him," I told Robin.

"It's not that simple," Robin said, shaking his head so adamantly that his bulky beard slid across the slick material of his jacket, sounding as if someone were zipping and unzipping their fly. "For all we know, you could be involved. That's why they sent me here, to check and see if anyone was poking around."

I rolled my eyes. "Oh, right, because I clearly have a motive for killin' one of me only friends, kidnappin' his wife, and returnin' to the scene of the crime," I replied. I didn't bother mentioning the fact that—if I'd planned to hurt Christoff or his family—they would never have stood a chance. Trust is a tricky thing; it's hard to live without giving it to someone, but at least then you didn't have to worry about a friend popping over to gun down you and your loved ones in your sleep.

Dark, I know.

But seeing that toy covered in blood...I realized being a pessimist had its advantages.

Like knowing exactly where to find your gun in the middle of the night. "Your sarcasm is noted," Robin said. "But I still can't take you to see him without permission."

I huffed, exasperated by the bureaucratic response. "Well, get your permission, then! Make the call, or whatever it is ye lot do."

"You're kidding, right?"

"Why would I be?" I asked, sliding my finger along the trigger of his gun, wondering if I could shoot his pinky finger off at this distance. I didn't want to do any permanent damage, or anything, just something to let him know I meant business.

"None of the Chancery's founders have cell phones," Robin explained. "They don't even have rotary phones. Most of us are old school like that. Why do you think we chose Boston in the first place?"

I blinked, wondering what that had to do with anything. Honestly, I'd never given it much thought; I'd always assumed the Fae had settled here because there were a lot of believers in this city—superstitious folk who dodged curses like they were speeding cars and threw as much salt over their shoulder as they put on their eggs. In my mind, it had always been a 'bees to honey' scenario. If you build it, Fae will come. When I explained this to Robin, he laughed like I'd said the funniest thing in the world.

I considered simply plugging a bullet in his jiggling belly, because I wasn't in the laughing mood, and gutshots were the ultimate buzzkill.

"Well, sure, but you've got it backwards," he said after his laughter died down. "We didn't settle here because of the believers, the believers settled here because of *us*," Robin said, wiping a tear out of one eye. He cleared his throat once he realized I'd raised the gun once more. "Listen, it's not your fault. Easy mistake to make. But you live here, right? Haven't you wondered why the bones of the old city haven't been tinkered with as much, here? Brick and glass and stone. That's what you'll find if you look hard."

"Why would that matter?" I asked, confused.

"Iron," Dobby interjected. "There's less of it here."

"See, Casper the Friendly Ghost gets it," Robin said.

What Robin said made sense, although I'd never given it much thought. The Fae hated iron, almost universally. Dealing with them individually was always tricky; you never knew which nonsensical thing would send a Faeling running—horseshoes, a branch from a rowan tree, the Holy Word of God. But you could typically depend on their aversion to iron. And Robin was right; after being declared historic landmarks, places like Beacon Hill looked more or less the same as they had in the early 1800s, which gave much of Boston an old, quaint feeling that encouraged tradition and super-stition in equal measure.

"Alright, fine. Let's say I believe ye. How do we get hold of your bosses?" I asked. "Because I don't t'ink I've got the patience to exchange letters."

"Hansel does like his letters," Robin said, then continued before I could respond. "It looks like you really only have one option, in that case," Robin said. "You go to them."

Of course, that's what he'd say.

Filthy goblins-es.

CHAPTER 11

The law office of *Hansel, Hansel, & Gretel* looked like one of those shabby townhomes you often find trapped between two buildings—the door too narrow, the steps too steep, the windows on either side like portholes on a ship. The cute little bronze sign displaying their name hung out front but drew no curious glances from passersby. Perhaps it was the curiously sad state of the place, or the fact that—as one of the many law offices that littered State Street—it hardly stood out among its peers.

"Did you bring it?" Robin asked, tipping his hat. He glanced at his fingers, which came away bloody, and popped them into his mouth.

"That's disgustin,'" I said, with a grimace. I hefted the bundle in my arms. "And aye, what d'ye t'ink this is?" I didn't bother mentioning that, along with the parcel, I'd brought Othello's disc—sort of like an insurance policy should the Fae try anything.

"Oh, please," Robin said, interrupting my thoughts. "This from the Manling who insisted on using a cell phone. You know how much bacteria you all carry on those things?" Robin shot me a disdainful look and took off across the street towards the law office, dipping between a lull in traffic. I rolled my eyes and followed, ignoring the curious gazes of more than a few people on the street. To be fair, we made an odd couple, Robin and I, especially with me carting around a bulky package. I tried not to think about what I had in my arms, or what I'd agreed to do, but it nagged at me even as I took the steps that led to the law office door.

After leaving Christoff's house nearly two hours before, Robin had given me the address to the Chancery headquarters. At first, I'd thought he was joking. But, after a quick Google search, I found out there was in fact a *Hansel, Hansel, & Gretel* office in Boston, though I couldn't track down a website or any images of the building from the outside. I wondered whether Robin had played a little fast and loose with his superiors' whereabouts, but —in hindsight—realized he was likely one of those old school Fae members he'd been talking about. It probably hadn't occurred to him that I might show up and launch a Molotov cocktail through the window for kicks. But then, most people didn't think like that.

They lacked the imagination.

Sadly, Robin had covered several other bases, including what I would and wouldn't be allowed to do once inside. In fact, he'd even gone so far as to tell me how to blend in, refusing to take me unless I agreed not to embarrass him. As if I would. Ordinarily, I'd have told him to fuck off, but with Christoff's life potentially at stake, I couldn't take the risk.

Concerned about Christoff's safety, Dobby had wanted to tag along as well, but—when he wouldn't tell me exactly why seeing the redcap had freaked him out so much—I'd vetoed the idea. I was getting tired of Dobby keeping secrets from me, no matter what his reasons were. If I couldn't trust him to tell me the truth, then I couldn't trust him to have my back, simple as that.

Besides, when Ryan had first asked me to take care of him, he'd mentioned the Chancery's unusual interest in spriggans, and warned me to keep Dobby out of their hands. The way I saw it, waltzing into their headquarters with him in tow would have been the same as gift wrapping him and leaving him on their doorstep.

So here we were, the fashionable arms dealer and the infamous redcap, about to enter a law office. There was a joke in there somewhere, but probably not a good one. "Do we knock?" I asked.

Robin nodded, then proceeded to knock nine times. Thrice at the top of the door, thrice in the middle, and thrice at the bottom. I shot him a curious look, which he noted only after the locks began to turn. "If you mess it up, the kobolds will try and eat you. It's not a good way to go."

I frowned. "Kobolds?"

"Shapeshifting sprites. Think boggart, or brownie. Only German, so they're always on time and they don't do small talk," Robin explained.

I glanced at my companion, trying to see if he was kidding, but couldn't tell. I hadn't come across a kobold before, but I'd heard of the other two from my aunt, who jokingly insisted we find one to clean our house for us —because that was something they did. Although, in this case, it seemed as though the kobolds' duty included taking care of a different kind of trash: unwanted visitors. "What about Regulars who stumble across this place?" I asked.

Robin glanced back at the people strolling down the street behind us and shrugged. "Well, at least they wouldn't have to worry about whatever legal trouble brought them here."

Before I could respond, the door opened, and a dapper older gentleman waved us through. He was a sprightly old man with shoulder-length hair, so blonde it appeared white in the dim light of the entranceway. His suit was tailored, but out of fashion by perhaps three hundred years. He checked a pocket watch—a real one, not a hipster knock-off—and smiled. "Right on time. Welcome. Hello, Robin."

"Hansel," Robin replied, ducking his head in acknowledgment. "Good to see you."

"And who is this young lady?" Hansel asked.

"Right. Quinn MacKenna, meet Hansel."

"Ah, yes. I believe we've sent a few notices your way, if memory serves." Hansel held out a hand to shake. "I hope our requests weren't too forward."

I stared at his hand, realizing the letters I'd received from the Chancery must have been drafted at this office. I briefly considered snubbing the man, if only to make myself feel better, but decided that would be childish. Besides, what would you do if a legend whose fairy tale you were raised on wanted to shake your hand?

Yeah, exactly.

"Don't ye worry about it. Although next time, I'd appreciate it if ye left it in me mailbox instead of puttin' it on me kitchen table," I said chidingly, as I shook his hand. "So, Hansel, eh? Like *the* Hansel?"

Hansel shrugged. "Well, one of them, at any rate. My younger brother and I have the same name. I assume you know our story?" he asked.

"Aye," I replied, though I hadn't known he had a younger brother. Hansel and Gretel in a nutshell: two kids are ditched in the woods by their parents, get kidnapped by a witch, do loads of clever shit, and come home to live happily ever after. Oh, but their mom dies. Because it's a German fairy tale.

"Well," Hansel continued, "after my sister and I were abandoned for the second time, our mother got pregnant. Sadly, she died giving birth to our younger brother, and my father—who was not a particularly imaginative man—gave him my name as a replacement."

Yikes. Imagine that, finding out your dad named your baby brother after you because he left you to die? "And the law office?" I asked, deciding to change the subject. "How'd ye end up here?"

"If you'll recall, we had a wealth of jewels at our disposal once we returned home. Practicing law has always been a noble profession...and it got us out of the woods. My sister has a particular knack for litigation, I believe you'll find. I, on the other hand, fell in love with copyright law. The fine print fascinates me. My brother's focus, interestingly enough, lies in genealogy."

"Is that so? And how much is your retainer?" I asked, idly, wondering what the going rate for a fairy tale lawyer would be.

Hansel's eyes widened. "Planning on needing a litigator anytime soon?"

I grinned wolfishly. "If there were no bad people, there'd be no good lawyers."

"Dickens!" Hansel exclaimed. "How delightful."

I nodded sagely, deciding not to reveal that I'd gotten the quote off a meme I saw last week while playing on my phone at the bar; in my experience, three-fourths of being brilliant was knowing when to shut the fuck up.

The rest was knowing when not to.

"Quinn wants to go below," Robin interjected.

"Oh, does she now?" The old man's eyes twinkled in amusement. He looked me up and down, then noted the parcel in my arms. "And you've explained the rules to her?"

"Most of them," Robin said, grinning. "I figured I'd let you do the honors."

Hansel nodded and waved for us to follow him. I fell in step behind Robin, feeling especially vulnerable walking around without my guns. That had been one of Robin's conditions. Weapons of any kind were forbidden, and I do mean any kind; Robin had given me a list. Like an actual paper copy.

I'd taped it to my refrigerator as soon as I got home.

Together, the three of us passed through a small waiting room and into one of the three offices, one of two with Hansel's name hanging on the door. "How d'ye know which is which?" I asked, pointing at the plaques on each.

"My brother's office can be opened remotely," Hansel said, indicating the other door, where I noticed a remarkably modern padlock." He's differently abled. To use the newest and most politically correct terminology." Hansel pulled a ridiculously ornate *Secret Garden* key out of his jacket pocket, unlocked his door, and waved us through.

Hansel's office looked like a turn-of-the-century lawyer's wet dream; leather-bound books lined the walls from floor to ceiling on all sides, each one a uniform height and color, their spines embossed with gilded lettering that might as well have been written in braille for all the sense they made to me. A thick oak desk—complete with a quill, a horrifically inaccurate globe, and a lantern—took up most of the room.

"To be certain you understand, Ms. MacKenna," Hansel said, shutting the door behind him, "let me review our expectations of you once more. The first rule is the most obvious; you will not reveal the whereabouts or entry conditions to anyone who is not already a member of the Chancery, knowingly or unknowingly."

"No talkin' about Fight Club, got it," I quipped.

"Quite. The second rule, which I'm sure Robin explained to you, is that no violence is permitted once you have descended into the lower level. Frankly, I'd prefer you keep the violence outside my building entirely, but one cannot have everything."

I snorted. "Aye."

"Lastly, to enter you must state your intentions, and you must do so clearly. I would recommend being as honest and forthright as possible with us, for your sake."

"Remember the kobolds?" Robin said, nudging me.

I grimaced, considering what Death by Housekeeping would even be like. Probably something involving detergent. And bleach. "So that's it?" I asked. "All the rules?"

"The ones worth mentioning, yes. Of course, there's social etiquette to consider. I trust you've come prepared on that front?" Hansel asked, gesturing to the bundle.

I sighed. I'd really hoped Robin had been lying about that part. I peeled off the tape sealing the parcel and unfolded one corner to reveal a racy black dress I'd bought on my way home—per Robin's suggestion. I'd always hated dresses, ever since I was a little girl; I'd always come home with tears in my skirts and bloody knees, begging my aunt to let me wear pants so I could play the way I wanted to.

Rough.

"So, where can I change?" I asked.

"First, state your intentions," Hansel said, idly studying the dress I'd chosen. "No sense ruining a perfectly good dress if you insist on lying. I'm sure Gretel would be glad to hem it, should you end up not needing it after all."

I couldn't tell if the old man was joking or not, but then maybe that was the point. I started to state my intentions, then hesitated. What *were* my intentions? Sure, I wanted to find Christoff, but that wasn't all I wanted. I had other questions for the Chancery. Like whether or not they knew about the recent killings, and what they wanted with me; before Ryan left, he'd warned me to stay away from them, that there were factions within the Chancery that would try and use me to their own ends. I didn't want to go down there and get sucked into a power struggle. I didn't have that kind of time. Or patience.

I took a deep breath. They'd asked me to be as honest and forthright as possible, after all.

"Me intentions," I said, staring down the two men across from me, "are to find me friend and his family so I can protect him from anyone who would hurt them, includin' ye Fae bastards. I plan to discover what ye lot know about the Jack the Ripper fucker who's out there killin' people in me town. And, most importantly, I plan to tell your superiors to go fuck themselves if they even t'ink about usin' me as a bargainin' chip."

The room was very quiet after that.

But I didn't end up getting attacked by malevolent housemaids, so…bonus?

CHAPTER 12

*H*ansel considered me for a moment, while Robin tried his best to pretend I didn't exist. Had I embarrassed him already? Oh well. The woodcutter's son barked out a laugh as he sat on the lip of his desk. "I think you and my sister would get along very well." He plucked a small white stone out of thin air and tossed it to me. "I think you may find much of that more difficult to accomplish than you think. Keep that, just in case."

I turned the stone over in my hands. It was smooth and round. Unremarkable. "What does it do?"

Hansel ignored me, walking around to the other side of the desk to fiddle with the quill and a bottle of ink. "Come, sign here, acknowledging you've understood the rules as I've explained them to you."

I frowned but did as he asked after briefly glancing over the contract, which seemed remarkably straightforward. I'd been prepared for a Willy Wonka style agreement, full of legalese and fine, nigh unreadable print. I signed it, awkwardly, flinging ink off the tip of the quill as I went, cringing at the scratching noise it made. Ironically, it reminded me a lot of the difficulties I faced when trying to sign an iPad with my finger.

Ballpoint pens for the win, all I'm saying.

"Now," Hansel said, after I finished, "once below, you may change in one of the adjoining locker rooms. I would, however, advise you not to wander into the shower area."

"The what?"

"Trust him," Robin said, nodding along, his eyes haunted. "There are some things you can't unsee." Then he physically shivered.

With that, Hansel spun the globe. I wobbled, gasping as the entire room began to descend. The mechanism made hardly a whisper as it took us down. For some reason, none of us spoke. The elevator effect, if I had to guess—the natural instinct to avoid potential conflict when in confined places with relative strangers.

We reached the bottom in under a minute, which didn't tell me squat about how far down we'd ended up. It didn't really make much difference, though; if I had to drill my way out, I was already fucked. Robin hopped off first, landing a foot further down on a hard marble floor that reflected light from up above. The chamber was otherwise dark.

I began to say something to Hansel but felt the old man's firm push at the small of my back, sending me over the edge. I stumbled off and, by the time I turned around, he was already heading back up, waving. "Don't wander off!" he called.

"Whatever ye say, Doctor Who," I muttered, under my breath. Now that Hansel was ascending, the light from his office was retreating, leaving us in a dim, cavernous space. I frowned. "Ye know I can't see in the dark, right?" I asked Robin.

"Give it a minute."

Once Hansel's platform had completely risen, shutting off all light, torches bearing balls of brilliant white light erupted in a wave along a long corridor that disappeared around a bend. I shielded my eyes, then glanced at Robin, who'd put on sunglasses. "Ye could've warned me," I hissed.

"You could have warned me you were planning to come here and start a war," he chastised. "I thought your business was with Christoff?"

"What can I say," I replied, "I'm a multitasker." I took a long look around, studying the beautiful, seamless marble floor and the elaborate torches. "Where does the smoke go?" I asked, looking for some kind of ventilation system.

"The smoke?"

"From the torches," I said, pointing.

"Oh. Yeah, not torches. Those are will-o-wisps."

I blinked, then approached one of the sconces on the wall and the ball of light floating above. It pulsed, as if sensing my attention. I drew back. "And they, what, work here?"

"They had to go somewhere," Robin said. "Modern electricity makes it impossible for them to run around on their own. Too conspicuous. Anyway, it's this way." He took off down the corridor, his sneakers squeaking as he went.

"So, what should I expect?" I asked.

"Once you get inside?"

"Aye."

Robin chuckled. "It's best if you don't have any expectations. You won't believe half of what you see, and you really shouldn't believe the other half. This is the closest you will get to Fae in the Manling realm." A thought seemed to occur to him. He glanced back. "Whatever you do, don't accept a favor. Of any kind. Even if someone offers you a glass of water, turn them down. You don't want to owe these people anything if you can help it." Robin turned back around.

"Is that how ye got involved, then?" I asked, sensing he had more to say on the subject.

"We all get roped into working for someone, one way or the other. If not for the Chancery, then for someone else. Keeping to yourself in this world isn't an option for one of the Fae. Eventually, the Manlings will cover every inch of this world, provided they don't destroy themselves, first. And then, we'll only have places like this left."

"So, d'ye like the way they do business, then?" I asked, genuinely curious. I wasn't sold on Robin Redcap's backstory. Sure, it was possible he worked for Christoff on Ryan's recommendation, even likely. But if I knew anything about the way the world worked, it's that everyone wanted something, even the Fae. Ryan had been all about the party; he enjoyed women and booze and making friends. Once you knew that about him, everything else fell into place. But I still wasn't sure what made Robin tick, or why he was helping me. And, call me a cynic, but unless I knew what was in it for them, every helping hand looked like a begging hand.

"I think you have a warped idea of what the Chancery is," Robin said. "You think we run this city, right? That we police it and control it?"

I shrugged, not disagreeing.

"Well you'd be right, but that's only one part of what the Chancery does.

We also offer asylum. We're basically our own nation, taking in refugees. Freaks and Fae alike. We find them jobs. Housing. And yes, the higher ups monitor activity in the city, but it isn't about playing Big Brother. It's about keeping us safe. Exposure is the enemy, but it becomes less and less of a concern every year. Manlings have made science their god, and science can't explain us, so we've been able to hide in plain sight."

"But isn't that a problem?" I asked.

"What do you mean?"

"A friend told me that ye lot draw your power from our kind, and vice versa. That, in Fae, Faelings tell Manling tales to their children the way we tell fairy tales to ours. If we cease to believe, won't ye cease to exist? Or lose your power, at least?"

Robin sighed. "That's a debate we've been having for decades, now. You've heard there's friction in the Chancery, right?"

I nodded.

"Well, some of us prefer anonymity to power. We'd rather live comfortably with Manlings than return to our former glory. It's easier for Fae like me," Robin admitted. "Before, I haunted castles and murdered people. It was in my nature. But the longer I've been away from home, the less murderous I've become. I don't live to kill or guard or serve. I live to live. And I don't want to give that up. But there are others among us, those whose power far exceeds my own, who crave their former glory."

"And who's in charge?" I asked, wondering which faction I'd be forced to contend with if I wanted to get Christoff back.

"In charge?"

"Aye. Like who should I speak to? Will I have to find a clerk or somethin'? Is there a judge I should speak to?"

Robin glanced back at me. "Sort of. But that's not exactly how the Chancery works. You'll see. You should get changed, though, before someone sees you."

I muttered obscenities under my breath.

These Fae and their riddles were going to be the death of me.

If I didn't kill them first.

 met Robin at the entrance.

"What the fuck is this, then?" I asked, indicating the double doors and the sign that hung above, which read *El Fae*. I'd changed into my dress and already felt uncomfortable, not the least of which because I'd had to conceal the disc, tucking it up into the underwire of my bra. I'd had to apply plenty of makeup to mask the bags under my eyes; even if I hadn't been hungover, I was sure I'd have woken up in a cold sweat, my skin clammy, my dreams lurking in my subconscious like a virus. Sadly, that was becoming more and more common lately; I'd begun drinking every night to cope. Still, I guess I looked alright because Robin—who'd donned a stylish pinstripe suit and a blood red fedora—whistled in appreciation upon seeing me.

"Ready?" he asked, ignoring my question.

I rolled my eyes but waved him forward. "Fine, then."

Robin turned, kicked the door with his heel—it didn't so much as rattle —and then stepped away.

"What, no kobolds?" I asked, mockingly.

Before Robin could respond, the doors swung open with a breathy whisper, and he urged me forward...into a different, heavenly world.

That looked remarkably like a bar.

A speakeasy, to be precise. If you've never been to or haven't heard of one, a speakeasy is a bar concept that was incredibly popular during the Prohibition Era—bars hidden in plain sight that could be converted at a moment's notice. When they weren't being used, they could look like anything: a gentlemen's lounge, a sitting room, a barber shop. But add a little liquor and a little music and suddenly you had yourself a speakeasy.

The *El Fae* had both. A live band played in the far corner of the room and a smoky haze permeated the place, adding to the atmosphere. Stunning— and by that, I mean truly ethereal—waitresses with excessively pierced, pointy ears dropped off drinks at tables whose occupants were hidden within the curve of the booths that encircled them. Clearly, privacy was a priority, here.

For those who preferred social interaction, a bar lined the far-right side, occupied by more than a few patrons, most of whom seemed content to enjoy the music and nurse their drinks, oblivious to Robin and me. A few, however, turned to look our way.

I'll admit, I wasn't prepared for what I saw.

I'd expected to run into a couple of odd-looking Faelings while I was here; they couldn't all look like Ryan and the waitresses, a shade too beautiful to be entirely human.

But I hadn't been prepared for this.

"It's the Irish girl!" a woman at the bar exclaimed, elbowing her companion, although the motion looked especially odd considering the woman's head hung in the crook of that very arm.

"Cassandra," I replied, waving slightly, surprisingly relieved to find a friend here. Well, somewhat. I ignored Robin's piercing stare and the questions warring across his face and focused instead on the headless horsewoman I'd met a few months ago—when she'd helped open the portal to send Ryan back to Fae. Back then, however, she'd been astride a horse. Now she straddled a barstool.

Cassandra hopped off her stool and sauntered over as the doors shut behind us. I noticed two ogres in standard bouncer t-shirts—all black and tight as hell—posted up at the entrance. Cassandra eyed Robin for a moment before dismissing him, turning slightly to introduce her companion, a woman with long, unruly black hair which obscured most of her face, including her eyes. "This is my girlfriend, Barbara. She prefers to go by Barb, though."

"Pleasure to meet ye, I'm Quinn," I said.

Barb said nothing. I realized Cassandra was weaving the fingers of one hand in the air, and eventually Barb did the same with two, her hands flying.

"Barb says it's her pleasure, and to tell you she loves your hair," Cassandra explained, grinning as she flicked a strand of my hair. "Very fiery."

"Oh, well, t'anks."

Cassandra conveyed my response, then turned to me, signing as she went so her girlfriend could follow the conversation. "Barb's deaf, you see. An occupational hazard that afflicts many Banshees who don't take their aural care seriously." Cassandra flashed her girlfriend a chiding look.

A deaf Banshee. A deaf, lesbian Banshee.

Rock on.

"What are ye doin' here?" I asked. The last time I'd seen Cassandra, she'd been escorting Ryan through a Gateway into Fae. After meeting her, I'd done some research on the Dullahan, the mythical headless horse riders, and discovered they had the unique ability to open portals from one realm to the other. Supposedly, that was their main duty when they weren't scaring the shit out of people on the Scottish moors. Cassandra, on the other hand, was the closest thing the Fae had to a media liaison; she monitored upticks in Fae and Manling interaction, which included overseeing various social media platforms. But, from what she'd indicated back then, she'd seemed less than impressed by the Chancery. Finding her here was definitely a surprise.

"I was invited, actually," Cassandra replied.

"I thought Cassandra might be interested to see what passes for entertainment here in the human realm," a man said, joining our conversation. He was about my height with medium-length, wavy hair, built lean and broad-shouldered, but trapped in the earliest stages of muscle growth—stuck in the body of a high school senior swim prodigy. He wore a thin v-neck cardigan that displayed far too much chest, a pair of light blue slacks, and boating shoes.

Oh, and he was blue.

Not uniformly blue, like a Smurf. But his skin definitely had a bluish tinge. His hair was two tones shy of navy and a full shade lighter than his lips, which were glossy and tinted, like black ice. By far what stood out, however, were his eyes—an icy, electric blue, several shades lighter than Robin's. He used these to look me up and down in a haughty, disdainful fashion that immediately rankled me.

"Quinn," Cassandra interjected, indicating the newcomer, "I'd like you to meet Jack."

"Jack Frost," he said, reaching out to shake my hand.

Robin hissed and even Cassandra seemed taken aback. Barb said nothing, but I got the feeling she, too, disapproved. I glanced at them and then at the proffered hand. "Why do I feel like I'm missin' somethin'?" I asked.

"Jack, that's very rude," Cassandra chastised.

Robin leaned in. "It's his power. He can use it to freeze you, turn you into a statue forever if he wants." Robin glared at the other man. "It would be very much frowned upon, but not technically violent. The ice would melt...eventually."

I didn't know whether or not to believe Robin, but if this really *was* Jack Frost, it wouldn't surprise me to find out he had that ability. Sometimes—especially when we're tucked away beneath blankets in front of a roaring fireplace with a mug of hot chocolate in hand—we forget what it means to freeze. We forget that winter used to be synonymous with death, and that it still is, in many places. That winter kept us locked away in our homes. It starved us out or stole our warmth away. The man in front of me represented all of those things—its cold beauty, yes, but also its cruelty.

I took a deep breath, deciding to give everyone something to talk about...

And accepted the bastard's freakishly chilly handshake.

CHAPTER 13

*N*othing happened.

Well, nothing happened to *me*.

Everyone else, Jack included, stared at me like I'd shoved a fork in a light socket. For a brief moment, I considered giving an Oscar worthy performance and acting like his frigid hand had frozen me solid but doubted I could win one by standing perfectly still in a dress. I mean, who was I, Keira Knightley?

"Nice to meet ye, Jack," I said, grinding his knuckles together for good measure. It was petty, but I'd taken a gamble by shaking the Faeling's hand, so I was feeling a little giddy, and maybe a little cocky that my field had worked as it usually did, for once. It felt like I'd leapt off a cliff into a frothing ocean and survived. "And to t'ink, I'd expected a chilly greetin' from ye lot...how silly of me," I said, eyes roving the room before settling on Jack.

He looked like someone had shoved an icicle up his ass.

Honestly, what I'd done was incredibly risky. But what you have to remember is that the Fae don't think like we do. Faelings might as well have coined the term "might is right." They respected one thing: strength. And I was stuck in a dimly lit bar underground with a host of beings whose abilities had earned them leading roles in children's nightmares.

Without weapons.

To them, I wasn't a threat. I was an oddity—a cat that could use the toilet. Jack's offer had revealed not only his disdain, but also what I could expect from many of the Faelings I was bound to run into in a place like this —subtle acts of mischief or malice that skirted the line between tomfoolery and torment. Manlings, even Freaks, were mere playthings to the Fae; our mortality made us cute, precious.

But I was no one's toy.

And now they knew that.

Jack stared down at our hands, blinking rapidly. Cassandra coughed into her hand. "Well, I'm glad to see the rumors weren't exaggerated. I'll admit, after watching Dorian Gray's latest Fight Night, I had wondered—"

"Wait, that was *you?*" Robin asked, incredulously, staring me up and down as if only just now recognizing me.

Jack finally pried his hand free and rubbed it self-consciously. "What are you all talking about?" he asked, clearly displeased to be left out, but eager for a change of topic from his frigid impotence. He folded his arms stubbornly—the first and only guest at his very own pity party.

"This young lady, whom I had the pleasure to meet once before," Cassandra said as she signed, making sure Barb could follow along, "took on Gomorrah. A Biblical entity. One of the Unclean."

Barb signed back at Cassandra, who nodded and replied with her own fingers, speaking as she went, "Yes, those. There's at least a dozen of them, from what I understand. Mercenary types. They don't serve any one individual for very long and can be contacted in various ways."

That was news to me. Until I'd run across Sodom and Gomorrah in New York City, I'd never even heard of the Unclean. Admittedly, the name sort of did all the work for me, but I'd done some research on my own. In fact, my Google search had netted a ton of results.

That was an hour of my life I would never get back.

At this point, I was simply glad I'd survived. Taking on a giant, millennia-old rock monster in a one-on-one brawl hadn't exactly been a walk in the park. If it weren't for the strange fluctuations of my anti-magic field and the overwhelming amount of firepower I'd had at my disposal, I'd be fertilizing a Master vampire's lawn right now.

"Contacted how?" Jack asked.

"Oh, you know, virgin sacrifices. Massacres. Betrayal of a loved one. Standard ritual procedures," Cassandra replied offhandedly, then patted

Barb—who'd flung her hands about in disgust—on the shoulder. "I know, very barbaric, I agree."

"Ah," Jack said, then thumbed at me. "And how did this Manling win against the creature she faced?" he asked in a tone that made it apparent he thought it a fluke—like the Unclean had tripped and knocked himself out by accident.

"I blew apart his leg and made him crawl on his belly," I replied, choosing to speak for myself. "He was rude and needed to be taught a lesson. Probably a side effect of bein' an immortal prick. Sound familiar?"

Jack sneered openly, lowering his arms aggressively, hoarfrost suddenly coating his knuckles.

"Quinn," Robin said eagerly, leaning in, "we should get moving."

I realized Robin was right; Christoff needed me, and I needed answers. The more time we spent delaying here, the less time my friend had. Besides, if this kept up, I'd be forced to knock Jack Frost flat on his ice-cold ass. "Right, lead on," I said.

"So soon?" Cassandra asked, pouting. "What're you doing here, anyway? Surely you don't make it a habit to visit this establishment."

"She's meeting with a Court representative," Robin replied. "Which means she's expected." His tone implied that this reason alone should satisfy Cassandra's curiosity, or at least convince her to leave us be.

"Oh? Which one?" she asked, unperturbed.

"Which one?" I echoed, suddenly curious.

"Well, yes. The Seelie or the Unseelie Court," Cassandra replied, as if I should know what that meant.

I turned to Robin, who appeared put-off.

"Oh, I see," Cassandra said. "You haven't explained how things work here, I take it?"

Robin grumbled something under his breath that I didn't catch. I frowned at him, then Cassandra, wondering why everyone was being so fucking weird. I was already here. I'd put on the stupid dress, and I'd pissed off Mr. Freeze. Couldn't we just cut to the chase already?

I mean, Robin was helping me, sure, but I still hadn't figured out what he was getting out of it. Meanwhile, Cassandra had already made it pretty clear what she wanted—the pleasure of my company, to put it politely. Of the two, however, she seemed the more straightforward, bordering on blunt.

"Would ye mind fillin' me in?" I asked.

"Certainly," Cassandra said, brightening. "As I'm sure you know already, there is a balance of power that must be upheld for any organization to function. Your government, for example, runs on a three-branch, essentially two-party model. The Chancery saw the wisdom of adopting a system to control their wilder impulses and, as a result, chose to mimic the governing arrangement of the Fae realm. Though they've done a truly shit job of it, I must say. They've become far too much like you Manlings with their politics and their compromising."

Barb signed something.

"Yes, yes, I know," Cassandra replied, sighing. "Sorry, I'll keep my personal opinions to myself. Basically, the Seelie court represents what you might call the 'good' Fae. The ones who don't actively try to eat you or ruin your crops or steal your children. The Unseelie are those you would try to avoid on a moonlit evening, or in a dark cave, or a forest in the middle of nowhere. They are less remorseful. In the Chancery's case, the two operate on a checks and balances system—all legislation requires a majority vote. In the Fae realm, however, one side or the other holds sway and it generally stays that way for a good long while."

"Which court is in charge right now?" I asked, curious.

"Mine," Jack Frost said, puffing out his chest, probably compensating for his weak ass handshake. He'd been surprisingly silent during our exchanges up until now, glancing at the door as if waiting for someone to arrive.

Cassandra eyed Frost skeptically. "At present, I don't know that either has complete control. As you'll recall, there has been significant upheaval lately."

I realized Cassandra was likely referring to the death of Ryan's father and the defeat of the Faerie Queens, both of which had taken place a few months ago; Ryan had been recalled from exile shortly thereafter as a result. I had no idea what the precedent was for such a thing, but—even glancing around the speakeasy—I could sense the unease, the palpable tension.

Almost like a war was coming.

Jack waved her comment away, leaving a trail of frost glittering in the air. "The Queens have everything in hand. King Oberon's allegiance has been secured. Soon things will return to normal. *Wylde*," Jack spat a phlegm-cicle at the ground as he said the word, "*the Manling born in Fae*, will be dealt with in due time."

"'That remains to be seen,'" a Faeling said from a nearby booth. I noticed the band of musicians had fallen silent, perhaps taking a quick intermission.

Jack stiffened, and both Barb and Cassandra whirled around.

"Regardless," the interrupting Faeling continued, "the Queens' servants will find no refuge here, Jack Frost. And neither will you, if you insist on picking fights in the *El Fae*. Winter has come and gone. No matter how hard you blow, you will not make it come a second time." The Faeling slid out from the booth, rising in a fluid motion that screamed inhuman.

I lost it, wondering if the double entendre there was intentional. "Please," I said, trying to contain my laughter, "if his punches are anythin' like his handshake, I'll be sure to leave the windows open."

Jack bowed slightly, lowering his eyes, ignoring me entirely. "That was never my intention, forgive me."

"It is not my forgiveness you should be asking for," the Faeling replied.

Jack turned a baleful eye my way and inclined his head. "Please accept my apologies."

I wavered back and forth; I knew it would feel really good to tell the infamous Jack Frost to go fuck himself, but I needed to cultivate at least a little goodwill if I hoped to find answers and being bitchy wouldn't do me any favors. "Apology accepted," I replied.

"Ladies," Jack continued, dipping his head towards Cassandra and Barb, "you must forgive me, but I believe it's time I take my leave. I hope you enjoyed your visit." He took a shuffling step back, then turned on his heel and rapidly headed for the doors. The ogre bouncers had to rush to let him out.

The Faeling who'd spoken watched Jack leave with half-lidded eyes and pursed lips, which gave me plenty of time to study him. Unlike Jack Frost, this Faeling had the body of a fully grown and powerful man, as aesthetically pleasing and proportionate as any I'd ever seen. He was also green. If Jack's aspect had been winter, then this Faeling's was spring; his beard was made of twigs and bushes, each strand of his hair a leaf, his teeth carved from the wood of birch trees. He wore a black button-up beneath green suspenders, the sleeves rolled up to reveal thick, veiny—make that viney —forearms.

"Sir," Robin said, bowing neatly, one hand securing his fedora, "let me introduce Quinn MacKenna. Quinn, this is the Green Knight."

The Faeling waved that away. "A pretentious title, from a different time. Please, call me Bred."

Okay, fangirling in three, two, one...I cut myself short with a quick breath.

Play it cool, Quinn. Play it cool.

Bredbeddle, or Bred for short. The Green Knight. As in *Sir Gawain and the Green Knight*. If you haven't heard the legend, let's just say he's a mysterious and powerful figure who—after interrupting festivities long enough to have his head chopped off—eventually judges the worth and loyalty of Sir Gawain, one of King Arthur's entourage. I had no idea what he was doing here, of all places, but I had to admit I was incredibly curious.

Unlike many of the myths and legends I'd had to research over the course of my career, I'd grown up on Arthurian tales of heroism and intrigue; while Dez was staunchly Catholic and exceptionally anti-British, she'd always had a soft spot for King Arthur and the Knights of the Round Table. When I was a little girl, I used to strip the broom down to its handle and jab at the empty air, fighting to defend Camelot from its dastardly enemies. Hell, I had a whole slew of corny King Arthur jokes at my disposal.

Who made the Round Table?

Sir Cumference.

"Sir Bredbeddle is one of the court Adjudicators," Robin explained. "He represents Fae interests and serves as their voice."

"Your voice, as well, Robin," Bred added.

Robin ducked his head. "Of course, sir."

"So, do we shake hands? Or will that get me turned into a tree?" I asked.

Cassandra barked a laugh.

The Green Knight grunted and extended his hand. "I swear on my power that I will not turn you into a tree."

I eyed his hand suspiciously. "That was remarkably specific. Ye could just as easily turn me into a bush."

Robin glared at me, but I was too busy having fun to care. The Green Knight didn't seem to mind. He seemed to surprise even himself by chuckling, then he rescinded his hand and bowed formally at the waist. "Better?" he asked.

"Aye, but I t'ink you'll be bent over for a good long while if ye expect me to return the favor," I admitted. "Pretty sure I'd tear this poor dress in half if I tried to curtsy."

"No harm in trying, dear," Cassandra chimed in, gazing at me lasciviously. "Manners and all that."

I shot her a look and she flung her free hand up. "Fine, fine," she said, grinning mischievously. "I can see we're only holding you up. We'll follow Jack's lead and get out of your hair."

"Cassandra of the Dullahan," the Green Knight said, drawing her attention. "I wasn't aware you sought entrance, or else I would have formally invited you long ago. Forgive me."

Cassandra shrugged. "No need to be so formal. We both know why I've avoided this place until now. To be honest, the only reason I took Jack up on his invitation was so I could try one of your famous cocktails."

I pointedly avoided dwelling on the physics of Cassandra drinking anything and focused instead on what a Faeling cocktail would even taste like.

Sunbeams and moonshine, I bet.

"I realize you've been mistreated by the exiles among us," Bred replied, sympathetically. "But you must understand, those who pass freely between realms are stark reminders of what our exiles have lost. They are like children lashing out."

The exiled Fae. Ryan had told me all about them, cautioning me to avoid them if I could. In essence, they were Fae who—for various reasons—had been forced to leave their home world. In fact, you could say the Chancery had become their haven, their sanctuary. Here, they could at least pretend to be what they once were. In that light, Cassandra's disdain for the Chancery made sense; nostalgia like that could be unhealthy, even dangerous.

I frowned as a thought hit me. "Are ye not an exile as well, then?" I asked Bred. It had occurred to me that he'd apologized on their behalf, but not as one of them.

"We take in our fair share," Bred noted. "But the majority of our people are asylum seekers, like Jack. Running from something or someone in the Fae realm. There are also those who came here and decided to stay, for one reason or another."

"Which were you?" I asked.

"The latter," the Green Knight replied.

"And why d'ye stay?" I asked.

"The only reason any of us stay," Cassandra interjected. "He fell in love."

Bred glanced at her in surprise. "That was a long time ago."

Cassandra shrugged, again.

"And now? Why are ye still here?" I asked.

Before he could respond, the speakeasy shuddered. The chandeliers swung, and the warm, refracted light pitched back and forth, spitting out shadows. As one, we gazed up at the ceiling, then back down at each other.

That's when the doors blew open.

CHAPTER 14

*T*he two beefcakey ogres went down first, crushed by the weight of the double doors. A howling storm blew through the gaping doorway, the gales strong enough to send more than a few patrons toppling from their seats. Many ducked for cover under the tables or behind the bar. Glass shattered and the Will-o-Wisps—clearly uncomfortable with the state of affairs—fled, leaving only the light from the distant hall to see by. Bred stepped in front of us, his broad back obscuring the view, but also providing shelter from the wind. I frowned and stepped around him, unperturbed by the vicious windstorm; unlike the rest of those present, it hadn't so much as ruffled my hair.

A Faeling stepped into the gaping doorway, her hands held out like claws, small cyclones of air spinning around each finger. She, like so many of her kind, had the face and body of a flawless supermodel. If that supermodel had been cast as the bitchy psycho in a remake of *The Craft*; with all that leather and punk rock angst, she looked like sex and violence had made a baby.

"Morgause!" Bred bellowed. "Enough!"

The winds died as abruptly as they'd begun and the Faeling, Morgause, lowered her hands. "I want to know who did it," she said, her voice husky and full-throated, engineered to deliver threats.

"You have broken the laws of this place, Morgause," Bred replied. "You cannot demand—"

"I do not care about your paltry peace, Bred! Tell me who brought him back," Morgause demanded. "Tell me who freed Mordred. Tell me who freed my son!"

Silence descended on the speakeasy like an atomic bomb. The faces around me paled, and even Bred seemed taken aback by her question. Mordred...I recognized the name almost immediately. According to the legends, he was the unfortunate offspring of King Arthur and Morgause—a legendary enchantress and Arthur's half-sister. Icky, I know. Mordred was also reputedly the man who killed Arthur. This was turning out to be quite the family drama.

Like a medieval soap opera.

And here I was with no popcorn.

"I swear to you I had no idea he'd been freed," Bred replied. "Where is he now?"

"As if I'd know that!" Morgause hissed. "I don't care what you say. If it wasn't you, it was one of your people. Who else would know where his cage lay? Who else could find him? Tell me, or I'll tear this place to pieces!"

I honestly couldn't tell who she was more pissed at, Bred, or her son, Mordred.

In the end, it really made no difference; Morgause, who was clearly enraged beyond reason, didn't even bother to wait for a response before lashing out once more. The winds struck again, only this time with enough force to send chairs and shattered glass flying. A martini glass swung around and clipped my arm, the stem breaking on contact. I cursed and hunkered down behind Bred. Maybe using him as a shield wasn't such a bad idea after all.

I heard chandeliers crash to the ground and the band's brass instruments collide with the walls, a clash of sound that made me put my hands over my ears. Which was convenient, because that was precisely the moment that Barb finally decided to rock out.

Or scream, rather.

Barb's shriek was inarticulate and full of rage. I glanced back and saw that Cassandra had been struck by some debris as well; her leg was bleeding from a shallow cut. But what captured my attention was the fact that the Dullahan had changed, somehow. Cassandra's once attractive face had become waxy and pale, her mouth leering and wider than I would have thought physically possible—teeth filed to wicked points and pressed together like the jaws of a bear trap. She cracked a whip in her free hand, its tip piercing the marble floor. The whip itself was garishly white and oddly shaped. I stared at it, then grimaced.

A spine.

Her whip was a human spine.

The wind changed direction the instant Barb's piercing scream hit the air. It began to form a funnel around Morgause, obscuring her from view within the eye of the storm. Brief flashes were visible as the funnel swirled, brief flashes of light barely visible. Morgause was using the wind to block out the sound of Barb's scream, I realized, and preparing a counterattack. Things were about to get real ugly.

I knew I should have brought my damn guns.

The Green Knight settled a hand on Barb's shoulder, and her screams faded. "Leave her to me and go, all of you," he said, roughly thrusting the banshee back towards her lover. "This is Chancery business."

Robin snatched my sleeve. "Come on, let's go!"

I shook him off. "Are ye serious? I can't leave yet. Not without knowin' where Christoff is." Granted, I had a bunch of other questions to ask in addition to that one, but most of them could wait until everything slowed down a little...once Mommie Dearest wasn't plotting to kill us all.

"We don't have that kind of time," Robin said. "We're a hundred feet below ground, and the last time I saw her this pissed off she took out half the northeast."

"And how d'ye figure we're gettin' out of here?" I asked, pointing towards the whirling storm clouds. "Last I checked, that's the exit. And, more importantly, me clothes are back there!" I growled, gesturing at the skintight, but ultimately inelastic dress that covered me like a second skin.

Robin grimaced, realizing I had a point. To flee, we'd have to walk through a thunderstorm with a cranky immortal enchantress on the other side. Not exactly high odds of success, there. "Well," he said, "you seem to be immune to her magic, maybe I could distract her while you—"

"While I run away in this dress?!" I asked, throwing my hands up and gazing towards the heavens as if God might be able to save me.

Turns out, I didn't need Him.

Because I had a not-so-secret admirer.

"Come on!" Cassandra shouted, suddenly yanking me by one arm towards a Gateway she'd created behind the bar. A host of other Fae had already poured through it and promptly disappeared. I noticed Cassandra's appearance had gone back to normal, and Barb was waving Faelings through like a stewardess on an airplane. On the other side of the Gateway, I could see a bright, open pasture upon which Cassandra's horse—a gorgeous, all black stallion—grazed. His enormous head popped up, ears flicking back and forth to chase off industrious flies, seemingly oblivious to the commotion behind us.

Robin bumped into me from behind in his haste to catch up, causing me to glance back over my shoulder. The storm still brewed, and it seemed The Green Knight had taken on the full weight of his title; armor, in layers so copious that I couldn't see how anything could get through it, had materialized over his whole body. Small tree limbs poked out here and there from between the plates, spiking outward like barbs, and upon his head he wore a crowned helmet which rose to a series of points like a deer's antlers. In his right fist was the cruelest, wickedest axe I had ever seen—looking at it made me physically cringe.

Robin thrust me through the portal and I fell onto the grass. Lightning struck behind us, crackling as it arced through the opening above my head, chased by the sound of thunder. Cassandra spun and released the Gateway, cursing. I rolled over and took a few deep, calming breaths.

Then I sat up and punched Robin in the stomach.

The redcap doubled over. "What was that for?" he asked, wheezing.

"What d'ye t'ink it's for, ye idgit? I followed ye into a death trap, I'm stuck in a dress in a field in the middle of nowhere, and ye didn't even get me Christoff's address!"

Robin hissed and nodded. "Guess I deserved that, yeah."

"Aye. Now, tell me what ye plan to do to fix it," I demanded.

"Well, I would say we meet with the Chancery's other Adjudicator, not Bred, but that's out," Robin said.

"Why's that?" I asked, glaring at the man as I fought to stand, my heels sinking into the grass.

"You just met her."

The string of profanities that left my mouth would have made anyone's ears burn.

But that was alright, because I was half-tempted to set the whole world on fire, anyway.

O nce I'd calmed down and found a nice comfortable rock to sit on, I weighed my options. I knew Christoff and his kids were being held somewhere in Boston, likely in one of the Chancery's safehouses. I'd counted on the Chancery's cooperation to get me in the door, but, without it, I was back at square one. Well, maybe square two—at least now I knew a little more about how the Chancery operated; Robin, probably fearing that I'd beat the living shit out of him if he kept anything else from me, had divulged everything he knew about the shady organization shortly after we arrived, while Cassandra made new Gateways for the Faelings who'd fled with us.

According to Robin, both Morgause and Bred were Adjudicators who represented Unseelie and Seelie interests, respectively. Each was responsible for maintaining their side of the fence—nurturing growth and pulling weeds as necessary. To my surprise, that meant the majority of the Fae in town were given their autonomy, although—now that I knew how their judicial system worked—that sounded an awful lot to me like they were being given enough rope to hang themselves.

Incoming Faelings—Fae exiles like Ryan, or remnants like my friend Paul the bridge troll—were swept up into their respective party, given a rundown on the do's and don'ts, and promptly given a place in society.

In Paul's case, that meant being given a bridge to sleep under in exchange for not eating people, and the occasional construction gig; I was betting he'd end up working overtime trying to repair the *El Fae*. For Ryan, it had meant working for Christoff at the bar and entertaining high-profile guests whenever they came into town.

When I asked him how he knew so much about my friends, Robin confessed that it had been his job to keep tabs on his fellow Fae. That, in fact, he'd never even met Ryan; his recommendation letter had been forged.

"Ryan being called back caused a bit of a stir," Robin explained. "Sir Bred sent me in to work for Christoff to find out what I could, to see what it meant for the Chancery. He was worried about the possibility of a mass exodus, should the exiles be allowed to return home in bulk."

"You're a spy," I hissed, angrily yanking my hair down from its artful bun. There were worse things I could have called him, but I'd done my fair share of intelligence gathering, and wasn't about to start chucking stones.

Robin nodded, then hung his head in shame. "It's not glamorous, I promise you." He looked up, his baby blues catching the light like sapphires glittering in his earnest face. "But I want you to know, I do want to help. Working for Christoff...he's a good guy, and a fair boss. Never asked me to do anything he wouldn't do himself. He knew what I was, who I was working for, right away, but never made a fuss about it. He even let me design a few cocktails and listened to my input..." Robin trailed off.

I grunted. "Aye, I get it," I finally muttered. And I did. I'd always been a bit of a loner, especially after I branched out on my own to start working as a dealer. I'd always told myself I preferred it that way, that getting close to people was a liability I couldn't afford. But then I'd met Christoff—a man willing to invite me to celebrate a holiday with his family. That's when I realized it wasn't getting close to people that bothered me, it was simply that I found most people repulsive. It had taken meeting Christoff—a truly good, worthwhile person—to redeem my faith in humanity.

And he wasn't even fully human.

"So, what now? Will you let me help?" Robin asked.

I sat back and pondered his question. Weirdly enough, I trusted the redcap now more than I did before. I'd known something was off about him from the beginning; after all, no one acts for purely altruistic reasons—even saints believe they're serving a higher purpose. So, Robin wanted to help because he felt guilty for spying on his boss, and because Christoff had shown him respect. That, I could buy.

"Tell me about the *El Fae*," I said, finally. "What's a speakeasy doin' beneath a law office in the middle of Boston? And ye do know it translates into 'the Fae', don't ye? Which means we're sayin' *the* the Fae...That'd be like me openin' a bar and callin' it 'The Human.'"

Robin cocked his head and stared at me, not comprehending.

I sighed. "Go on," I mumbled, giving up.

"The name is based on one of the original speakeasies in New York City," Robin replied, shrugging—clearly not concerned with cultural sensitivity. "I didn't pick it. Anyway, the *El Fae* is neutral territory," he explained. "A place for both sides to meet and share a drink, gossip, maybe talk a little trash."

"So, what keeps either side from attackin' the other?" I asked.

Robin grunted. "Typically? The Adjudicators. The threat of being disciplined by them keeps most Fae in line. Ironically, that means—if the two don't kill each other this time—Morgause will walk away from this with a slap on the wrist."

"Why the fuck would ye want those two in charge?" I asked, baffled.

"It's not about what we want. It's just how things are. Hansel and his sister handle the sentencing, but either the Green Knight or Morgause execute the punishment. When and if someone more powerful comes along, the mantle and the responsibility transfers to them," Robin explained. "Theoretically."

Of course. It made sense, given the fact that the Fae believed that power defined status, not the other way around; it didn't matter whether Bred or Morgause were qualified, it mattered whether they could enforce their laws. Whether they were scary enough. "How long have those two been Adjudicators?" I asked, a sneaking suspicion whispering in the back of my mind.

"Since the Chancery was founded."

"Well that's just fuckin' brilliant," I cursed. In essence, the Adjudicators had run the show, unopposed, for centuries. Robin nodded in agreement, but I could sense he was holding something back. "Out with it," I said.

The redcap sighed and settled on a rock of his own. "Remember when I said there were members of the Chancery who want to amass power? To step back into the light?" Robin asked, staring out at the horizon.

"Aye."

He met my eyes. "Bowing to power has never been a perfect system, but things have been that way for ages, long before we came here. Lately, though, there have been rumors that things are about to change. Cassandra's right, many of us have been seduced by Manling ideals, especially equality. Some Fae believe, if they can gather enough power, they can revolt. That they can change the system. Make it fair and give everyone a voice."

"And how about ye?" I asked, not missing the wistful gleam in Robin's eyes. "I thought ye said ye prefer your anonymity."

"I do. But you saw how casually those two began throwing their weight around. How long before we get caught in the crossfire? Many of us fled the Queens' influence so we wouldn't have to fight and die for causes we didn't believe in."

I was beginning to understand why Ryan had warned me to stay away from the Chancery before he left. Until a moment ago, I'd thought the factions he'd been worried about were the Seelie and Unseelie—the good and the bad—but now I knew better.

This wouldn't be a war between good and evil, but between ideologies. The Chancery was on the verge of a rebellion—possessed by the very same revolutionary spirit that had toppled governments in my world. It made sense now that Ryan, who had suspected things would escalate eventually, knew I would end up on their radar, because if there was one thing you could count on in a revolution, it was that both sides would want to be armed.

And guess who could cut them a deal?

A thought I should have entertained long ago occurred to me. "Wait, so how d'ye lot die, then? I thought ye were supposed to be immortal."

Robin shook his head. "There are different degrees of immortality. The weaker you are, the greater the risk. That's why most joined the Chancery to begin with. For protection. Compared to how fragile Regulars are, it may seem that way, but being exceptionally long-lived and damage resistant isn't the same as being immortal. Though there are some among us, like Morgause and Sir Bred, who can withstand so much damage and live so long that it may as well be true."

"And where d'ye fit in?" I asked.

"He's a deserter," Cassandra chimed in, clomping over on horseback with Barb perched sidesaddle in front of her. "But I suppose that makes him a survivor, too, in a way."

Robin hung his head for a second time.

"A deserter?" I asked.

"Indeed," Cassandra replied. "No one leaves Fae forever without a reason, after all. Your friend Robin here was once Captain of the Redcaps. Their leader. Many years ago, he and his people fought for the Winter Queen. Her personal guard. Then he left and abandoned his people to roam the Scottish moors."

"It wasn't like that," Robin said.

Cassandra shrugged. "I'm not judging. Although I must say I think it's pathetic, what you've done with yourself since. Spying for the Chancery... it's beneath you."

"I wanted to have a life, that's all," Robin whispered, his expression pained.

The regret in Robin's voice surprised me. He sounded so human. But then, why shouldn't he? I frowned, realizing I'd always thought of the Fae as *other*, as an alien species—their wants and needs somehow different than my own. That's why I'd always kept Ryan at a distance; you can't trust someone you fundamentally don't understand.

But the Faelings I'd met recently had proven time and time again that they really weren't that different from us: Paul was mortally afraid of falling asleep without a structure over his head, like a child without his nightlight; Ryan had missed home so much he'd chased women like it was his job; and Robin, it seemed, had gotten so tired of war that he'd run away from the world, willing to do whatever it took to make his own decisions.

Turns out the Fae were people, too.

Weird-looking, obscenely powerful people. But people.

"Cassandra," I said, opting to change the subject before I ended up over-whelmed by any other epiphanies, "where are we, anyway?" I'd tried to call Christoff once we arrived on the off chance he'd gained access to his phone, only to discover I had no bars, which was odd since I'd gotten my phone from a tech guru friend of mine. My guess was Cassandra had found us a remote spot in the Massachusetts wilderness—someplace where even satellites were out of reach.

Cassandra took a quick look around and sniffed. She stuck a finger in her mouth and held it in the air, then peered up at the sun. "Somewhere in Wales, I think." She patted her horse's flank. "He prefers their grass."

Wales.

We were in fucking Wales.

"What's the matter?" Cassandra asked, marveling at whatever she saw on my face. I held up a hand. How could I explain to Cassandra that she'd inad-vertently taken my international traveling virginity?

On second thought, maybe I'd keep that to myself.

"I hate magic," I growled, finally.

assandra's Gateway snapped shut behind Robin and me a moment
after we stepped into Christoff's living room. At first, I'd planned
to have Cassandra drop us off at my apartment. But, after considering the
possible consequences of the flirtatious Dullahan knowing where I lived, I'd
vetoed that plan. Besides, I had to be careful not to let anyone find out
about Eve if I could help it; I'd promised Johnny Appleseed to keep the
budding Tree of Knowledge a secret, to keep it safe, and I planned to keep
that promise. Besides, if Cassandra poked her head in and Eve started
spouting out equestrian facts for the next two weeks, I'd probably leap out a
window.

After some careful deliberation, I'd given Cassandra the only address
that made sense: Christoff's house. The scene of the crime. I glanced down
at our feet and the muddy imprints we were leaving on Christoff's carpet
and grimaced. We really had to rescue him and his family; otherwise I was
pretty sure the Russian werebear and his wife were going to kill me.

Russians were sticklers for having pristine house shoes so as not to track
filth onto the floors.

"So, what are we doing here, exactly?" Robin asked.

I held up a finger, retrieved my phone, and dialed.

"Agent Jeffries," a voice on the other end said.

"It's Quinn MacKenna, Agent Jeffries."

"Oh! Quinn," Jeffries was quiet for a moment. "That was fast. It's only been a few hours. Did you find anything for us?"

"Well, no, not exactly."

Jeffries cleared his throat. "So…"

"Is it true the FBI handles kidnappin's?" I asked.

Robin shot an alarmed glance at me, which I ignored; it was his turn to be left in the dark for a change.

"Sometimes, yes," Jeffries replied. "That's really not my squad's forte, though."

"And if the kidnappin' in question were to involve, say, a werebear and his family?" I asked, trying my best to sound flippant.

Jeffries cursed. "This is the part where I really wish I knew if you were being serious or not." He sighed. "Why do you want to know?"

"How about if I said it's because I'm standin' at the scene of the crime and there's too much blood and too many bullet holes for me to make sense of it, and I need people who can help me track the werebear down…would ye believe me?"

"That's a remarkably specific hypothetical, Ms. MacKenna."

Uh oh. Jeffries was giving me his best cop voice, and we were no longer on a first name basis. "And," I said, raising a finger in the air even though he couldn't see it, "if I were to assure ye that I had nothin' to do with it, but that the werebear was a good friend?"

I could practically hear Jeffries massaging his temples. He took a deep breath and blew it out. "Alright, tell me everything."

So, I did.

Well, you know, almost everything.

A girl has to keep some secrets, after all.

*W*arren held his hands out, his palms hovering inches from the wall, and performed slow wax-on, wax-off motions. On the other side of the crime scene, Jeffries and Hilde compared notes, studying the overturned furniture and blood spatter patterns. Lakota was too focused on Robin to be doing much of anything else; I doubted the younger FBI agent could look more surprised if Robin started singing showtunes out of his anus. Admittedly, part of me was really curious about what the soul of a Faeling looked like…but the rest of me knew better than to ask.

I'd had enough nightmares without looking behind that particular curtain.

I, meanwhile, was doing my best to stay out of everyone's way now that I'd changed into something more comfortable. I'd practically begged Jeffries over the phone to bring me a new set of clothes that fit; both Christoff and his wife were tiny people, and nothing they owned would have suited me. When Hilde showed up with a plain white t-shirt, a pair of black jeans, boots, and a leather vest, I'd threatened to kiss her. Remarkably, the clothes themselves hugged my body perfectly, as if tailored to my unique proportions.

"Ye know," I said, sidling up next to the Valkyrie and her boss, "I'd expected to end up wearin' FBI-issued sweats." I admired the outfit, adjusting the leather vest a bit. "I have to say I'm impressed ye knew me size."

Hilde acknowledged my statement with a slight nod, still studying her notes. "They're Valkyrie-issued. One size fits all."

My eyes widened. "D'ye mean these clothes turn into armor, like yours?" I asked eagerly, sounding like a kid on Christmas morning.

Hilde snorted, then glanced up at me. "Oh, you're serious. How cute. No. They only do that for us. But they are handy. Here, watch." Hilde tapped the shoulder of my vest and I watched in amazement as sleeves appeared and lengthened, stopping at my wrists. I marveled at the leather vest, now a leather jacket.

"I take it back," I whispered, hugging myself, but also checking to make sure Othello's disc hadn't disappeared in the process; I'd pocketed it while changing. "Magic, I love ye, ye beautiful fucker."

"They'll change color, fabric, and style according to your need, and will self-repair if torn," Hilde explained. "It seemed less cruel than making you wear Warren's *obviously* unused gym clothes."

"I heard that," Warren called out from across the room.

"Good," Hilde replied. She grinned at me. "I'd intended to get them back from you at some point, but it's not like I need the extra set. You're welcome to keep them."

"Are ye sure yer a Valkyrie?" I asked. "Because right now ye look more like a saint."

Hilde rolled her eyes. "Anyway, Leo filled me in on what you told him..." She checked her notes. "Your Russian friend is a werebear who runs a bar in the city. He's safe, but hidden, and they have his wife." Hilde flicked her eyes up at me. "So, you think they're what, holding her hostage? Any chance this is related to his job? Maybe he owed money to the wrong people?"

"Ye could ask his bar manager," I said, jabbing my thumb towards Robin, who sat on the stairs trying to ignore Lakota's intense scrutiny. "But from what I know about Christoff, I doubt it."

"You want us to ask the Fae, you mean?" Hilde asked, eyeing Robin.

I cleared my throat. "Uh, right. About that..."

"We know about the Faerie Chancery," Jeffries interjected. "A Freak we came across early on gave up the name, but that's all he could tell us. We were hoping you'd fill us in on the rest but decided to wait to press you about them..." Jeffries looked at me expectantly.

I muttered under my breath. I'd been so careful to keep information on the Chancery from his team, not wanting to spill any secrets, and all along Jeffries had known. "I'm afraid I can't tell ye much more than he could," I replied, hesitantly.

Jeffries clicked his pen, thrust his notebook in his suit jacket, and gave me the best cop stare I'd ever seen—and I'd been arrested once or twice, in my time. There was a weight to it that couldn't be faked; the gaze of a man who was used to having things go his way, one way or the other. Ordinarily, that would have rankled me, but I could tell Jeffries wasn't the type to abuse his authority—if he asked a question, it was because he figured the answer could save lives.

Which meant I was probably the asshole, here.

"Well, I should say I *won't* tell ye much more, not about the Chancery, anyway," I clarified, averting my eyes. "Listen, I met with 'em on your behalf. That's why I was wearin' that stupid dress. I went, hopin' to find out more about your killer, but t'ings went to shit before I could find out what I wanted to know." I held my hand up to stop Jeffries' retort. "That's the truth, I swear. But ye have to understand, you're better off leavin' t'ings be right now. Drawin' the Chancery's attention at the moment could be dangerous, and if your killer is one of 'em, it'll tip him off."

"She may be right, Leo," Hilde said, resting a hand on her superior's arm. "I'd rather not have to track this son of a bitch to another major city."

"How about him?" Jeffries asked, thrusting his chin at Robin. "Can he tell us anything?"

"About your killer? To be honest, it hadn't even crossed me mind. We've been a little busy, as ye can see." I showcased the room, raising both arms like I was on *The Price is Right*. "But you're welcome to grill the Faelin', as soon as ye can tell me where me friend is, or where they took his wife."

Hilde cocked an eyebrow. "And what do you plan to do then?"

Shit. It occurred to me that I hadn't thought that far ahead. Now that I'd involved them, I doubted Jeffries and his team would let me walk away and handle shit on my own—especially the way I preferred to solve problems. Fortunately, Warren spoke up before I had to come up with a believable lie.

"You said your friend was a werebear, right?" he called out.

"Aye."

Warren frowned. "And you're sure he wasn't killed?"

"He definitely escaped," Robin replied.

Warren glanced over at Jeffries.

"He's telling the truth," Jeffries confirmed.

So, the FBI's Special Agent in Charge could tell when a Faeling lied... that was pretty damn convenient. Over the years, I'd heard all sorts of nonsense about how the Fae never lied, but the truth was the Fae were some of the most capable liars I'd ever met. In fact, the only way to get one to tell you the whole truth and nothing but was to put them under your power, typically with a binding or some sort of contract.

My guess was the origins of that myth—that the Fae could never lie directly—could be traced to previous millennia, back to when the Fae first began crossing over into our realm. Factually, it wasn't that the Fae never lied, it's that—at that point in time—they hadn't even bothered.

We weren't worth the trouble.

If you want to know how all this came about, start by imagining you're a peasant in the distant past. You live in a hovel, still fascinated by the miracle that is fire, and a Faeling—one of the most gorgeous beings you've ever seen, tall, with a full head of hair and all his teeth—offers to trade for something you value. You agree, because when a god wants to do business, you do business. But as time goes on, fire loses its appeal. You've moved on to a villa with indoor plumbing. Then carriages. Trains. The gods are long gone and civilization teaches you the value of getting the better end of the deal—something the Fae always knew. So, you begin to lie and to cheat, and soon they return the favor, and before long neither side can trust the other.

Bet they didn't teach you that in your Social Studies classes.

"Well, then we may have a problem," Warren replied after a moment's hesitation.

"A problem? Besides the obvious?" I asked, eyeing the devastation around me with an arched eyebrow.

"Yeah," Warren replied, closing his eyes. A stiff wind blew through the house, ruffling his shaggy hair. Goosebumps pebbled up my arms once I realized the door and windows were all closed. "Two people were killed here," Warren said. His eyes snapped open. "And they were both werebears."

Robin and I exchanged looks. What the hell had happened here? What exactly had Christoff gotten into?

"Can you track him?" Jeffries asked.

Warren adjusted his spectacles. "Of course, I can."

Well then, it was time to be *vewy vewy quiet*.

Because we were now hunting werebears.

CHAPTER 16

*W*arren's tracking skills left something to be desired. I'd been expecting a bloodhound approach—like a psychic GPS telling us when to turn or to let us know when we'd gone too far. Instead, we hopped into a car and he pinged off certain areas, playing the *hotter, colder* game for the better part of three hours. After the first hour, I mimicked Hilde's shoulder-tap magic on my new clothing and was surprised to find I could turn my leather jacket into a fur coat. I balled it up, tucked it against the window, and fell asleep for the first time in what felt like eons.

*S*omeone patted my shoulder, waking me. I jerked upright, my heart hammering in my chest, instincts on high alert; something was wrong. "Easy, you were having a bad dream," Robin said, leaning through the car's open window.

I waited for my breathing to slow before taking stock of my surroundings. I was in the backseat of a car. We'd stopped. I sighed, then peered out the window, and immediately felt my heart rate speed back up; I had no idea where we were just by looking at the street, but my hard-earned Southie instincts told me we sure as shit shouldn't be there.

The thing is, if you grew up in Boston, you knew it could be a rough town. Hell, even the upscale, renovated parts are full of mouthy, feisty fuckers eager to pick a fight with the cardigan-clad Harvard barneys. But it's also a beautiful place, full of history and charm; when you're walking the Freedom Trail, it's easy to forget that crime rates exist. To forget that, on the other side of the city, drugs and guns and sex are being trafficked in dodgier parts of Roxbury, Dorchester, and Mattapan. Or—as the locals sometimes call them—Glocksbury, Deathchester, and Murderpan. Still, I'd learned not to jump to conclusions, because I knew better than most what lurked beneath a neighborhood's bad reputation—that good, hard-working people lived there, shelling out every month for shabby little places because the rent was cheap, and their job paid shit.

But this wasn't one of those neighborhoods.

From where we'd parked, I could see at least a half-dozen warning signs that sent alarm bells clanging inside my head. The building next to us, for example, had a burned-out room in its center that stood out like a gaping wound, not to mention several shattered windows and a kaleidoscope of spray-painted gang tags marring the walls. No cars lined the road. Down one alley a group of homeless people huddled over a trashcan fire, warming their hands despite the comfortable weather. The streetlights were busted out in places, leaving behind pockets of shadow that the waning sunlight hardly touched.

I glared at Robin. "This is where the Chancery put a safehouse?"

"You expected a penthouse hotel room?" Robin replied drily.

"It's fine," Jeffries said in a hard tone as he clambered out of the van he and Hilde had followed us in. I could tell he was as on edge as I was. "We'll find your man and get out of here as quickly as we can."

Warren, looking particularly nervous, ducked out of the car. "He's close. I apologize for the delay. Locating psychic energy is tricky at best, and the false reads kept drawing us off course."

On the way over, I'd coerced Warren into confessing how he planned to track Christoff. Apparently, people left residual psychic energy all over the place, but it tended to gather most in locations we had strong connections to, like our homes. Warren had managed to pick up the unique frequency Christoff's energy emitted and then hunt down its source. Unfortunately, it had taken us a while to realize that Christoff's bar—his home away from home—had soaked up the very same energy.

"Can ye tell us exactly where he is? Now that we're close?" I asked.

Warren shook his head. "I can't narrow it down any further. He's in this area, but that's all I know."

"Guess we'll have to go old school and knock on doors," Jeffries said, looking less than pleased. He rapped his fingers on the car's window. Lakota rolled it down and leaned over the console, one hand on the wheel. "Keep an eye on the vehicles," Jeffries said. "I'd rather not come back to find our tires missing."

Lakota flashed him a thumbs up, blew a ridiculously large bubble, and let it pop.

"So, divide and conquer?" I asked, eyeing the dilapidated street. "Or strength in numbers?"

"I'll take Warren and the Fae," Jeffries said. "That won't be a problem, will it?"

"Not at all," Robin said, exchanging looks with me. I shrugged. It was clear Jeffries didn't trust either of us; he wouldn't have split us up, otherwise. But I didn't care. As long as we found Christoff, I could handle the Special Agent's skepticism.

"Hilde," Jeffries continued, "you and Quinn take the building on the right. The one that isn't abandoned," he added, pointing past the ramshackle structure I'd noticed when we arrived towards a battered apartment complex further down the road.

"Alright," Hilde said. "Be careful."

I nudged Robin. "Dibs on your hat if ye die."

"You want my bloody cap?" Robin asked, dubiously.

"I'm bettin' I could fetch a decent price for it, if I find the right buyer," I quipped.

"Cute," he said, rolling his eyes.

With that, we went our separate ways.

Hilde took the lead. The clip of our heels on the cracked pavement echoed in the near silence. Despite the warm weather, I felt a bit conspicuous in a plain white t-shirt, so I slid my fur coat over my shoulders and tapped it once more. The fur flattened and coarsened, binding together to become denim fibers. Brass buttons burst along the jean jacket's center front.

"Ye know, ye Valkyries should have your own brand," I said, admiring the finished product.

Hilde shook her head. "Those fibers are woven from the hair of Skadi,

forged from the scales of Jormangund, and infused with the spirit of Ymir."
She glanced back at me, emphasizing the value of her gift with a stiff nod.
"Mass production isn't exactly doable. Besides, we'd ruin the entire
infrastructure. You'd never need to buy clothes again, and the whole
industry would collapse."

I considered that as we walked, then nodded. "You're right. These
threads are like an Everlastin' Gobstopper."

"A what?" Hilde asked.

"Ye know, from *Willy Wonka?*"

Hilde snorted. "Has anyone told you that you're strange, even for a
Freak?"

Not that rudely, I thought to myself.

But yeah.

"Aye," I replied as we ascended the steps that led to the apartment building's entrance.

Hilde froze mid-stride. She whirled towards me. "Get *down!*"

"What? I—" I began. But Hilde tackled me to the ground before I could
say anything else. I landed in the dirt with her on top of me, more than a
little dazed and winded from the fall. I hip-thrusted her off me, prepared to
go toe-to-toe with the mythical warrior...until I caught the din of bullets
tearing into the stone steps we'd left behind.

"Down! Now!" Hilde urged again, pushing me back.

This time I didn't argue.

CHAPTER 17

*H*ilde rolled off me and drew her arm up, producing a shield out of thin air, then hunkered down behind it. "Get behind me!" she yelled over the sound of bullets shattering the glass behind our heads. I did as she asked, staying low to the ground and balled up behind her. I tried to peer past her shield to see who was shooting at us but was forced to duck back as rifle fire blew past me.

Curiosity wasn't about to kill this cat.

I could hear more yelling down the other side of the street, where Jeffries' group had gone to investigate. Had we stumbled into the middle of a gang war, or was this some sort of ambush? Either way, I desperately wished I was armed; playing possum during a shootout is a pretty pathetic way to spend your evening.

"Hilde!" I yelled. "What are the odds you'd be willin' to give a girl a gun?"

Hilde flicked her eyes back at me, then returned her attention to protecting us from the bad guys with guns, angling her shield to block most of the fire. "Zero!"

"Ah, come on! Why not?"

"Can't risk you killing someone with my gun! Policy!"

"Can't ye like, I don't know, deputize me, or somethin'?" I yelled back, my voice hopeful.

"This isn't the Wild West!"

"Tell *them* that," I argued.

"We have to move before they decide to flank us," Hilde said, ignoring me. "On three, we stand. Stay behind me, as close as you can. I'll get us to cover and then go after them, myself."

"Aye!" I called. I pressed a hand against Hilde's back to let her know where I was, and felt the cool, metallic surface of her armor beneath my hand—armor I seriously hoped was bulletproof...and me proof, I realized, with a start.

I let out a shiver of relief when the armor didn't disappear.

She gave the order and we rose, together, and made for the rundown building we'd passed earlier. Its brick and mortar walls were shoddy at best, but they'd provide more shelter than Hilde's shield. No matter how durable the shield seemed to be—unless it could magically transform into a damn tank—I doubted we'd last much longer huddled on the ground.

"Try and look behind us as we go," Hilde said. "Make sure there's no one down that alley."

I glanced back, noticing the alley we'd passed for the first time. She was right, we'd be sitting ducks if any of the shooters were lying in wait; they could come at us from both sides and mow us down. "I'll keep an eye out!" I yelled. I kept my hand on Hilde's back and swiveled my eyes back and forth between what lay behind us and the next several feet in front of me.

Tripping right now would be embarrassing.

Not to mention fatal.

We cleared the edge of the apartment building, and I stared down a narrow, lightless alley. I cursed, realizing I couldn't make out a thing beyond the first few feet. A killer could be lurking in those shadows, within striking distance, and I'd never even know.

"How we doing back there?" Hilde called.

"Fine," I lied, still pressed tight up against her, moving as she moved. Frankly, explaining the situation to Hilde would take too long, and I didn't want to risk her taking her attention away from keeping us safe. I kept my eyes on the alley, praying I'd catch the glint of a muzzle before it was too late.

I could still hear the bullets pinging off Hilde's shield, making my shoulders twitch spasmodically with each strike. Whoever was firing had an absurd amount of ammunition, and they were good shots; if Hilde weren't covered head to toe in armor and shielding us, we'd have been gunned down almost immediately. That's when I saw it, the glint of a gun barrel at the far end of the alley where, luckily, a lone streetlight from the next street over was still operational—the faint light enough to reveal a dim silhouette.

"Hilde!" I yelled. "Company!"

Hilde snarled. "Duck!"

I did, squatting down just as Hilde whirled, one hand clutching the shield and the other toting a short sword. She reared back and, I shit you not, flung the sword down the alleyway as if it were a Bowie knife. It spun end-over-end before burying itself hilt deep in the gunman's chest. The gunman crashed to his knees, his gun clattering to the pavement, before he fell into the shadowed alley between us and the streetlight behind him.

"Let's go!" Hilde snatched me by my jacket collar and drew me upwards. But, before we could continue our flight, three more men appeared in the alleyway. "Shit!" Hilde cursed.

Shit, indeed. At this point—unless Hilde could pull some crazy shit out of her ass—we were going to end up gunned down from both sides. Of course, she wasn't the only one who could do that flinging thing.

"Hilde, be ready!" I yelled. I reached into the pocket of my jacket. I clutched Othello's disc between my fingers like a playing card I was preparing to throw. I'd played horseshoes as a kid, and I was hoping it would be about the same. Just get it near the target—and pray.

"Ready for what?" she asked, grimacing as the newcomers raised their rifles.

"Anythin'!" I screamed. I tossed the disc. It rose into the air and then fell, skidding across the pavement, to land at their feet. Where it stayed. Unmoving. I hung my head.

Well, it was worth a shot.

The man in front barked out a command I could hardly hear over the sound of intermittent gunfire coming from behind. They crept forward, clearly hoping to fire on us at close range. But, before they could move more than a few feet, I noticed the copper disc begin to glow. So did the men. Another barked command, and they pointed their guns, not at us, but at the disc.

It was too late.

The disc, glowing red as if it had been left in a furnace, spiraled into the air, freezing in midair above their heads. The men whipped their rifles up, shouting, but unsure whether to fire or not. The stench of burning ozone

96

assaulted my nostrils, acrid and bitter. Then, in a flash of brilliant light, a bolt of lightning came careening from the sky, colliding with the disc, which burned white hot. I covered my eyes an instant before the electricity leapt from the disc to the earth in the most convenient path it could find, the air sizzling from its descent.

Fun fact: metal is a conductor.

And guess which dumbasses were standing beneath the storm generator?

When I glanced back, the three men were on their backs twitching next to their impaled comrade. Small arcs of lighting rode their bodies like snakes. The air smelled worse now, like burnt hair and cooked meat. But I could live with that; I preferred my bad guys well done.

"What the hell was that?" Hilde hissed.

I shrugged. "Ye aren't the only one who has nice t'ings," I quipped.

Another bullet pinged off Hilde's shield. She cursed, snatched my collar, and thrust me behind her. "Any more toys I should know about?" she asked, as we left the alley behind.

"Fresh out!" I called back.

I felt the wall of the run-down building at my back, a moment later. We'd made it, for whatever that was worth. I thrust my hands back and felt along the wall, sliding my fingers across jagged stone, careful not to cut myself.

"Look for a way in!" Hilde commanded, pausing.

I scoured the building, scanning left and then right.

"There!" I said, pointing to a hole at the base of the wall. A chunk of brick exploded a foot from my hand and I drew it back, cursing. As we approached, I realized the hole was actually a basement window that had been removed, leaving a gap hardly big enough for a child to slip through comfortably.

"Get in!" Hilde yelled.

"You're jokin', aren't ye?" I asked.

"Now!"

I swore, muttering as many derogatory things as I could think of about Scandinavians—mostly badmouthing *IKEA*—as I knelt and crawled towards the hole. I thrust my feet through first and wriggled until the lower part of my body cleared the space. The backs of my thighs burned from having to scrabble against the brick, and I could tell I'd torn holes in my jeans.

Looked like I'd be testing out my self-mending clothes sooner than I thought.

But at least there was no broken glass. I held my breath as I squirmed, inching through the hole, praying my ass didn't get stuck. My legs dangled and—for a moment—a wave of panic hit me; what if the basement floor was further down than most? I didn't want to work this hard just to break my legs when I fell. I inched myself further in, reaching down with my toes, praying I'd brush the basement floor.

"You good, yet?" Hilde yelled.

I glanced back to see the legendary warrior hunkered down on one knee, her shield tucked tight against her side. I groaned, took a deep breath, and forced myself to scuttle further in. If I fell, I fell; I'd rather have shattered legs than be a burden. I raised both arms above my head, pulled in my shoulder blades, and dropped through the opening with a squeal.

I landed on both feet, a mere foot below the window.

I hissed in pain as the adrenaline from dodging bullets wore off, probing my side where a shard of brick had dug in. Once I confirmed I wasn't bleeding, I rose onto my tiptoes and peered through the window. I could see Hilde's legs, and, beyond that, the moonlit street—the remaining streetlights that had worked when we'd arrived had been shot out in the exchange. Soon the sun would fall and we'd only have moonlight to see by.

"Are you in?" Hilde yelled.

"Aye!" I called. I briefly took stock of my surroundings. I knelt in a room, probably an old office judging by the cubicles and the ancient computer equipment stacked up against the far wall. Either way, I knew I had to find higher ground. My entrance hadn't exactly been stealthy, and I'd make an easy target down here—all they'd have to do was stick their rifles through the hole and fire until their clips ran empty. Murphy's Law would take care of the rest.

"I'm going after them," Hilde yelled. "Find somewhere to hide!"

"Will do. Give 'em hell!" I cheered.

Hilde's resounding laughter made me cringe; in the timbre of her maniacal cackle, I heard the unrestrained glee of a woman about to mow down her enemies and play Double Dutch with their intestines. For a moment, I almost pitied the assholes who'd decided to use us for target practice.

Almost.

She clomped off, the clanking of her armor rattling against itself disappearing beneath the clamor of burgeoning gunfire. I cursed and headed for the door, ducking low, doing my best not to get shot now that I'd made it relatively out of harm's way.

I found the door that led to the stairs only to find the building had no power. Surprise, surprise. I flipped the switch a few times to be sure, then poked my head into the murky stairwell. I knew the apartment that had gone up in flames was somewhere above me, near the center of the building. I didn't want to end up there; I'd be as likely to fall through the floorboards to my death as to get shot by a vigilant gunman.

But if I went a few stories up, I might be able to get a better look at what was happening outside. From there, I might be able to do something. Of course, I knew the cops would show up sooner rather than later; no shootout goes down without some reaction from the police. But this was a bad part of town, and the ladies and gents in blue knew better than to drive right into the middle of a turf war—going in early would only get you killed. Sadly, I had a feeling that by the time reinforcements arrived, it would be too late; either we'd be dead, or they would.

Whoever *they* were.

I sighed, propped open the basement's rusted door, and headed upstairs. From within the stairwell, the sound of the fighting outside dwindled to nothing but white noise; the sound of rifle fire little more than pebbles skittering across the ground. I had to feel my away around in the pitch-black darkness, testing each step and holding tight to the railing. The doors to the first two stories were jammed shut, either locked or too warped in their frames to move.

The third-floor door, fortunately, was unlocked. But when I tried to push it open, I noticed something had been stacked up against the door, something which made it hard to budge. I set my back against the railing, confirmed it was firmly attached, and lashed out with one foot, slamming my heel against the door. I kept at it until I had a few feet of space to work with, wincing at the startlingly loud noise I made each time my boot slammed against the metal. Once I had enough room to fit, I slid through the opening, only to stumble over a pile of what turned out to be bricks. I held on to one of them, just in case.

I began carefully feeling out the confines of the room; I was in a hallway with doors on either side. I tested the knobs, hoping to find a room with a window I could look through, but the doors were all locked. Based on what

I'd seen from the outside and the basement, I was guessing this had once been an office building—the kind used by small start-ups hoping to have a space of their own, but without the means to take on a whole structure's worth of bills.

As I jiggled yet another doorknob, a flickering light caught my eye. I crouched low, trying to judge where the light had come from. Maybe light from outside was drifting in, somehow? I took stock of my surroundings once more, mapping out how far I'd gone towards the center of the building, and realized the burnt-out apartment had to be close by, which meant I'd have to double back and go up another floor if I didn't find an unlocked room soon.

I rose to my full height, and that's when I saw it. The light. It wasn't coming from outside, but from the edges of a doorway, lining it in a soft, pale yellow glow. Now that I knew it was there, it practically stood out like a candle's flame. How had I missed it before?

I edged towards the doorway, toting the brick in my hand. I flattened myself against the wall the way I had when I thought someone had broken into my apartment and tested the doorknob. Locked. But beyond, I swore I could hear something. I pressed my ear against the door, listening. Murmured voices. Whispers. There was definitely someone in there. Several someones, even.

The sound of something careening down the hallway drew my attention away from the door. I whirled towards the noise. The world went white, and pain flooded my senses. I fell back, my ears ringing. Memories, flashbacks of my days spent training alongside my mentor—a sadist if ever there was one—reminded me what caused this sort of pain.

A flash grenade.

Someone must have tossed a flash grenade down the hall, hoping to stun anyone who happened to be nearby. I tried to rise, but I was too disoriented. A boot heel slammed into my shoulder and drove me backwards, pinning me to the ground. More light hit my eyes, emitting from a small flashlight mounted on a much bigger machine gun, a modernized version of the AK-47 which I recognized as the AK-12—a gun I'd heard about but had never actually seen in person before. A Russian military-grade assault rifle. I hardly had time to process what that meant before I felt the pressure of the boot increase, the pain driving me to scream. The man spoke, but I barely heard him, my ears still not fully functional. I desperately felt for the brick with my free hand. If I ended up shot, so be it, but I wasn't about to go down without a fight.

At the exact same instant, I found the brick, I felt the weight of the boot disappear. A loud crash. More light, only softer, less brilliant. Someone bent down over me. I lashed out, swinging the brick at my assailant, but my wrist ended up in someone's grasp.

"Quinn!" I heard a man call out. "It is me."

"Christoff?" I asked, blinking rapidly, wondering if the flash grenade had actually struck me in the head before detonating, and now I was imagining things. But the older man's stoic features began to make themselves clear, and the pounding in my ears receded somewhat. I swung my eyes around, trying to find the man with the gun, then realized he was sitting against the wall. Well, most of him. His arm lay further down the hallway and half his guts were piled up on his lap like an offering to some ancient, primordial god. His eyes were sightless, unfocused—the eyes of a dead man.

"What happened?" I whispered.

Christoff pried the brick free from my hand and tossed it behind him. "I heard grenade, then your scream from the other side of door," Christoff explained. "Then his words." He jerked his head towards the dead man.

"Did ye kill him?" I asked.

Christoff nodded. "Come, we must go inside." I peered past the older man and saw a well-furnished room with two beds, a dresser, and a small table laden with bread and fruit. Beneath the table, hidden behind a couple of chairs, were Christoff's two children. His son, the older of the two, held his tiny sister, who stared at us with an open, toothless mouth. Christoff drew me inside, then fetched something from the hallway before shutting the door.

I fell back against the wall and studied the room, trying to figure out where we were. It was clearly one of the apartments, but the lights were on and there were two windows overlooking the street; we'd definitely have noticed something like that when we pulled up. Maybe he'd just turned the lights on? But how? I'd tried the lights a little while ago, without success. I shook my head, still trying to clear it.

Christoff, meanwhile, had urged his children to abandon the table and sit against the far wall, between the two beds. I realized he'd snatched the dead man's rifle and had its strap slung across his body. He expertly checked the weapon over, running his calloused hands along the barrel to make sure the muzzle was still straight, inspecting the bedding of the barrel and all its screws—even examining the stock for any cracks. He grunted his approval and tested the weight of the weapon, drawing it to his shoulder. I frowned; I had no idea Christoff had ever fired a gun, let alone handled a military-grade rifle. But he'd handled it with a practiced familiarity approaching boredom.

"Where are we?" I asked.

Christoff glanced over at me. His gaze, so much colder than I was used to, sent shivers up my spine. This was not my friend, the exuberant bar owner. This was someone much...scarier. "This is hideout," Christoff replied. "Where Chancery places us. A safehouse. What are you doing here?"

"Shouldn't ye turn off the lights?" I asked, ignoring his question for the moment. "They're bound to come up here."

Christoff shook his head. "There is no need. No one can see from outside. The Chancery used Faerie glamour."

I fought the urge to slap my forehead and cause more brain damage than had already been done. Glamour, the ability to make something seem different than it was—basically illusion magic—was a special kind of Fae magic, and the Chancery was no ordinary organization; it had plenty of members who could produce a glamour strong enough to mislead any passersby. That was why they'd chosen such a shady location—who would go out of their way to investigate some hovel in a bad neighborhood? In fact, as I compared the room's location to what I'd seen from the outside, I realized I was likely standing in the burnt-out apartment. The Faeling who'd created the illusion must have woven it over the outside of the building but left the inside intact. Otherwise we'd all be standing around, comfortable, in a burnt-out shit hole.

I turned my attention back to Christoff, only to find the barrel of the gun pointed squarely at my chest. "Oy," I said, raising my hands innocently, palms out, "what d'ye t'ink you're doin'?"

"Please. Answer question. What are you doing here? How did you find us?" Christoff growled in a very cold tone.

"I came to save ye," I said, scowling. "I found out ye were in trouble and I wanted to help."

"So, you did not lead them here?" Christoff asked, jerking the muzzle of his gun to indicate the dead man in the hallway.

"If we did, it wasn't on purpose," I admitted, after a moment's hesitation.

Christoff could be right, after all. Maybe we had been followed. But followed by whom? Who were these bastards, anyway?

"We?" Christoff asked, hiking the barrel up further.

"Oh, ye know, me and a few ragtag members of the FBI," I replied.

Christoff's eyes widened.

I sighed, deciding it was best to start from the beginning and tell him everything before he put a bullet in me. I quickly fed him the highlight reel, explaining how I'd met Robin at his place, gone to the Chancery, and eventually called in the Sickos. "They helped track ye down. I was hopin' to get ye and the wee ones somewhere safe and to help ye find yer wife. That's all."

Christoff lowered the muzzle slightly and glanced over at his children, who remained eerily quiet. Maybe they were in shock from watching their father kill someone? Or maybe he'd trained them to behave that way. If so, Christoff should probably teach a class or something. Russian Parenting 101: Shut Up or Else. I shook my head. I couldn't afford to let my mind wander with one of my very few friends pointing a gun at me. Also, now that I could hear better, I realized that the gunfire from outside had ceased.

I wasn't sure whether that was a good or a bad thing.

That's when my phone started buzzing in my pocket.

"Give me phone," Christoff said, keeping the gun trained on me as I handed it over. I noticed on the caller ID that it was Jeffries' phone number. Christoff answered the phone and put Jeffries' on speaker, holding it out so we could both hear it.

"Quinn, it's Leo. Are you alright?"

Christoff nodded at me to respond.

"Aye, I'm fine."

"Where's Hilde?"

"She ran off to hunt down whoever was attackin' us," I replied. "Is everyone alright on your end?"

"Yeah, I'm pretty sure their attention was focused on you and Hilde. We were able to sneak up behind and chase them off."

Christoff was shaking his head. "You did not chase them off," he said. "They are still there, somewhere. You should get away."

"Who is that?" Jeffries asked. "Is that your friend?"

"Aye, I stumbled on him by accident, he—"

"Agent Jeffries," Christoff said, cutting me off, "you must listen to me, they will be coming for you. They do not run from anyone. Not ever. You must hide."

"Who's they?" Jeffries demanded.

The sound of gunfire rippled through the phone an instant before I heard it coming from outside. The call ended. Christoff cursed in Russian, tossed the phone back to me, and moved to the window, staring down at the street below.

"Papa?" the boy said, speaking for the first time. He held his sister's free hand. She had the other in her mouth, fingers wriggling against her gums.

"It will be fine," Christoff said, "do not worry."

I edged toward the window, beyond which I could make out very little. But I swore I could hear sirens in the distance. The police were finally on their way. Reinforcements for Jeffries and his squad? Maybe enough to scare off the enemy. The gunfire continued in small spurts, reached a crescendo, and then cut out. I faced Christoff, fear and anger churning in my gut. "What the hell is goin' on?" I asked, recalling Jeffries' question from a moment ago. "Who came after ye? And why?"

Christoff adjusted the rifle so it hung at his side and pressed his palms flat against the window frame, the muscles in his thick forearm tense and corded. This time, when he looked at me, his eyes were softer, the lines of his face less cruel. This was the face of the man I knew...or thought I knew.

"They are *ghosts*," Christoff growled, finally.

"I hope ye aren't bein' literal," I replied, frowning. I would love to say nothing surprised me anymore, but ghosts wielding automatic rifles would have taken the cake for the day.

And I'd met Arthurian legends this morning.

"No, though at times they have been called this. I mean they are ghosts from my past..." Christoff drifted off, then shook his head as if to clear it. "There is no time to explain. We must leave this place. We are not safe here. Not anymore. They will be coming for us."

"The car we took is down there," I said, peering through the gloom until I could make out the four-door Sedan. I wondered if Lakota was still inside, or if he'd gone to help out the rest of the team. "If we can sneak down there, we can—"

"No," Christoff said. "See there? The car is being watched." He pointed to a rooftop on the other side of the street. I squinted. Christoff was right. A figure in all black knelt along the edge of the rooftop, peering through the scope of what I assumed was a sniper rifle; from this distance it was hard to make out much more than that. "The only reason you and your people are still alive is because they have not found me yet. But that will change soon. They will know their man is missing and come for him." He took a deep breath and blew it out slow. "You must take the children and hide. Once they have me, they will leave."

"Well, I for one t'ink that's a stupid plan," I replied, frowning. "I'm not about to let ye run off after I worked so hard to find ye. Besides, ye know I'm no good with the wee ones," I joked. Then a sudden thought hit me, and I grinned. "I have a better idea." I scrolled through my contacts list as the pitch of sirens grew louder. Luckily, it didn't take long to find who I was looking for and hit the call option.

"Who are you calling?" Christoff asked.

"A friend," I said, distractedly.

Christoff looked dubious.

"Oy, I have friends!" I snapped defensively. "Well...I say she's a friend. But she's more like a drinkin' buddy, if I'm bein' honest," I added.

"Ah, this makes sense," Christoff said, nodding emphatically as if all were now right with the world. Apparently, my having an actual friend wasn't nearly as believable as my having a drinking buddy.

Rude.

I scowled at the grizzled Russian as the phone rang. On the fourth ring, it finally clicked over, and a woman's soft, low voice warbled out of the speakers. "Callie Penrose," she said. "Who's this?"

CHAPTER 18

I turned from the window and took a seat at the table, snatching an apple to keep me distracted. I wasn't nervous, per se, but I did worry about whether Callie would be willing to help. We'd only just met a few days ago, after all, and it was awful early to be calling in favors. Still, if anyone could help us right now, it was her. "Callie, it's me, Quinn," I said.

"Quinn, who?"

"Quinn," I repeated, forcefully. "Quinn. Tall, red hair. Drank ye under the table."

"You must have called the wrong person," Callie said, sounding drowsy, as though I'd woken her up from a nap. She yawned. "No one drinks me under anything."

"I canno' be playin' games right now, Callie Penrose," I said, shaking my head. "Lives are at stake. I've got kids here."

"Tell me where you are," she suddenly demanded, no longer sounding the least bit tired. I could hear her getting around, probably shuffling out of bed and putting on clothes. I cursed, realizing I had no idea where we were; I'd taken my own nap on the way over and hadn't bothered to ask for the address.

"Christoff, I need the address and the room number," I said, holding one hand over the phone. He rattled it off and I repeated it to Callie, whose voice grew tinny and barely audible, "Alright, I'll be there in two minutes."

Christoff flinched and spun towards the door, sniffing the air. "They are coming."

"Hate to rush ye," I said, "But can ye make it one minute?"

"See you soon," Callie said, then ended the call before I could confirm whether or not she heard me.

I thrust my phone into my pocket and held out my hand. "Give me the gun. I'll cover ye if they get in before she gets here," I said.

"No," Christoff replied. "Keep the children safe. I will take care of the rest." He hefted the rifle in one hand, then brought the other up to keep it steady—except his other hand had become a massive bear paw. His claws raked the metal of the assault rifle, slightly scarring it. I noticed his pupils had expanded and darkened to a deep, chocolate brown. The eyes of a bear.

I heard footsteps down the corridor.

"Will they be able to find us?" I whispered. "What about the glamour?"

"Their comrade will give us away. Once they are outside door, they will be able to see through glamour, as you did," he replied. Christoff nudged me towards the children. "Stay between beds."

Right at that moment, a portal hemmed in silver flame appeared, causing Christoff to twirl around. I pushed the muzzle of his assault rifle down, hoping to avoid friendly fire as a beautiful, white-haired woman stepped through. She wore a purple sash with a red cross tucked into a dark blue leather bomber jacket and a pair of grey denim jeans that hugged her hips salaciously. Callie Penrose took one look around the room, gauged the situation, paused to study Christoff's paw for a moment, then flicked her eyes towards the door. "Follow me if you want to live," she said in her best Schwarzenegger impression, waving us towards the portal she'd created.

I could hear Russian being spoken down the hall. Christoff seemed to waver, but finally tossed me the gun, snatched up his children, and bolted through the portal. I followed, tight on his heels, then waited for Callie to do the same. Except she didn't. Instead, I watched her study the door, head cocked to one side, rolling her shoulders as if preparing for a fight.

"What d'ye t'ink your doin'?" I hissed.

"I don't like it when people threaten kids," Callie said, as if that explained everything. "And hangovers make me bitchy."

Too late, I realized that—of all the people I could have called in to de-escalate the situation—Callie Penrose was probably the worst possible candidate. Sure, she could create Gateways; I'd learned that much in Vegas a few nights ago when Othello had coerced me into a girls' night out with a few of her friends.

But that's a tale for another time.

During our whirlwind trip to Vegas, I'd also learned that Callie had originally been trained by the Vatican to become a Shepherd—one of the twelve supernatural bogeymen and women responsible for protecting God's Chosen from Freaks and demons alike—before branching out on her own to become the sole arbiter of justice in her hometown of Kansas City. From what I'd seen during our brief stint in Sin City, she had scary ties to all things cosmic, including a Fallen angel wrapped around her finger.

And I don't mean that metaphorically, either.

A condensed ring of shifting shadows encircled her thumb, rotating lazily of its own accord.

"Well, ye can give 'em a piece of your mind later," I hissed. "Right now, I need ye to take us to Alaska."

Callie blinked, then turned, head tilted quizzically. "Alaska?" She considered the door once more, blew out a regretful sigh, and then stepped through the portal. It snapped shut behind her just as someone, or something, broke down the door. Callie didn't even seem to notice. Instead, she stared past me, at Christoff. Her eyes flicked to his hand, which had reverted to normal. "Ah, the bears. So, he's the one?"

I nodded. While in Vegas, Callie and I had exchanged tales of our most recent adventures. Our mutual run-ins with angels and demons. My role in Boston as an arms dealer. Hers in Kansas City as a peace-keeper. I made her promise me that she'd knock Dorian Gray flat on his ass for the Fight Night he'd put me through while I was visiting New York; apparently, they were friends. She made me promise that if I ever ran into any ancient religious artifacts, I'd give her a call.

Oh, and she told me about her city's sizable werebear population.

Including where they liked to vacation.

"Aye, the bears," I replied, grinning.

Christoff growled, hoisting his children a little higher against his chest. "What bears?"

"The bears in Alaska," I explained. "Weren't ye listenin'?"

CHAPTER 19

A half-naked woman stepped out of what I could only assume was the bedroom before I could explain to Christoff what I was referring to. And by half-naked I don't mean in lingerie, but naked from the waist up. I glanced back and forth between her and Callie and cleared my throat. "Oh, I'm sorry. I didn't realize ye had company..." I said, drifting off uncomfortably.

Callie glared at the woman, while Christoff did his best to ignore her and her assets. His attempt at fidelity was admirable, really. "Claire," Callie hissed, "put some clothes on! There are kids in here."

The woman, Claire—a petite, curvaceous blonde—blinked owlishly at all of us. "When did we start taking in strays?" she asked. She took a deep breath as if to huff at the inconvenience of dressing, then froze, staring at Christoff's turned back. She sniffed the air and growled, the sound low and menacing and inhuman.

Christoff glanced over his shoulder, and I realized his eyes were that same, chocolatey brown from before. Callie held a hand out towards both of them, "Now, now. Play nice, you two. I just bought this apartment. Claire, this is Quinn. She's one of the girls I met in Vegas this past weekend."

Claire pouted. "The trip you wouldn't let me go on, you mean?"

"It wasn't my place to invite anyone. *I* was invited," Callie replied, rolling her eyes. "Quinn, this is Claire. As you have probably already figured out from the fact that she's still not wearing clothes, not to mention the fact that she sounds like a lawn mower when she's riled up, Claire is one of the local werebears. She's also my best friend."

Claire's face wavered between irritation and pride as if she couldn't decide which part of Callie's introduction to focus on. Pride won out. "Pleased to meet you," she said, waving. "Now, who's your friend?"

Christoff sighed and turned. His son dipped his face into his father's neck shyly, while the daughter gurgled and stared around the room, head lolling. "I am Christoff."

"Christoff...runs a bar in Boston," Callie explained, as if recalling the details, I'd shared with her for the first time. Frankly, given how drunk we'd been by the time we talked about our mutual werebear friends, that wasn't particularly surprising. Now that Claire had been properly introduced, in fact, a few hazy details were resurfacing on my end. Like the fact that Callie's best friend turned into a Polar Bear when she shifted.

Which was pretty fucking cool.

Pun intended.

"And he's a werebear," Claire said, sniffing pointedly.

"And he's a werebear," Callie replied tiredly.

Claire sized up the short, muscular Russian man with his greying temples and his stoic features. Her gaze flicked back and forth between his two children and, at last, she smiled. "Well, welcome to Kansas City."

Christoff's eyes widened, clearly panicked. "We are in Kansas City? We have to go back. I have to find my wife before they..." he drifted off, realizing he held his children in his arms. "Please, we must return home," he said, imploring me.

I nodded but held up a hand. "That's why I called Callie, here," I explained. "But we can't go back until your kids are safe. That's where the bears come in."

Claire waved her hands. "Wait a second, what about the bears?" She glanced at Callie, who seemed bothered by something, though I wasn't sure what.

"I think Quinn plans to ask the bears for help. To take in the kids. But this is the first I'm hearing about someone *else* being in danger. And you two still haven't explained who I saved you *from*," Callie added, making sure I knew that she'd done us a favor by pulling us out.

"Your guess is as good as mine," I said. "He still hasn't filled me in on the details."

Christoff hung his head. "This is a lot to explain."

"Well," Claire said, wandering back into the bedroom, hopefully to put on a damn shirt, "you'd better be ready to spill your guts when we get to Alaska, then. Armor isn't going to let you walk away until we've heard the whole story."

"Armor?" I asked.

"He's the Alpha of our Cave."

"Cave?" Christoff asked.

"I guess you could call us a sleuth, technically," Claire yelled. "But it just sounds weird."

"But you are bears," Christoff said, brow furrowed. "Bears do not do this. We live alone."

"Not us. Don't worry, you'll see for yourself soon!"

"So, you're alright with me taking them?" Callie asked.

"Sure. But we should both go." Claire poked her head around the doorway and gave Callie a level look. "Beckett's there, getting a handle on things." Callie's face immediately darkened about a dozen shades, making me momentarily nervous, but Claire continued on. "Besides, Armor might get upset with you for bringing in strangers without warning."

Callie took a deep breath, and then slowly nodded. Then she folded her arms over her chest. "You just want to see Kenai," she said, barely concealing a grin.

Claire blushed and ducked back into the bedroom. "Whatever. You all should put on some layers," she called out. "It's gonna be chilly."

"Yes, because clothes are important," Callie muttered, rolling her eyes.

"I heard that!" Claire yelled over the sound of a blow dryer turning on.

Callie sighed and held out her arms, a wide and gleeful smile on her face. "Alright, well, while she's getting ready...gimme the baby." Christoff hesitantly passed his daughter over and watched first in surprise, and then amusement, as Callie bounced the little girl, making funny faces and noises at her.

"See," I said, nudging Christoff. "She's a much better babysitter than I would've been."

"Yes, much," he agreed, too quickly.

I scowled at my bartender, ignoring his giggling daughter being thrown into the air in front of me.

That was it, no more tips for Christoff.

CHAPTER 20

*T*rue to Claire's word, Alaska was cold. It was also bright; the sun had yet to fall on this side of the country by the time we arrived, which was a little off-putting. I shivered the instant we stepped out onto the wide, white plain, then tapped my jacket, shirt, pants, and shoes. Within seconds, I looked like a *North Face* cover model—sans stocking cap—and breathed a sigh of relief. Claire and Christoff seemed oblivious to the cold, wearing little more than windbreakers. The children, meanwhile, had been bundled up in a couple of Callie's bulky sweaters and were both clutching their father tightly. Callie herself had thrown a thick fleece coat over her leather jacket and her boots had given way to galoshes, though I hadn't seen her change shoes. I caught her glaring suspiciously at me.

"What?" I asked.

"Where did you get those?" she asked, pointing to my clothes.

"Oh, these old t'ings?" I said, twirling. "A little present from a Valkyrie. No big deal." I frowned as I finished, still wondering where Hilde and the rest had ended up and whether or not they were alright. I'd tried calling before we left for Alaska, but Jeffries' phone had gone straight to voicemail. Unfortunately, I didn't have anyone else's number. All I could hope for was that we'd come back and find them safe and sound when our business with the bears was concluded.

Callie's eyes narrowed, assessing my clothes. "Well, do they tell you when demons are approaching?" she asked, imperiously.

"No," I replied, cocking my head. She looked pleased. "But they do repair themselves," I added, noting how the tears had mended after I'd ducked through the hole to the building where I'd found Christoff.

"How about bullets?" Claire asked, folding her arms, fidgeting with a bracelet of pale leather etched with dark symbols of some kind on her wrist. "Do they protect you from bullets?"

"No," I admitted, turning from one to the other. "Apparently, though, there's a way to turn 'em into a badass suit of armor. I simply haven't figured that bit out, yet." I didn't care what Hilde said; I was definitely going full-on She-Ra at the first opportunity. I mean, what's the point of having magical threads if you can't roleplay in them?

Callie turned and whispered something to Claire, who nodded. "We've decided you owe us for helping you," Callie said. "You're welcome to pay us back in clothes."

I chuckled. "I'll see what I can do. They're a wee bit hard to come by, from what I've been told."

Two figures emerged from behind a snow bank that glittered in the sunlight. I took stock of our surroundings and realized that Alaska was far from the desolate landscape I had imagined. Mountains rose up in the distance, and a crystal-clear lake spread out for miles behind us. It was breathtaking...although that might also have been the altitude; the thinner air was noticeable at this elevation.

Claire took a step forward and waved to the newcomers.

Callie frowned.

"What is it?" I whispered.

"Nothing. That's Kenai," Callie said, nodding towards the larger of the two men. "Claire's been crushing on him for a few weeks now."

"I'll *cut* you," Claire threatened out of the side of her mouth, still smiling at the newcomers.

"And the other?" I asked, staring at the smaller man. He was handsome and obviously fit—even beneath his jacket I could tell he had an athlete's body. I'd have even called him attractive if it weren't for the brooding, angsty expression on his face.

"Beckett," Callie replied, though her tone suggested she had nothing to add on that front. Or maybe a whole helluva lot to add.

"Play nice," Claire urged.

Callie shrugged stiffly and thrust her hands in the pockets of her coat. Kenai, the bigger of the two newcomers, waved us forward—a broad, bulky, bearded man with a deep tan and an easy smile—and threw his arms wide. "Welcome," he said. "Claire, who are your friends?"

The other man, Beckett, stayed a step back, studying his boots. Tension was suddenly thick in the air. There was the obvious strain between Callie and Beckett, of course, but also a fair amount surrounding Kenai—who seemed like the jovial, let's-grab-a-drink type, but who was also clearly wondering whether we were friends or foes.

"This is Christoff," Claire said, indicating the older Russian man. "And his children. He wants to talk to Armor. He has a request. Bear-to-bear."

Kenai's eyebrows rose. "Ah, I see. And this woman?" he asked, eyeing me up and down.

Claire bristled. "That's none of your business, you big furball."

Kenai laughed and held out his arm for Claire to take. "It doesn't matter. Armor will find out. Come on, I'll escort you." Claire scowled but eventually took his arm, resting her head on his shoulder as they walked back towards the snow bank and whatever lay beyond. Beckett trailed them, leaving us to take up the rear.

"So," I said, trekking alongside Christoff and Callie, who had insisted on taking Christoff's little girl for the duration of our walk, "what's the story with Beckett?"

"Former cop. Betrayed me. Betrayed us all. Joined up with a group that hunts down Freaks and sold us out." Callie replied, her tone clipped and cool. She spoke softly, but I could tell Beckett—with his enhanced hearing—heard every word; his head hung lower and lower as she filled me in. If Callie noticed, she didn't seem to care. "He came to his senses, but not before taking a blow from Claire in her werebear form. He's here learning how to control his baser instincts and avoiding me. Which is for the best." She said that last bit a little louder, just in case.

I nodded in understanding; neither of us were the type to let things like that go—very much the never forgive, never forget types. Although she and I had clashed more than once upon meeting each other for the first time, I'd come to appreciate her no-fucks-given attitude and her irreverent sense of humor—even if it routinely toed the line between sarcasm and spite.

"So, d'ye want me to kill him?" I asked, teasingly, knowing I couldn't even if I wanted to; I'd left the assault rifle back at Callie's place.

Showing up armed for bear when you're about to ask a bunch of bears for a favor?

A bit counterintuitive.

Callie grunted, then grinned thoughtfully. "No, but if you get a chance to dick punch him like you did that poor kid..."

"That was an accident!" I hissed, glaring at her.

Callie shrugged, but I could tell she was in a better mood, so I let it be. "Oh," Callie said, "keep in mind that things may be a little different here than what you're used to. And don't stare. They don't like it when you stare."

"Who?" I asked, eyebrows knotting.

"Them," Callie replied as we cleared the bend. Down below, in a bowl-shaped valley ringed by huts and cabins, stood a host of people milling about, exchanging small talk, most of them completely butt-ass naked.

Oh. Right.

Eyes to myself.

Got it.

CHAPTER 21

*A*rmor, the Alpha of the Kansas City werebears, lounged on a massive throne in the middle of the room like some sort of bear deity. Below him, next to the throne, a tiny, adorable bear fastidiously cleaned his paws. His son, maybe? Other than those two, Kenai and Claire were the only other werebears present; Beckett had wandered off shortly after we entered the basin the werebears called home. Callie had taken the children to the far side of the room and was busy playing peek-a-boo with the little girl, giving her giggle fits. The slightly older boy sat and stared at the massive bear, eyes wide as dinner plates. Christoff hadn't wanted to part with them, of course, but Claire had insisted.

"Armor will have questions," she'd explained. "They'll be safe with Callie. Safer, really, if he doesn't like your answers."

I wasn't exactly sure why I was being called up to the front of the class, too, but decided not to rock the boat. Maybe they wanted a character witness, or maybe they wanted to vet me and make sure I wasn't a threat. Either way, I had nothing to hide.

Well, less than most, anyway.

Armor hunched forward, settling his titanic paw on the arm of the throne with a thud. "I've been informed that you have a request to make of us," Armor said. "But we do not know you, and therefore do not trust you.

SHAYNE SILVERS & CAMERON O'CONNELL

We don't make a habit of aiding those we do not trust. What do you suggest?" The Alpha's snout swung around, and his eyes met mine.

"Me?" I asked, jerking my thumb towards my chest.

"Yes, you," Armor replied, lips curling back in what I hoped was amusement.

I frowned at Christoff, who seemed as surprised as I was that they'd asked me and not him. I noticed the small bear had perked up and seemed unusually interested in my response—his beady little eyes locked on my face. I considered Armor's question and finally shrugged. "Well, assumin' knowin' someone leads to trust, I suggest ye lot get to know each other and go from there."

Armor nodded. "My thoughts exactly. So, stranger," he said, swiveling his gaze to the man beside me, "tell us about yourself."

Christoff nodded, though his head hung so low afterwards that he may as well have been sentenced to the gallows. "My name is Christoff Peterson," Christoff began. "I am—"

"That won't do," the diminutive bear said, his words a little garbled as he gnawed on a rock. "If you can't at least tell us your real name, you will always be a stranger."

I held up a hand, frowning at the bear I'd taken to be a child. "No offense to the Snuggle Bear," I said, "but that *is* his name." It was a ridiculous thing to accuse Christoff of, as if they were looking for an excuse to tell him no.

Armor bristled at my comment, like an overprotective father, but the tiny bear held up a paw.

"It's alright," the tiny bear said, chuckling at me good-naturedly. "But please, call me Starlight from now on." The bear, Starlight, rose to stand on his hind legs, maybe half as tall as I was, at most. "You should know that Starlight is the name I go by, but not the name I was born with. Just as I know that Christoff Peterson is the name he has chosen for himself but was not the name he was given at birth." The bear's eyes twinkled mischievously, and I suddenly had the impression that he was older than Armor, despite his stature. It was something about how he stood—that hunched, bow-legged stance that afflicts the elderly.

"He is right," Christoff said, flicking his eyes at me before staring at the ground. "I swore off my name, the name given to me, long ago."

"But it haunts you," Starlight said. "Your name is at the heart of why you have come."

Christoff marveled at the little bear as if he were some sort of prophet. "How do you know this?"

Starlight waved that away and settled back down on his haunches. "Tell Armor the truth from now on, if you want him to help you. Remember your proverbs. The burden is light on the shoulders of another."

Christoff flinched and bowed his head. "Yes. You are right." He raised his chin and the hard, fierce gaze of the man who'd held a rifle on me settled on Armor, who growled in response to the sudden change. "The name I was given, along with my comrades, was Alexie Stepanov," Christoff said. "It means Defender of Crown."

He glanced over his shoulder, ignoring my dumbfounded expression, to stare back at his two children, who Callie had corralled into making a miniature snowman. He seemed relieved they weren't listening. "Today, I own and run bar. But, many years ago, I fled from Russia. I left behind who I was, hoping to find better life. I did this. I changed name. I found wife and had children. Made family." He bowed his head. "But they have found me, somehow."

"Who found you?" Armor asked.

"The *Bor'ba Medvedi*," Christoff said, turning back to face the throne. "The Fighting Bears. Soldiers and spies trained from birth to fight for Mother Russia."

While Starlight bobbed his head in understanding, the other werebears in the room exchanged baffled glances. The tiny bear tapped Armor's leg. "May I?"

Armor nodded.

"Who did you serve under?" Starlight asked, seemingly unperturbed by Christoff's change in demeanor. I, meanwhile, wasn't sure how to feel. Part of me felt betrayed, but I wasn't sure why; Christoff didn't owe me his life story, and I certainly hadn't given him mine. But it was there, all the same, lingering like a bad aftertaste.

A child's abrupt laughter distracted me—Christoff's son was tossing snow on Callie, who had fallen back with a moan, pretending to be mortally wounded. I frowned, realizing I was being silly, blaming Christoff for not being the consummate family man I'd taken him for; it didn't change what he was willing to do to protect his family, or what I was willing to do to help him.

Still, I wish he'd have told me.

"So that's why you left," Starlight said, and I realized I'd missed a huge chunk of the conversation while dwelling on my mixed feelings.

"Yes. I saw an opportunity and took it," Christoff replied.

Starlight glanced up at Armor. "You heard the man. What do you think?"

Armor propped up his enormous head with one paw, studying Christoff. "What is your request?" he finally asked.

Christoff cleared his throat. "I do not wish to part with my children, but I can see no other way. I would ask you to guard and protect my children while I go and search for their mother."

"Your former comrades have her?" Armor asked.

Christoff dipped his head in acknowledgment.

Armor settled back against the throne, considering the situation and Christoff's request. "We will protect your cubs," Armor said, but then held up a single, viciously sharp claw. "But first I'd like to see you take on one of my bears. I believe you, but I have no desire to send a fellow bear to his death. If you aren't up for it, I will insist you stay behind and let the human authorities look into her whereabouts. I have no interest in raising your children for you."

"I'll take him on," Kenai called.

Claire punched his arm. "No one asked you."

"I will do this," Christoff said off-handedly, as if Armor had asked him to take out the trash.

"Good, now that we've settled that," Starlight chimed in, "what can we help you with?" His grizzled, teddy bear face swung towards me.

"Who me?" I asked, for the second time. "I'm along for the ride with Bearnedict Arnold over here, that's all," I insisted, jerking a thumb towards Christoff, who grimaced at the reference.

Starlight grunted and slid off the dais, tottering over to me with the help of a small staff. He stopped a foot away and stared up at my face. "How does it feel to be so broken?" he asked, cheerily.

My eyebrows shot up. "*Excuse* me?"

"You know, you should pay attention to your dreams, every once in a while. And drink less."

"Callie could always take her to AA!" Claire called, being obnoxious. Kenai cuffed her on the arm. She immediately cuffed him right back, then she nuzzled against his chest.

"I don't have a drinkin' problem, Paddington," I replied, ignoring the bizarre couple and the likelihood of their relationship devolving to domestic abuse. "What d'ye know about me dreams?"

Starlight spun and wobbled back towards the throne. "Wrong question."

Wrong question? What the fuck did that mean? I thought back to the numerous times I'd woken up over the last several weeks in a cold sweat, my heart pounding, my senses on fire. I ran a hand through my hair, before realizing Starlight was waiting for me to ask another question. The right one this time. I sighed. "Can ye help me?" I took a guess, biting down my Irish pride in hopes that he had something good to tell me. Some kind of answer.

Starlight tapped his staff against the ground. "Much better. And sure. It'll take some time for us to prepare you, of course, to know we can trust you with our secrets, otherwise—"

"Can't I just fight a werebear to prove meself, like Christoff?" I interrupted, half-jokingly.

Armor huffed. "I don't think—"

"I mean, unless you t'ink there should be a different standard for men than for women," I said, glaring at the Alpha and his wee sidekick.

Armor clearly looked uncomfortable, shuffling his big, hairy butt on the throne. He exchanged looks with Starlight, who seemed amused. Finally, Armor cleared his throat, the sound startlingly loud in the tiny hut coming from the mouth of a bear. "Well, I suppose that would be alright. Although, I should warn you, it can be dangerous—"

"I want Beckett," I declared.

Even Starlight seemed surprised by that; his beady little eyes widened comically. Armor shook his shaggy head. "He's still learning control. That wouldn't be wise."

"You pitted Beckett against Claire when she was newly turned," Callie called out as she offered Christoff's daughter a snowball to chuck at her squealing brother—obviously having followed our exchange much closer than she had let on. She pinned Armor with a judgmental glare. "What's the difference?"

"Will you vouch for her safety, then, Callie Penrose?" Armor fired back, his tone clearly warning her not to overstep.

Callie and I exchanged looks. We hadn't really discussed our abilities, but—over the course of the weekend—we'd seen each other in action; Callie with her angelic powers and preternatural reflexes, and me with my hand-to-hand fighting skills and violent, no-holds-barred tendencies. Still, she had to know feeding me to a werebear came with potential consequences, and I could see doubt warring across her face.

"Please," I insisted, "I'll do anythin' to get a good night's sleep. And I owe the bastard a dick punch," I added, smirking.

Callie snickered. "I'll vouch for her," she said, finally, "but keep an eye on Beckett. We all know how far he's willing to go when he goes up against a Freak."

Oh, that tone was cold. So, so cold.

The werebears in attendance grudgingly accepted her comment, though I could see her choice of delivery didn't sit well with most. The truth hurts, I guess. Starlight, of course, hardly seemed to have heard. Instead, he studied Callie, head tilted quizzically.

What an odd fucking bear.

"Very well, then," Armor said. "Kenai, gather the bears."

CHAPTER 22

One thing they neglect to tell you about fights between werebears: clothing is most definitely optional. While I'd been surprised to find out that the Kansas City bears' Alaskan retreat doubled as the United States most low-key nudist commune, I honestly hadn't expected that to apply to the fights as well. I mean, even male gladiators got to put on skimpy leather numbers to protect their junk from flying all over the place. Naturally, Christoff hadn't even batted an eye at the custom; he took his clothes off one article at a time, folding each neatly in a pile on a nearby rock. I, meanwhile, waived the honor of getting naked in front of a bunch of strangers—the Alaskan wilderness sure as shit wasn't my kind of strip club.

Besides, even if it were, they couldn't afford me.

"You sure?" Kenai asked me, winking at my apparent prudishness.

"I'm pretty sure Claire *will* kill ye, ye know, if ye keep that shit up," I replied, glaring.

Kenai laughed and began untying the laces of his boots. "She's cute when she's jealous. But she knows I don't mean anything by it. So, your friend, the Russian spy..." Kenai said, jerking his head towards Christoff, who stood naked on the other side of the makeshift arena, hemmed in by a horde of freshly transformed werebears. "He any good?"

Frankly, I had no idea. I knew Christoff had put down a bridge troll, but I'd been too busy climbing out of the ruin that was my car to watch it all go down play-by-play. Still, no matter how badly I felt like lashing out at Christoff for lying to me, I wasn't about to pass up an opportunity to mess with Kenai's head. "He's old," I said, finally. "He's got kids. And he runs a bar. And his old friends just took his wife..." I shrugged and left the rest to Kenai's imagination, although I had to admit, Christoff didn't look like your average bar owner; he looked like a fighter, his muscles taut and firm, with silvered scars dancing across his body. He looked dangerous, and Armor had given him a lot to fight for. "Good luck," I said, patting Kenai's shoulder before walking backwards to see his reaction as I headed towards Callie and Claire. "Ye may need it."

Kenai frowned, but continued getting undressed until he stood in all his nude glory.

Basically, a man-sized Brillo pad made of hair and muscle. He strutted to his side of the clearing and bellowed, joined quickly by many of the bears in attendance. I nudged Claire and pointed. "I see what ye see in him," I quipped, earning a fierce scowl. Callie chuckled, and I was about to join in before I noticed Beckett sitting on a rock by himself, far removed from the crowd. Callie tracked my gaze and then pointedly turned back towards the fight.

"He's good, you know," Callie said, sounding as if she was gritting her teeth to admit it. "Beckett came here as a human and fought Claire to a standstill."

Claire crossed her arms over her chest and huffed. "He cheated."

"Cheated?" I asked.

"He stripped down before they fought. Claire got...distracted." Callie tried her best to keep a straight face, but I could tell she was struggling.

Claire muttered something under her breath that I couldn't make out. I frowned, realizing the kids weren't in sight. "What happened to the wee ones?" I asked.

"Armor had one of our mother bears take them to a cabin. She'll keep them entertained," Claire explained. "We thought it would be best if they didn't see their dad fighting."

"Ah," I said, "makes sense." I didn't bother mentioning that they'd seen their father disembowel a man a few hours before; if the KC bears wanted to be conscientious, more power to them.

"Bears!" Armor called out, emerging from the hut we'd left behind, Starlight marching behind him. The Alpha's wide shoulders brushed past his fellow bears, and soon he stood at the front of the crowd. "Today, a stranger strives to become known to us. Christoff, of the Russian Fighting Bears, will take on Kenai, of the Kansas City Bears. Let it begin."

Kenai sprung forward and, with a stupendous roar, exploded into his bear form. A grizzly weighing in around a metric ton. He shuffled forward on all fours, angling his body sideways towards Christoff like a cat prepared to strike. Christoff never even blinked; he simply stood in human form, waiting for Kenai to come closer.

"What's he doing?" Claire asked. "He's not planning on taking Kenai without shifting, is he?"

Callie shook her head, unsure.

I tried my best to act like I knew what Christoff was about to do, planting a smug smile on my face for all to see. Inwardly, I cringed. If Christoff ended up losing here, there was nothing he could do but stay behind with his kids. Callie was our ride, after all, and I doubted she would defy Armor's ruling. Which would leave me to hunt down Christoff's wife.

Maybe the Sickos would help me...

If they were still alive.

Kenai bellowed once more, drawing my attention back to the fight. As close as he was to Christoff, the roar actually ruffled the old bartender's hair. Kenai pushed off the ground to stand on his two hind legs, his shadow falling over Christoff, and raised a meaty paw. When the man still didn't move, Kenai brought it crashing down, throwing the full weight of his body into the swipe...and was stopped short.

Christoff, naked as the day he was born, held Kenai's paw between two of his own—his arms abnormally, disproportionately large and covered in mounds of dark brown fur. The older man snarled, turned his body, and pushed off from a deep squat, tossing Kenai to the side. By the time Kenai rolled and came up on all fours, Christoff's arms had returned to normal. I briefly wondered why Christoff hadn't gone after his opponent, but then I noticed the stunned reaction from the crowd of bears.

"He can *partially shift?*" Claire whispered, her eyes wide. She spun and grabbed me by my jacket. "Did you know he could do that?"

I eyed Claire's dainty hands, wondering how she'd get by in life once I sliced them off at the wrist. Fortunately, Callie cut in before I had time to react, nudging Claire with her hip. "Let her go, Claire. Quinn's touchy about her personal space. And Kenai signed up for this."

125

Claire glared at me, but finally let go. I readjusted my jacket and, after a moment's hesitation, decided to answer Claire's question. I could tell she was simply frightened and lashing out, even if she didn't want to admit it. I wouldn't hold that against her...well, not for long, anyway. "He's always been able to do that. But he's the only werebear I've ever met, so I didn't know it was rare," I admitted.

"I've never seen any of the bears do it until I came to rescue you two and I saw his paw," Callie admitted.

"*You* knew?" Claire demanded, ringing her hands nervously.

"Suspected. I know two werewolves who can pull it off," Callie said, thoughtfully, "but it never occurred to me to ask if the bears knew how."

"It's a lost ability," Claire said, watching as Kenai circled the older man, clearly warier now than he had been. "Bears rarely come together the way we have, but some of the older members claim to have known werebears who could do it. Their ancestors, mostly. But even then..." she drifted off.

I nodded in understanding; by showing off his ability in front of the Cave, Christoff had proven there was truth behind the legend—a werebear who could shift parts of himself at will. The question was, how much of an edge did that provide?

And did that make him Legend-Beary?

Christoff, seemingly tired of being on the defensive, answered that question in record time. He ran at Kenai, who backed up and rose on his hind legs, instinctually. Kenai swiped a paw at the man, but Christoff was faster; he ducked beneath the paw and stepped in close. In an instant, Christoff grew, his thick, muscular legs giving way to the hind end of a Kamchatka brown bear—a breed of Russian bear found in Siberia, said to be the ancestors of the Kodiak. The rest of his body shifted in a lightning-fast wave—faster than Kenai could react—that rippled upwards until his entire body was covered in fur.

Of course, some of that fur was Kenai; for a brief moment, the massive grizzly lay across Christoff's shoulders, implausibly held aloft, his paws hanging a few feet off the ground as Christoff spun in a slow circle. Then Christoff tucked one shoulder and tossed the grizzly to the snow where he landed with a sickening crunch. Kenai raised his head for just a moment, roaring in pain, then let it fall back into the snow. I wasn't sure what, exactly, but I was pretty certain he'd broken something.

No bear was meant to be thrown like that.

"Enough!" Armor roared. I could tell even the Alpha was shaken by Christoff's werebear form; from where I stood, I couldn't tell which of them was taller, or larger. If the two clashed, it would be like watching titans go at it. Fortunately, Christoff didn't seem the least bit interested in asserting dominance over Kansas City's Bear Lord. The older man shifted back to his human form in an instant, not even winded, although I could see a sheen of sweat on his brow.

"Will you keep my children safe, as promised?" Christoff called out, not-so-subtly making sure his deal with Armor was known to the rest of the Cave.

Armor nodded. "Until you return to claim them," he said, staring down at Kenai, "which I have little doubt you'll manage." The Alpha scanned the crowd, then waved. "Claire! Come and see to Kenai!"

Claire rushed forward, sliding in next to the grizzly.

"She used to be a veterinarian. One of the best," Callie explained. "She'll make sure he's alright."

I nodded, not trusting myself to speak, but Callie caught my expression. "What is it?"

I shook my head. "Just wonderin' who me friends really are, that's all," I said, staring at Christoff as he retrieved his clothes.

"I know what you mean," Callie said, watching as Beckett approached, the chip on his shoulder practically visible.

Oh, right.

Guess that made it my turn.

CHAPTER 23

*B*eckett kept his clothes on, which I was almost upset about. Unlike Kenai, who'd been nearly as furry naked as he was as a bear, Beckett struck me as the manscaping type; I was willing to bet there was a six pack under all that hostility.

He and I waited for Claire to help Kenai back to his feet before stepping forward; the big bastard had likely broken a few ribs, and seemed to be favoring one leg, but he managed to wink at me as he passed—earning another solid blow from Claire—so he couldn't be hurting too much.

I realized the crowd seemed less interested in our bout, for some reason. Many of the bears pointedly looked away. Maybe the novelty of a human facing a bear had diminished after witnessing Christoff's little show? Beckett noticed as well, the skin around his eyes tightening in anger, but said nothing. Starlight appeared at my side as if by magic, slipping in under the forepaws of a nearby bear as he gnawed on a small branch. He glanced up at me, then at Beckett.

"Some of our bears were targeted when the Templars came to town," Starlight said. "The Templars were the ones who recruited Beckett. Freak hunters. An old religion." He licked the tip of the pine branch and grimaced, tossing it aside. "Sap," he explained as he pawed at his tongue to remove the sticky residue. "Anyway, he hasn't received a warm welcome. And he refuses to shift. That's mostly why Armor didn't want you fighting him."

I stared at the man across the clearing, noting the warning signs for the first time—the tightly balled fists and the way his muscles seemed in a constant state of tension, like a prize fighter the day before the bout. What I'd mistaken for anger was, in fact, a man at war with his nature. The other bears sensed it, too, their eyes averted as if avoiding the powder keg sitting at the center of the room. Because he *would* blow, eventually. No shifter could fight their beast indefinitely. At least none that I'd ever met.

"What d'ye suggest?" I asked Starlight.

"Suggest?" The little bear cocked his head at me, quizzically. "I was just trying to tell you that you made a dumb decision. Have fun!" Starlight waved and sauntered off.

I glowered at his retreating back.

"Bears!" Armor called, for the second time.

"No theatrics," Beckett yelled, before Armor could go on. "Let's get this over with." He marched towards me. "I heard you asked for me, personally. I'm flattered," he snarled, self-loathing dancing in his eyes.

I didn't bother responding. Anything I said was guaranteed to make him angrier, and I didn't want that. Usually, I would welcome a pissed-off opponent; anger blinded most fighters, leaving them vulnerable. But someone who was on the verge of shifting for the first time?

That would be like poking the bear.

I crack myself up.

What I needed, instead, was to drop Beckett before he could Hulk out on me. My field would protect me from his werebear form, of course, but a shifter's first time could be unpredictable. He could end up getting himself seriously hurt, and maybe me, too—even Regulars can do some crazy shit when their adrenaline is up.

Unfortunately, Beckett seemed to have the same idea.

The former cop broke into a run, charging me, dropping his shoulder to catch me at the knees. Fighters called this practice "shooting," because the whole goal was to lift your opponent and bring them down. Hard. Fortunately, I'd seen men use the same approach time and time again whenever they sparred with a woman; men always tried to grapple first, hoping to overpower the woman and end the fight without throwing a punch. Which is how I knew to splay my legs out wide like I'd been trained, using gravity and my own bodyweight to prevent him from lifting me off the ground.

We collided, and I brought my elbow down, solidly connecting with the back of his head. He grunted, fell to one knee, and rolled away, probably choosing to distance himself from me and come up with a new strategy.

But I wasn't about to let that happen.

I rushed the man before he could get to his feet, kicked snow up into his eyes to blind him, and then swung my other foot across his face. The thick edge of my rubber boot slammed against his jaw, and blood hit the snow.

I aimed another kick at his exposed midsection, except, this time, Beckett was prepared. He caught my foot, trapped it, and rolled, sending me flying face first into the ground. I flipped over, prepared for another exchange, but Beckett had already scrambled away. He rose, tonguing his busted lip. I did the same, groaning, my knees aching.

I was getting too old for this shit.

"Ye shouldn't have let me up," I said, brushing powder off my jacket.

Beckett shrugged. "Ready to go again?"

I fell back into a comfortable stance, my legs akimbo, arms bent. "Aye, whenever ye are."

Beckett approached with a lot more caution this time around. He feinted in like a boxer, dipping to his left and firing a stiff jab that I slapped away. He sidestepped again, trying a one-two combination—another jab and a straight. I knocked those away as well. I could tell he was testing my reaction time, trying to get me to open up, but I'd been in too many fights for that tactic to work. Beckett smirked, feigned a punch, and fired off a kick aimed at my thigh. I took it. Then, as quickly as I could manage, I dropped to one knee and blasted the poor guy right in the crotch with a jab of my own.

Beckett crumpled, groaning as he clutched his family jewels.

A collective grumble greeted me when I stood—I guess even bears despised low blows. I waved and bowed a little, then flashed Callie a thumbs up. Her eyes were wide, as if she hadn't really expected me to punch him in the nuts, but she returned the gesture, although very discreetly. Beckett, meanwhile, had risen to his knees, coughing.

"Oh, c'mon," I said, patronizingly, "I didn't even hit ye that hard."

"I appreciate the restraint," he said, between gasps.

I started to respond, but was interrupted by Beckett's headbutt, his forehead slamming into my abdomen with a surprising amount of force. I fell back onto my ass, gasping, holding my poor stomach. We both lay there for a minute, gathering ourselves. I wondered what we looked like to the bears —probably ridiculous, us fighting with our fists like Neanderthals.

Together we staggered to our feet. I eyed Beckett, acknowledging his speed and general wiliness; it took balls to headbutt someone while cradling your...well, balls. From our brief exchanges, I knew I wouldn't catch him napping, which meant I had to hit him hard, and often, if I wanted to win. I waved him forward. "Anytime, pretty boy. Just be sure to *protect* those stones, or I'll *serve* ye another helpin'," I quipped, playing on the policeman's motto—to protect and serve.

Low blow, I know.

Beckett's eyes flashed.

Sadly, making him angry didn't seem to make him any less capable. He rushed me, leading with a series of punches—jabs, hooks, uppercuts. Anything to keep me off balance. It was a good strategy; if even one connected, I'd be dazed enough for him to finish the job. It helped that he was disciplined, drawing his forearms back after each punch to protect his head. But if there was one thing I knew about fights, it was that the longer they went on, the sloppier you became—and Beckett had spent an awful lot of time and energy on offense.

Which meant it was my turn.

I began trading punches, leaning back to dodge a hook, then springing forward to land a body shot. When Beckett brought his arms down to shield his ribs, I struck with a hook of my own, twisting my torso and hips so hard I almost slipped in the snow. Thankfully, my new boots had plenty of tread and I was able to stay upright. Beckett, however, took the shot right on the temple and dropped to one knee, reeling from the blow. I dug my fingers into his hair and, savagely, rammed my knee in his face. He fell back, bleeding from his shattered nose.

I danced away, massaging my knee, cursing under my breath. I always found it ironic how action movies portrayed fights, especially the one-sided brawls where the main character whoops ass, takes down like ten people, and goes on about their day. The truth was, contrary to what most people think, even winning a fight like that comes at a cost. Tomorrow, my knuckles would be swollen and my knee bruised—you can't hit anything that hard without consequences, after all. Hell, I routinely woke up with bruises I couldn't explain even when I *hadn't* gotten into a fight. Of course, that still meant I'd be better off than Beckett, who was only just now coming to.

"Oy!" I called, scanning the crowd until I found Armor. "D'ye t'ink that's enough?"

Armor nodded, curtly, and began to speak, but was cut off by Beckett, who sat up with a groan. "I'm not done yet," he insisted. He thrust one leg forward and stood, listing a little, then raised his fists. "Come on, then."

I frowned, but Armor didn't seem inclined to deny the man—he actually looked pensive—so I did as Beckett wished. I took two quick steps forward to cover the distance, dodged a lazy kick, and blasted him with a straight cross, knocking him flat on his ass yet again. Before I could step back, however, he grabbed hold of my leg, pinning me in place. I brought my heel down on his chest. Once. Twice. He finally let go, his right eye swollen shut, nursing a few shattered ribs, blood spilling out of his mouth and nose. I turned to walk away.

"I'm...not done," Beckett said, leaning on one elbow. He managed to get onto all fours. "Finish it," he said, voice cracking. When I didn't make a move, he propped himself back onto his knees, his fists hanging limp at his sides. "Do it!" he screamed, blood and spittle spewing from his mouth. "Come on!" He fell forward, panting, glaring up at me out of his good eye. The clearing was eerily silent, and a brief look around confirmed that every single bear was now paying very, *very* close attention.

A man on a ledge will always draw a crowd.

"Are ye sure?" I asked. "Ye look like shite."

He continued giving me the evil eye, his face locked in a grimace of pain and hate. But I knew now it wasn't me he hated—not really. This whole show wasn't Beckett being a tough guy, it was a man in pain, whose self-loathing had grown to the point that he felt he deserved to be punished. The disgraced cop wanted me to play judge, jury, and executioner.

Most would have walked away...

But I was from Boston, not the Midwest.

I obliged him.

I whirled and fired off a side kick, driving my foot into Beckett's shoulder, connecting with enough force to send him sprawling on his back. But I wasn't done; if Beckett wanted to be punished, then I was prepared to go as far as I had to. I mounted his upper body, fending off his feeble attempts to grab me, and punched him in the face. Then again. And again. Eventually, his arms fell limp. I finally drew back, my knuckles bloody, shaking.

Beckett, on the verge of losing consciousness, stared blearily up at me from a face so mangled it no longer looked human. He smiled through blood-stained teeth. "You punch...like a girl," he rasped.

I snorted. It was now or never. "Shut up before ye pass out, ye idgit. Ye know, if ye don't shift soon, your face will stay like this," I said, jerking my chin towards his broken mug.

Beckett grimaced. "No more magazine covers for me, I guess." He started to laugh; I could feel his body shaking beneath me. Except it didn't stop. His eyes rolled back, and blood frothed at his mouth. His limbs began to twitch and spasm.

"Claire!" I screamed. "He's havin' a seizure!"

I felt something tug at my pant leg and realized Starlight was by my side. "He's not seizing," Starlight explained. "He's shifting. He can't hold it at bay any longer. Too much damage...but I suspect you *knew* that would happen," he said, studying the torn skin of my knuckles. "Come on."

I followed him, crossing over to where Callie stood, her expression smug. A small contingent of polar bears fell in to the space we'd left, circling around Beckett as he twisted and turned, shifting in pieces. I could tell it hurt. "Is it always so violent?" I asked.

"He's fighting it, still," Starlight replied, shaking his head sympathetically. "He's suffering a great deal."

"Good," Callie chimed in.

Starlight swiveled his head around, eyes narrowed. "You've seen the detective's soul, Callie Penrose. Have you forgotten what you saw there? Can you so easily cast the first stone?"

Callie grunted, her expression haughty—disdainful even. "I would never betray my friends. Not like that. Besides, *no one* uses me and gets away with it."

"I wouldn't be so sure," Starlight said, enigmatically. "We all have our limits. Our flaws. Like seeking vengeance," Starlight said, nodding at Beckett's writhing form. "Or forsaking mercy."

Callie started, lips parting wordlessly for a few seconds. Then she spun on her heel and marched off. Starlight didn't even bother watching her leave. Instead, we watched as Beckett tottered like a baby deer in his brand-new form: a sun bear, barely clearing five-feet, his chest covered in a U-shaped patch of golden fur like a super hero.

He was...*adorable.*

"Well, *that's* unexpected," Starlight said, after a moment's hesitation.

"Well, at least now ye aren't the only height-challenged bear, here," I quipped. "Maybe ye two could start a club."

Starlight thumped me with his staff. "Alright, show's over. Let's go get you cleaned up and see what twisted things you have floating around in your head," he said.

I cringed, remembering why I'd opted into this fight in the first place. As I followed the tiny bear, I found myself praying my subconscious wasn't as messed up as Starlight suggested.

As if.

CHAPTER 24

*C*laire met us on the fringes of the bear's refuge. Starlight and I had walked for what seemed like an eternity, weaving between the trees in silence, leaving me plenty of time to dwell on whatever was about to happen. I had no idea what the bear had in store for me—some form of hypnosis or psychotherapy that would bring my subconscious to the fore, maybe—but I wasn't eager to figure out what had been waking me up in a panic the last several weeks. Some nightmares were better left alone. Still, I needed a good night's rest something fierce, and I wasn't going to get it by chickening out now. I'd had to break a pretty man's face just to get here— the least I could do was stick around to see what I'd paid for.

That said, I was worried about Beckett. Sure, according to Callie, the guy was a world-class shitbag who had betrayed his friends and hunted down Freaks, but you get a read on a person when you fight them—an insight into who they are and what they're about. And, from what I could tell, Beckett was a decent guy. Angry, yes. Self-loathing, definitely. But honorable, willing to let me stand when he could have attacked, even going so far as to come at me like he meant it, which few men have the guts to do. Despite all that, if he didn't get his shit together, soon, he'd end up throwing himself in front of a bullet meant for someone else, or go charging into a no-win situation that was guaranteed to get him killed.

In fact, that's why I'd gone after him so hard.

Sometimes the only way to make someone see reason is to blind them to everything else.

"Jesus," Claire said, sniffing the air and noting the blood spattered across my knuckles and on my clothes—most of it Beckett's. "What happened to you?"

"Beckett's a sun bear," I said, ignoring her question. "You're welcome."

"A what?" Claire glanced at Starlight, who'd settled next to a small campfire. Kenai lay on his side in bear form, sleeping, his snores threatening to put out the fire. When Starlight didn't answer, Claire huffed and held out a hand. "Alright, well, let's get you patched up."

I shook my head. "All I need is a wet towel and some antiseptic," I said, then glanced down at myself. "And maybe a washing machine. Most of this blood is his."

Claire looked a little alarmed at that but decided not to comment. "Wait, so your clothes aren't self-washing, too?" she said instead, sarcastically.

I glared at her, then cocked an eyebrow. "Ye know…" I tapped and held my finger against my shoulder and watched as it became the same shirt, sans the blood spatter.

"Oh, come on!" Claire said. "Starlight, make her share!"

Starlight leaned in to sniff my shirt, testing its material between his paws, and even went so far as to try and lick it.

"Oy! Easy there!" I said, swatting his paw away and drawing back.

Claire chuckled. "I remember when I had boundaries."

I rolled my eyes and tapped the remainder of my clothes, discarding Beckett's blood and returning them back to normal. "Towel," I growled.

The bouncy blonde giggled and fetched a pack of alcohol wipes from a small First Aid kit lying next to Kenai. She tossed it to me, grinning. "All we have, I'm afraid."

I sighed, tore open the packet with my teeth, and began swabbing down my hands. I didn't cry. Not even once. Because I was a big girl.

"You should stop making that face," Claire advised, "or no one is ever gonna love you."

"Shut it," I hissed through clenched teeth. Starlight, meanwhile, wandered over to the campfire and began fiddling with a pipe that rested on a rock. Claire's eyes brightened upon seeing it.

"Oh! Is that how you're going to help her?"

Starlight nodded his furry little head, put the pipe to his lips, and took an experimental toke, the sudden aroma immediately recognizable, although slightly unique.

"Seriously?" I asked. "Your solution to me problem is to smoke me up?" I tossed the alcohol wipes and wrapper at Claire, who caught them and immediately looked sick to her stomach to be holding the bloody remains of my fight with Beckett. I grinned. "Talk about a face no one could ever love," I quipped.

"It's a ritual!" Claire argued, ignoring my jab as she tossed the wipes in a plastic sack next to the kit. "A sacred ritual. I swear, you and Callie can't help yourselves. Always jumping to conclusions."

"Excuse me?" Callie called, stepping out from between the trees. Claire stuck out her tongue, repeated herself, and thrust her hands on her hips as if challenging Callie to disagree. Callie sighed and glanced over at Starlight. "Yeah, well," she began, "it's a good thing I have people around who can set me straight, I guess."

Starlight dipped his head and blew a smoke ring as big as my head. "So, are you ready?" he asked me.

"Taking Quinn on a vision quest?" Callie asked, folding her arms over her chest.

"There are things she needs to see," Starlight replied in a mellow, distant tone.

Callie leaned in and whispered loud enough for us all to hear, "You know you have to get naked to smoke that, right?"

I gaped at her, realized she was serious, and whirled on the tiny bear. "Absolutely not!"

Claire raised her hands in a helpless gesture. "It's part of the ritual."

"Listen here, ye wee little pervert, I will not be gettin' naked, ye hear?"

Callie laughed and held out a hand. "I told you," she said. "Fork it over."

"Fine," Claire growled, shoving a ten-dollar bill into Callie's outstretched palm.

"Ye bet I'd say no?" I asked.

Callie shrugged, smirking. "Took a shot in the dark, that's all."

Claire grumbled something about insider trading but left it at that. If Starlight was bothered by my refusal, he certainly didn't look it. In fact, the little stoner bear seemed content to watch us banter back and forth until the sun exploded. Of course, depending on the potency of his shit, I'd probably be cool with it, too. He burped, and a puff of smoke drifted out of his mouth. "Excuse me," he said.

"So, what now?" Callie asked.

"Well," Starlight said, staring up at me with a puzzled expression, like I was some sort of abstract painting, "there is another way. But it'll hurt. A lot."

"Another *way*?!" Callie interrupted. "Seriously? You felt me up, you little—"

"Callie!" Claire interjected. "He said it *hurts*. Didn't you hear that part?"

Callie scowled at her best friend, but finally rolled her eyes. "Sure, I heard."

I weighed my options. I sure as hell wasn't about to get undressed and let Starlight cop a feel while he dosed me with whatever he was on—I didn't give a shit whether Claire labeled it a "ritual" or not, it sounded an awful lot like date-rape to me. But the idea of putting myself through torture struck me as an equally shitty option. Hadn't I gone through enough already, today? I realized they were all looking at me expectantly and sighed. "Alright, guess I'll be takin' the red pill," I said. "Bring the pain."

Because when asked to decide between sex and suffering, one would always trump the other.

I'd been raised Catholic, after all.

CHAPTER 25

*S*tarlight led me to a grove and a patch of what he called wildflowers, but looked suspiciously like weeds, poking up through the snow. The grove itself was secluded, hemmed in on all sides by stone. I doubted I'd have found the place on my own, even if I'd had a year to look; forests were like that—a world unto themselves, full of hidden treasures. We'd left Claire and Callie behind with Kenai, who was still recovering. I could tell Callie was still caught up in her thoughts—Beckett, maybe, although there was no way to know for sure, what with everything else she had on her plate.

Like protecting an entire city.

Personally, I thought she was crazy for claiming jurisdiction over Kansas City; it was a major city, for Christ's sake, not some military compound where you could impose strict rules and monitor ingress and egress. Her ambitions were bold, though, I had to give her that. If I was being honest with myself, I'd have loved to play Sheriff in my own hometown, but Boston had a long, bloody history of powerful figures—mostly mobsters like Barboza and Bulger—taking over the city under the pretense of "building a better tomorrow," and I wasn't keen to add to that legacy. See, I didn't mind being put in the corner…no one can knife you in the back if you're in the corner.

"So, what now?" I asked.

"Pick one that speaks to you," Starlight said, showcasing the grove and its overgrowth.

I took a brief look around, found the wildflower nearest me, and plucked it from the ground. "Now what?"

Starlight looked nonplussed, which I found amusing. In my mind, a plant was a plant. Well, except for Eve—I wasn't sure what the fuck she was, besides a receptacle of random facts and a total pain in my ass.

"Alright, now eat it," Starlight said. He plopped down and put his back against a boulder, urging me to do the same with a wave of his paw. I frowned but did as he suggested. My ass would end up wet, but, considering I was about to go on some sort of drug-addled vision quest, it was probably the better alternative. I didn't want to end up dancing off the edge of a cliff, mistakenly thinking I was out for a night on the town.

"What then?" I asked, dubiously eyeing the plant.

"Then you will find your answers," Starlight replied.

"Not that part," I clarified. "Like, how will it feel?"

Starlight shrugged a furry shoulder. "Usually? The experience is pleasant. But that's if you consume it the way it was intended. In its raw state? Probably not so much. Do you want a list of the possible side effects?" Starlight asked.

I grimaced. "No, as long as none of 'em are permanent, I'll be fine."

Starlight snorted. "You're about to see into your own subconscious, and you think there won't be permanent side effects?" He grinned. "There are no such things as *safe words* in your subconscious, you know."

I rolled my eyes. "Whatever, ye know what I meant," I said, holding the plant this way and that. "Which part do I eat?"

Starlight scratched his head. "The ritual helps bring out the flower's natural properties," he said. "So, I'm not sure. Probably best to eat the whole thing. I'll get you another one if it doesn't work."

"You've never done this before?" I asked, eyes wide.

"Eaten a flower off the ground?" Starlight replied. "Please, I'm a bear. Of course, I have."

"Aye, but this flower?" I asked, pointing at the glorified weed.

"Oh, absolutely not. That would be monumentally stupid. But you didn't want to take part in the ritual, so..."

I stared at the bear, slack-jawed. He mimed an eating motion and flashed me a thumbs up with one dainty claw. "Fine," I growled, and took a hefty bite of the cleanest part of the flower. It was rancid. Bitter. I swallowed and could feel it working its way down, destined to fester in my gut. I took another bite. And another.

Finally, it was gone.

I used snow to wash it all down and clean the dirt off my mouth. Starlight, meanwhile, looked at me in awe. I realized at some point he'd snuck forward, his eyes comically wide, like a child watching an adult light a cigarette. "Wow," he admitted. "I didn't really think you'd do it. You must really hate getting naked."

I shot him a stern look. "How long before it takes effect?"

Starlight stared up at the sky, which had finally begun to darken, as if judging the time of day. "No idea."

"Has anyone told ye that you're useless?" I asked, clutching my stomach, which was already beginning to ache.

"Not to my face," Starlight said, his tongue flapping loose in his mouth like a dog's, grinning.

"Well ye are. Totally...completely...useless..." I managed, before the Earth spun on its axis and sent me flying off the edge of the world, colliding with clouds filled with mist, drifting past stars that shone like glittering jewels encased in flame, time a concept that had yet to be invented...

Guess the drugs were working.

*E*ventually, I landed. I lay on a cool surface, feeling...odd. I couldn't describe the sensation, other than to say it wasn't euphoric or painful. It just was. I rose onto all fours, then to one knee, and finally stood. Moving was hard, the air thick and heavy, as if gravity had been taken up a notch. I felt my joints complaining as I took one plodding step forward, and then another. And another.

Was this it? Was I doomed to wander around a dreamscape until I lost my mind? Or had that awful plant actually killed me? Did that make this Heaven? Or Hell? At that precise moment— almost as if wondering where I was triggered my ability to see my surroundings—I saw them.

Doors.

No, not doors. Windows, I realized. Windows so large I'd mistaken them for doors, anchored on nothing, they hung, suspended in thin air, in the hundreds. Maybe thousands, I realized; they hung as far as the eye could see in either direction, forming a hallway of sorts, a corridor in space. I took another lumbering step, this time towards one of the windows—an urge I couldn't describe compelled me to open it, to see what was on the other side. Fast as thought, I had my fingers curled around a handle, moments from twisting and pulling it back to reveal another world.

"Stop," a voice commanded.

I froze, unable to move, trapped in a sliver of time—if this *was* a dream, it suddenly no longer felt like my own. My skin broke out in a cold sweat. Maybe this was Hell, after all; maybe it was my fate to stare at a window for all eternity, never to see what lies on the other side.

"Turn," the voice said, the authority in it almost too much to take. I did as I was told, pivoting slightly, releasing the handle to look upon the speaker, and felt my legs turn to jelly.

My eyes burned, refusing to close, even to blink.

I knew that face.

I knew it almost as well as I knew my own—the slow curve of her cheek, the freckles that dotted her nose, the locks of auburn hair that fell freely over her shoulders. Only her eyes—a bluer, less green version of my own— were unrecognizable; instead they burned, smoke billowing out from her sockets as if a wildfire raged behind her eyelids.

"Ma..." I whispered, disbelieving, recalling the pictures Dez had shown me of her. Why was she here? Was this my subconscious trying to tell me something about my mother? What kind of sick joke was that? Except, it wasn't a joke. I realized this didn't even feel like a dream, really—it felt like I had wandered into another realm, a corridor that existed outside time and space, filled with gravity-defying windows.

The woman with my mother's face scowled and shook her head. She approached in a white gown, the edges of her dress trailing across an invisible floor, the cosmos visible far beneath her feet. I saw comets go soaring past planets I didn't recognize. Planets of all different colors which spun, ever so slowly. I lost sense of time as meteors drifted lazily along currents I couldn't see. Her hand at my chin brought my head up, and I realized I'd been staring—literally—into space.

She locked her gaze on my face, her eyes still smoldering. I marveled to see that her frown, like mine, turned her face into something bratty and petulant. For some reason, that made me smile.

"What are ye?" I asked. "Where are we?"

"You've come too soon," she replied, finally. She stepped away. "Leave."

I felt her will tug at me, like someone had hooked a finger in my belly button and yanked it towards my spine. But, despite that, I stayed rooted to the cosmic floor. Her forehead crinkled. "What did you do?" she demanded.

"I've been havin' dreams," I explained. "I couldn't sleep. A...friend, offered to help, so I ate a nasty plant and came here. Wherever this is..." I drifted off, staring at the window I'd almost opened, again feeling that strange compulsion to peer through to the other side.

"The dreams should not have begun, yet," she replied, stepping forward once more. She passed her hands along my body, not touching me, but close.

And that's when I saw my anti-magic field for the first time.

No longer invisible, it hovered over me, glowing faintly, encasing me in an aura of dim light. She ran her hands along it, and—wherever her fingers trailed—the light grew brighter, the field more perceptible. Soon, it was practically opaque, which was when I first noticed them.

The cracks.

"This is how the dreams got through," she hissed, staring at the cracks as if they were some sort of vermin, or infestation. "What have you done?" she asked, pointing at them in accusation.

"Nothin'!" I insisted. But deep down, I suspected that wasn't true. Brief flashes of not-so-distant memories—an angel's power smashing against my field, Johnny Appleseed's hand in mine, Hemingway repulsed and perched on the rear legs of his chair, Gladstone staring at his perfectly ordinary hands, and more—assaulted me. Meaning the cracks weren't cracks at all, but fissures—pieces of my field that no longer aligned after having been pulled apart and shoved back together over and over again.

Which meant the dreams were my fault.

"I see," she said, reading my guilty expression. She sighed and reached out, resting her hand on one of the smaller fractures. She pinched the edges of my field together, then drew back; it looked good as new.

"How d'ye do that?" I gasped.

She scoffed. "Who do you think put it there in the first place?"

I frowned, wondering yet again who this woman was. And, more importantly, what she wanted. I pulled away. "If you're not me Ma, tell me who ye are," I demanded. "What are ye doin' here?"

She frowned, staring at nothing before returning her attention to me—

almost as if she were looking at something I couldn't see. "It's too soon to have this conversation. Let me fix your cage, and your dreams will cease."

"Me cage?" I asked, wrapping my arms around myself.

The woman frowned harder. "Never mind that. Come."

I refused to move. "No, I want answers," I said, heatedly. I took a step forward, prepared to confront her. Or at least I thought that's what I intended. Instead, I found myself at the window, clutching the handle once more.

"Stop," she commanded.

I froze a second time. Talk about déjà vu. What the hell was going on? I saw her approach out of the corner of my eye, only this time all her attention was fixated on the window, not me. She rested her hand against it, eyes closed. "Why this?" she muttered. "Why do your dreams bring you here?"

I tried to speak but couldn't. I couldn't stop her as she began remolding my field, either. She took her time securing it, pressing the shattered sections back together until they were a seamless whole. "It is not yet time," she said enigmatically as she worked. "If they find you now, you will not be free to choose." Once finished, she folded her arms across her chest, glowering at the window as if it had presented her with an unsolvable math equation. "Move," she demanded.

I got out of her way as she reached up and yanked on the handle, freeing the window. It opened to reveal another world, as I'd suspected—a murky, desolate place smothered in fog and despair.

"London, November 9th, 1888," she intoned, ignoring the slight chill in the air now that the window was open. The hairs on the back of my neck stood up. "The Whitechapel District. The hunting grounds of the man known as Jack the Ripper. This, for whatever reason, is what your dreams were trying to show you."

That's funny, I thought to myself.

Because that sounded like the prelude to a nightmare to me.

CHAPTER 26

A woman came tearing out onto the street, singing an Irish ballad at the top of her lungs, clearly drunk. She didn't, or couldn't see us—but, given the oppressive fog that swirled about her feet and drifted in the morning air, that wasn't particularly surprising. The fog was so thick, in fact, that I could barely make out her features. Her hair seemed dark one moment, and light the next, especially as she passed beneath the gas lamps, the glow around each warped and hazy. And yet, no matter how surreal the setting, I knew the truth.

What I was seeing was real.

Because that's the thing with simulations; you always know you're in one. No matter how high resolution the graphics, no matter how accurate the representation, reality has an intangible quality you can't fake—the sights, smells, and sounds that your brain processes in an instant. But I could see, smell, and hear everything through the window—the acrid stench of coal and the blast of fog horns—which meant I really was looking at London in the 1800s.

Unfortunately, that meant the woman dancing her way between run-down buildings under the cover of fog was going to die. Because, if the woman next to me didn't have her dates mixed up, and this was the Whitechapel District, then I was likely looking at Black Mary on the morning she met Jack the Ripper.

Part of me wanted to reach through the window and warn her, but for some reason I knew that wouldn't work. I was looking through a window, not a doorway. What lay on the other side had already happened, long before I was born; nothing I did could save her.

And so Black Mary, as she would later be known, continued to stumble through the street. She passed by one or two figures in the gloom, emerging from the fog like wraiths, only to be swallowed up again. It was a nightmarish landscape, fit for monsters and men alike. Which, a moment later, is exactly what I saw.

A man stepped out between two buildings, appearing as if from thin air, dressed in a thick coat, the lip of his top hat obscuring most of his face. Black Mary tried to skirt around him, but he sidled sideways to stay in front of her, then again when she dipped the other direction. Black Mary's song died out as she laughed. She rested her hand on the man's chest, using him to stay upright.

They spoke, the fog doing strange things to their voices, bouncing sound around so all I could make out were individual words, like "price" and "come." Black Mary offered her arm, slipping it between his as the two turned, about to walk away. But then a fierce gust of wind blew, forcing Black Mary to pin her dress down with one hand, shielding her eyes with the other, and the man's top hat soared into the air. I was sure he was going to lose it in the fog, but then his hand shot out—impossibly fast—snatching it from the air and returning it to his head. But not before I'd seen the briefest glimpse of what lie beneath.

Lips like black ice.

And electric blue eyes.

"What is he doin' there?" I asked, struggling to put two and two together.

The woman next to me whirled, then slammed the window shut, sealing Black Mary's fate in an instant. "You met the Frost child? When?"

I fumbled for words, still trying to process what I'd seen. Jack Frost in London, escorting Black Mary the morning she was found in her bedroom, mutilated. I didn't know many of the victims, or even that much about Jack the Ripper, but Black Mary's story had always held fascination for me; hers was easily the most confounding murder, drawing speculation from a host of scholars.

The woman reached out and shook me. "Tell me."

I pulled away. "Ye seem to know so much, why don't ye tell me?" I replied, heatedly.

She closed her eyes and the smoke stopped spewing from them, cut off as if she'd shut the chute of a chimney. I saw her eyeballs flicker and dance beneath her lids. She pursed her lips. "You're at a crossroads," she said, finally. "I cannot see beyond that. What I've done in restoring your..."

"Me cage?" I finished for her, glaring.

She nodded, eyes popping open, the smoke returning instantly. "What I've done will keep you safe, but not for much longer. What you do next will determine how much time you have."

"And I'm guessin' ye won't be fillin' me in on what that means?" I asked, sarcastically.

"I cannot...but I *can* see you will need help. You've used the bars of your cage like a weapon," she said, shaking her head, "which is something no one could have anticipated. Unfortunately, I believe you will do so again without power to call your own."

Somehow, I knew exactly what she meant. Although I'd always thought of my field as a shield of sorts, protecting me from the things that went bump in the night, it had never felt like one. You could depend on a shield. You could see it. It had mass and a breaking point. But still, I'd tried to use my field like one—taking on beings with far greater power under the assumption they'd be reduced to my level. But—if my field really was a cage after all—what was locked inside?

"And what power would that be?" I asked.

"Here," the woman said, removing a silver bracelet I hadn't noticed dangling from her wrist. She held it to her mouth and breathed on it, the way you might to remove a smudge on glass. The bracelet shone as if it had been thrust into a furnace. Before I could ask what she was about to do, she snatched my arm and slid the bracelet over my hand. I cringed, prepared for it to burn, but it was surprisingly cool. Three charms hung loose at equidistant points.

"Ravens?" I asked, studying the tiny silver birds.

"Crows," she replied, tersely.

"What's it do?" I asked.

"It does what it was designed to do. Save you from yourself," she said, before pivoting to walk away. "Beware loosing the third crow," she called. "The moment you do, they will find you."

"Who will find me?" I yelled after her.

She floated away, back turned.

"Wait, please! Can ye at least tell me are ye me ma...or somethin' else?" I asked, desperately. I knew how pathetic I sounded—like a little girl calling out for her mother—but, in a way, that's exactly what I was.

"Your mother is dead," the woman replied, so softly I could barely hear her. A moment later, the floor gave out beneath me.

I couldn't have cared less.

CHAPTER 27

I came to and found Starlight tucked up next to me, napping, his furry head tucked up against me, using my breast as a pillow. Night had settled in and I could see the moon floating high above us. I considered thumping the bear upside his head, but decided against it; my body ached, I'd sweated through my clothes, and I honestly didn't feel like picking a fight.

Instead I sat up, groaning, my gut on fire. Starlight woke and rubbed at his beady little eyes, yawning, his tongue curling up into his mouth in the process; I had to admit, when he wasn't talking, he made a pretty damn adorable bear. I reached down and plucked at my shirt, grimacing as I peeled it off the clammy skin of my chest. Guess I'd have to change again.

I tapped my shirt.

Nothing happened.

I frowned and tapped it again. Then my jacket. My pants. Shoes. Still nothing. I groaned again and flopped back onto the ground. Starlight loomed over me a moment later, his face obscuring the moon overhead. "So," he said, "how'd it go?"

"A woman with me ma's face ruined me magical clothes," I said.

He blinked. "Well, that's a new one."

"And I saw Jack the Ripper...turns out he was Jack Frost, all along."

Starlight eyed the wildflowers dubiously. "Maybe ingesting them wasn't the best idea..."

"But at least she gave me a bracelet," I said, raising my arm. The sleeve of my jacket slid down my wrist, the silver bracelet exposed.

Starlight took a startled step back. "Where'd you get *that?*" he asked, his little teeth bared.

"I told ye, the woman who guards the windows gave it to me," I said, surprised by his reaction. It was just a bracelet, after all—nowhere near as nifty as shapeshifting clothes. I felt another wave of sadness hit me as I mourned all the outfits that would never be.

Starlight padded over on all fours, sniffing the air near the bracelet. He inched closer, then, before I could pull away, licked the metal surface. He sneezed and fell back on his furry ass, pawing at his nose like a bug had flown in it. I, meanwhile, did my best to clean his saliva off my psychedelic consolation prize. "Serves ye right, ye weirdo," I scolded. "I mean, lickin' someone's jewelry? Who does that?"

"What did he lick?" I heard Claire call out from the edge of the grove.

"None of your business," I replied.

"So, she wouldn't get naked, but she's letting him lick her?" I heard Claire ask someone, probably Callie.

"I heard that, ye trollop," I muttered, clambering to my feet. I wobbled a little, but followed the sound of her voice to the edge of the grove. I had to rest, however, before attempting to climb over the rocks; my body was rebelling, clearly tired of putting up with my shit. A hand descended into my line of sight, and I followed it up to find Callie, offering to help me up and over. "Are you alright?" she asked.

I shook my head.

"Do you want to talk about it?"

I thought about it. "Maybe later. Some day. It's still a little raw, and I've got shit to do."

"Oh? Like what?"

I took her hand and scrambled up and over the rocks. Claire and Starlight were talking a dozen feet away, oblivious to the two of us, although I caught Starlight looking my way every so often, his eyes glinting in the moonlight. I avoided eye contact, choosing instead to study Callie, who seemed calmer than when I'd seen her last—like she'd made up her mind about something.

"I'm goin' to fetch Christoff, or Alexei, or whatever name he wants to go by," I said in response to her earlier question, "and we're goin' to save his wife. Then I'm goin' after Jack Frost before he murders anyone else in me town."

"Jack Frost," Callie said, as if double-checking she'd heard me right.

"Aye."

"Jack Frost is murdering people in Boston?" she asked.

"All over, actually," I replied. "From one coast to the other...although, I t'ink he skipped over Kansas City. And St. Louis." I scowled, realizing there may have been some merit in declaring ownership over a whole city; the fucker hadn't dropped any bodies in Nate and Callie's territory, after all.

"Do you want help?" Callie asked.

"Aye," I replied, immediately. "Ye can get me a change of clothes."

Callie looked relieved not to have to leap into the fray alongside me, then concerned. "What happened to your..." she tapped her own clothes, making a goofy face.

I sighed. "I'm pretty sure they only worked because me field was all out of whack. But, now that it's fixed, I'm pretty sure that's over with."

Callie took a long look at me and draped her arm around my shoulder, tucking her head in next to mine, our hair intertwining like hot blood on fresh snow. "It's okay, sweetie," she said. "The next time you come for a visit, I'll take you to see my tailors...they'll hook you up." The mischievous twinkle in her eyes didn't lift my spirits.

I nodded, morosely.

Claire came upon us like that, still huddled together, and frowned. "Everything alright?" she asked.

"Quinn's magic clothes stopped working," Callie explained.

Claire's eyes went wide, then her face fell. "Oh, honey...it's okay," she said, coming in for a hug.

And I let her.

CHAPTER 28

I woke to a text from Jimmy the next morning which sent me scrambling off Callie's couch, waking Christoff instantly. He and I had stayed over at Callie's apartment the night before, trying to get at least a couple hours of sleep before heading back to Boston to track down Christoff's wife. Claire had decided to stay behind and play nurse with Kenai.

Because he *needed* her.

Christoff tracked me with his eyes as I paced the room but said nothing. He had kept to himself the night before, acquiescing to my request that we get some rest before heading back to Boston to save his wife; I think he could see how worn out I was. That, or he didn't want to pick a fight, considering we still hadn't hashed out his having lied to me for the past several years.

Sadly, it didn't seem like we'd have that kind of time.

"Callie," I called, after rereading the text message Jimmy had sent, "I t'ink I need ye to drop us off at the hospital."

Callie poked her head out of her bedroom, eyebrow raised, her hair a fluffy mess. "Your stomach still bothering you that bad? I have a bathroom, you know."

I rolled my eyes. "No, me stomach is feelin' better. But Christoff and I need to get back. We have...unfinished business, at the hospital," I said, deciding it would take too long to explain, and I was in a hurry; according to Jimmy's clipped and very uninformative text message, one of Jeffries' team was in critical condition at Boston Memorial.

Christoff's jaw clenched, but he didn't argue, which I appreciated. Honestly, we probably *could* have avoided the hospital altogether and gone straight after the werebears who'd attacked him and his family, but Jeffries and his team had put their necks on the line to protect me and find Christoff.

We owed them.

"Alright. But did you want to change first?" Callie asked. "You might be a little warm in the snow gear. Plus, it smells."

I caught Christoff nodding and glared at him. "Aye," I replied, finally, with a sigh. "D'ye have anythin' that'll fit me?"

Callie grinned.

*C*hristoff and I arrived via Gateway a half hour later. Callie waved and closed it behind us, leaving us in the dark confines of a hospital's storage closet. I reached for the handle, but found the doorway blocked by Christoff, whose face was invisible with the light at his back. I felt more than saw him fold his arms over his chest.

"Quinn, we need to talk," he said.

"We don't have time," I said, trying to edge past the much shorter, but much broader man.

"This is only time we have," he argued.

"Ye don't owe me anythin', Christoff. Or, should I say, *Alexei?*" I hissed, sounding more hurt than I'd intended, inadvertently banging my shoulder against a shelf as I folded my arms over my chest.

A box fell at our feet, the glass inside shattering in the ensuing silence. We held our breath, waiting for someone to come yank us out of the closet and demand what we were doing there, but no one did. Christoff spoke first. "Please, do not call me by that name," Christoff insisted. "It comes with bad memories. Things I am not proud of. This is who I am, now. Christoff, the bar manager. Not Alexei, the killer."

"Were ye ever goin' to tell me the truth?" I asked, knowing it was an unfair question.

But I couldn't be rational all the time.

"No," Christoff admitted. "If they had not come, I would have told no one. Ever. In this country, only my wife knows what I was before. No one else."

I frowned, seeing an obvious flaw in that assertion. "So how did they find ye?" I asked.

Christoff shook his head. "This I do not know. But this does not matter, now. What matters is I get my Elena back. The things they will do to her if I do not come looking…I do not wish to think about."

"I t'ink you're forgettin' an important detail," I said. "I'm comin', too. Not for your sake, either," I clarified, "but for hers. And because no one shoots at me and gets to walk away."

"It will be dangerous. Very much dangerous," Christoff countered. "Before, when you and your friends come for me, they let you live. They wished to draw me out of hiding, that is all. Had they wanted you all dead, they would have made it so."

With a sinking feeling, I realized Christoff might have a point. Granted, the Sickos were a tough bunch, but dodging that many bullets and making it out alive? I mean, sure, I had a Valkyrie in Valhalla-mode shielding me, but the odds of making it out without so much as a flesh wound were pretty astronomical. I knew better than most that professionals didn't leave loose ends, which meant—if Christoff was right—we hadn't gotten lucky, we'd been let go.

"How many of 'em are there?" I asked.

Christoff's shrug was hardly visible. "This I do not know. Once, there were many. But as years go by, less and less. They will not have all come, however. Some will stay behind to protect the homeland."

"Protect it from what?" I asked. It finally occurred to me that he was talking about a government-sanctioned force of Freaks—something I'd never even thought possible, let alone heard of. Especially since it meant someone in Russia's top brass knew Freaks existed…or was a Freak themselves.

Was Vladimir Putin really a werebear?

"Protect it from all things," Christoff replied. "Some days this means fight in wars, some days fight insurgents, some days become insurgent." He shrugged again.

"Wait, so ye were a spy? With that accent?" I asked, cocking an eyebrow.

He stared at me for a long moment, and then let out an even longer sigh, relaxing his shoulders. "Aye. I speak seven languages, ye know," Christoff said, in a freakishly perfect imitation of my accent. No more of his broken English. Had that all been... a ruse? Even *that* had been a lie?

"Of course, ye do, ye fuckin' parrot," I muttered. "Well, I'm comin' along anyway. I don't care how many of 'em there are. Just because ye lied to me doesn't mean your wife should suffer havin' to see your ugly mug first t'ing."

Christoff grunted. "I am sure she will be pleased to see you." He reached out, resting his hand on my arm. "Quinn, I am sorry I lied to you, and got you involved in this. Please, forgive me. And thank you for help."

I narrowed my eyes suspiciously, but the apology seemed both sincere and heartfelt. "Alright, I forgive ye," I replied, finally. "Although, ye should probably t'ank Dobby for comin' to get me in the first place, or I'd never have come lookin'. He was worried about ye."

"Dobby?" Christoff said, surprised. "Why would he be worried? I say goodbye to him before I left for safehouse."

I slowly turned to stare at Christoff, a faint buzzing sound in my ears, as if my brain was doing a hard reboot. Dobby had...already *known* what happened with Christoff? Then why the runaround? Before I could dwell on that, however, I heard the door handle jiggle.

Someone had found us, after all.

"I thought I smelled magic!" Hilde hissed as she threw open the door and flipped on the lights. Her eyes widened in shock, either at finding someone she knew behind the door, or at finding a man nearly old enough to be my father with his hand on my arm in a dark, intimate space.

"Oy, I heard ye were here," I offered, raising my phone as explanation, hoping she'd play it cool and pretend like this had never happened.

Instead, Hilde snarled, grabbed me by the front of the jacket Callie had loaned me, and shoved me up against the wall. Hard. Then, before I could so much as cuss her out, she let go, wiping her hands on her pant legs as though she'd touched something repulsive. "Oh, bulging thighs of Thor, what are you *wearing*?"

I saw Christoff silently repeating Hilde's curse with a confused look on his face; I left him to it.

I winced a little as I came off the wall, adjusting the horrendously orange faux-leather jacket with a scowl. According to Callie, the jacket was the only thing in her closet that would fit someone with arms and a torso as long as mine—she'd worn it a few Halloweens back, part of a slutty traffic cone costume that included nothing but the jacket and an orange party hat.

Super classy, I know.

"What the hell was that shove about?" I demanded, ignoring her question. Ordinarily, I'd simply have come back swinging, but between my battered body and the fact that I wasn't entirely sure I could go toe-to-toe with a Valkyrie to begin with, I figured talking things out might be for the best. It would also decrease the chances of us getting booted out of the hospital; several staffers and patients were eyeing us after Hilde's little stunt.

"Is this talk we should be having here?" Christoff asked, poking his head out of the closet.

Hilde whirled on Christoff and charged into the closet, pressing him up against a row of shelves with one very shapely forearm. "Are you one of them?" she demanded, arm raised, the tip of her sword appearing inches from Christoff's throat.

"I am not," Christoff said, too calmly.

"Hilde," I hissed, realizing one of the nurses had broken off to make a phone call—probably to security. I ducked inside the closet behind the Valkyrie, shutting the door before someone reported seeing a woman with a fucking sword on the loose in the hospital. "Put the weapon away!"

A shield appeared in Hilde's other hand, and she swung it out at me in an attempt to smack me with the flat of it and send me flying. I braced myself for the blow, but her shield disappeared the instant it collided with me, leaving her arm bare and unadorned. I caught her forearm with my left hand and dug my nails in, hard—a little payback for the shove.

"Hilde," I said, leaning in to whisper as I slid my right hand up and over her shoulder, "I don't t'ink you'll be needin' that." I briefly tapped the pommel of Hilde's sword and watched it vanish into thin air. Hilde froze, like a startled cat, prepared to run or fight as necessary. I stepped away. "Let's walk and talk," I suggested, opening the door once more. I motioned Christoff to join me, which he did, excusing himself as he crept past the overly aggressive agent.

Hilde's arms fell to her sides, but I could tell she was still on edge. "How did you do that?" she whispered, finally, sounding very troubled.

"Come on out of the closet," I urged, "and I'll tell ye."

Hilde took a look around, realizing that she was the only one still standing in a storage closet. "Oh, right." She slipped out and shut the door, stared at us for a moment, then started walking. "Come on, we're on the fourth floor. Leo will know what to do with you, and you can tell me why my weapons fled from you on the way."

Christoff and I exchanged looks. "Well," I said, finally, "I don't know about makin' 'em flee from ye, but let's just say me abilities recently got...reinforced."

Hilde seemed to take that in stride, although it seemed she was having a much harder time with my choice of attire; she kept glancing back at me like I'd committed some sort of crime against all things right and decent. Once we were on the elevator, she reached out and tapped my jacket, thumping me hard enough to make me rub at my shoulder. When nothing happened, she frowned, and did it again.

"Knock it off!" I hissed.

"What is this woman doing?" Christoff asked, his whisper loud enough for us all to hear.

I sighed. "She t'inks I'm wearing the clothes she gave me, and that I chose this jacket. What she doesn't know is that I'm not and I didn't."

Hilde's frown threatened to pull the corners of her mouth to the floor. "What happened to the clothes I gave you?" she asked.

I winced. "Well, ye remember that reinforcement I was talkin' about earlier?" I asked, trying to sound upbeat.

"Did you lose them?" Hilde asked, her tone practically glacial.

"More like I broke 'em, I t'ink," I admitted. "But not on purpose!" I added, hurriedly. "Technically it wasn't even me. It was some sort of fortune tellin' goddess who looked like me ma. Or, ye know, an unfortunate representation of me subconscious...I'm still workin' that bit out."

Hilde glanced over at Christoff, dismissing me entirely. "You're the one Quinn asked us to find. So, tell me, why do you smell like the men who attacked us?" she asked. I hung my head; after ruining the priceless gift Hilde had given me, I suppose it only made sense that I was dead to her.

"Many years ago, I was one of them," Christoff replied. "We are...related. We share much. Same genes, even same blood, in some cases."

"Ye didn't tell me that," I interjected.

"It was not important," Christoff replied. "I have no more family left in Russia. My brothers died, long ago, before I come here."

"Those men shot one of mine," Hilde said, her tone promising vengeance. She flicked her eyes at me. "We were able to get out, but not before Warren took a bullet. When we couldn't find you, we assumed the worst. But, then I saw you here, unharmed, and it crossed my mind that you might have led us into a trap. *That's* why I attacked you."

Oh. Well, when she put it like that, it at least made sense. Didn't make my aching back feel any better, but hey—apologies weren't exactly FDA approved. Not that she'd offered one. "We fled," I explained. "I found Christoff and his kids and a friend got us out before they could find us. I tried to call Agent Jeffries, but he didn't pick up. Then t'ings got a little...hairy."

Oh, puns.

Christoff shot me a nonplussed look but said nothing. Hilde chewed over my explanation and nodded, stepping out onto the fourth floor the instant the door opened. "His phone was destroyed. We're working on it. Anyway, come on, Leo will want to talk to you."

"Oh, aye, I need to talk to him, as well," I said, hurrying to keep pace with her. "I found out who your killer is, after all."

Hilde jerked to a halt so quickly I bumped into her, bruising my hip in the process.

"Motherfucker," I hissed, rubbing my side. "What d'ye do that for?"

"Did Miss MacKenna just say she found our killer?" Jeffries asked, rising from one of the waiting lounge chairs.

"Aye," I replied, turning to face the Special Agent in Charge, prepared to brief him on everything I'd found out since we last saw each other, but the look on his ravaged face stopped me; his eyes were red-rimmed, and he looked every bit as old as the grey in his hair would suggest.

I realized from Hilde's expression that she hadn't stopped because of anything I'd said; she'd stopped because she'd seen her boss, shoulders bowed, looking down at his feet like a man carrying a burden he couldn't handle. Her hands were balled into fists at her side. "What is it, Leo?"

"It's Warren. He survived the surgery," Jeffries explained, "but he didn't wake up. He's in a medically-induced coma." Jeffries tucked his shoulders back and lifted his chin. "So, Miss MacKenna, how about you fill us in on everything you know about the soon-to-be dead men who attacked us. Then you can fill me in on who we're after for the murders, and we'll sort him out, too." He locked eyes with Hilde. "Off the fucking books, as Temple would say. I'm beginning to see the method to his madness."

I nodded, dumbly. Jeffries knew Nate Temple? But now wasn't the time. "Aye...I can do that."

And I would.

Because if I didn't, the look in Jeffries' eyes told me I'd be added to his *off the books* checklist.

I was secretly happy that the red tape had just gone up in a blazing inferno, and that the Sickos were finally ready to do things my way.

Because why play touch when you can tackle?

CHAPTER 29

$\mathcal{I}$ told Jeffries and his team everything I knew while we snacked at
the hospital's cafeteria, though admittedly I had to leave out a
few details—like how I'd consumed a hyper-hallucinogen that had sent me
soaring through the cosmos to another dimension under the supervision of
a stoner bear named Starlight. Or, you know, how I'd beaten the living hell
out of a former cop in a sanctified fight ring in Alaska. But, by the time I
was finished, they had all of the relevant details. Lakota and—to my surprise
—Robin joined us quickly enough to catch the tail end of my explanation.

"So how do you know Jack Frost is our killer?" Lakota asked, settling in
beside Hilde and popping a crouton from her salad into his mouth. The kid
shook his head, a lock of shoulder-length hair falling in front of his eyes. "I
can't believe how often I end up saying fairy tale shit like that," he confessed,
once he'd swallowed.

"Call it an anonymous tip," I replied. "I don't expect ye to string him up
without vettin' him for yourselves, first."

"It's possible," Robin interjected. "He came to town in the last couple
months, stirring up trouble. He's kept a low profile since, though."

Lakota shrugged. "If he's our guy, I'll know. Leo, too. Not even the Fae
can lie to him." The kid leaned in close to Hilde. "Do you wanna kill a snowman..." he sang in a pitch perfect impersonation of Anna from *Frozen*.

Hilde scowled.

"You're no fun," Lakota said.

Robin ignored Lakota entirely, fixated as he was on Jeffries, who seemed too grief-stricken to bother explaining his gift. "Jeffries can tell when someone is lyin'," I told the redcap, making sure Christoff heard me as well —it wouldn't do to have the older man go and say something that contradicted what I'd told them. "Well, most people," I added.

Robin grunted. "That explains a lot, actually."

My eyes narrowed. "Why, what d'ye do?"

"The Fae saved us," Jeffries interjected, catching my eye. "Without him and Hilde covering our retreat, we'd have all been goners."

"Huh," I said, glancing sidelong at the redcap. There was something different about him, I realized, aside from the fact that he'd changed from his suit and fedora combination back into Red Sox gear—which I appreciated. He looked beefier, somehow, his beard bushier, cheeks ruddier. Before I could analyze him too much, however, he and Christoff rose as one and walked off together without so much as a word.

"What's that about?" Hilde asked.

"Employee meetin'?" I suggested. My guess was Robin had something to say that he didn't want the FBI to overhear. Or maybe he wanted to apologize for his organization's role in keeping Christoff and his children "safe" by keeping them locked up. Either way, I found myself fascinated by their interaction now that I knew both their backgrounds; it turned out the two men weren't all that different. Both had left war and their pasts behind to start new lives. Perhaps that's why Christoff had hired Robin in the first place—maybe he'd seen something of himself in the would-be spy.

The two of them returned shortly thereafter. Christoff shot me a look that said we'd talk later—which of course every FBI agent in the room also read. I sighed. For spies, neither he nor Robin were particularly subtle.

"Spill it," Hilde said, as soon as they'd sat down.

"They know where his wife is," Lakota said, staring at them. "Or think they do."

Christoff's eyes widened, and Robin stared up at the ceiling as if he hadn't been paying attention. Worst. Spies. Ever. "So, does soul-gazin' let ye read minds, too?" I asked Lakota, ignoring the two men.

Lakota shook his head. "No, I'm just good at my job. His energy," he pointed to Christoff, "or whatever you want to call it, was erratic when he first sat down, which made sense. His wife has been taken. But the minute they sat back down, his energy had changed. He's more resolute, now. He has a direction. My guess is the Fae knows something about where his wife is and told him."

"Is that true?" Jeffries said.

Christoff bowed his head. "I am sorry for your loss, Agent. But this is my problem now, not yours. Please, leave me to my work."

Jeffries studied the older man. "You believe what you're saying. But there's a lie in there, somewhere...you don't know if you'll be able to take them on by yourself. Is that it?"

Lakota nodded, pointing to Christoff's chest. "Got it in one."

Jesus Christ, what a scary duo those two made. Between the human lie detector and the soul decoder, it was a wonder any bad guy ever got away with anything. "Well, he won't be by himself," I interjected, finally, sensing the mood at the table. "He'll have backup."

"I'm going," Robin said. "I owe the man a favor. And my kind honor that."

"If you know where they are," Hilde growled, "then I'm going, too. I owe them. For Warren."

"Guess we're doing this together," Lakota said, swiping at his bangs.

"No, we're not," Hilde replied. She leveled her gaze at Lakota, then swung it around to her boss. "You two should track down Frost, see if Quinn is right before the bastard has a chance to hunt down anyone else."

Lakota frowned. "You think we'd be liabilities," he accused, finally.

Hilde reached out and flicked his ear. "What did I tell you about using your abilities on me?"

Lakota rubbed at his ear, glaring at her. Jeffries watched the exchange with a hint of amusement; it was a welcome change. "She's right, though," the Special Agent in Charge admitted, "we would be a liability. How about it?" he asked Christoff. "Do you think the four of you will be enough?"

Christoff frowned, realizing now that there was no point lying to the man. "I do not know. It will be difficult. But, with four, maybe." He shook his head.

Jeffries grunted. "Close enough. Alright then, it's settled. You four will go after this man's wife. Lakota and I will see what we can track down about this Frost character. Hilde," he met his partner's eyes, "make them pay."

Robin coughed and held up a hand before Hilde could respond. "If Frost really is the one behind these murders you say have been taking place, my

162

people will want to know. To judge for themselves. My organization likes to keep things...tidy, here in Boston. I would urge you to consider coordinating with them before you make any moves."

"The Chancery, you mean?" Jeffries asked.

Robin nodded, though it was obvious he had little else to say on the subject of who he worked for.

"So, you're saying that, if and when we find him, we'll have to turn him over to you?" Lakota asked. "Well that's a shitty deal. How do we know he'll end up paying for what he's done?"

Robin locked eyes with Jeffries. "If he's guilty, he'll pay. My kind still believe in cruel and unusual punishment as a deterrent." Jeffries didn't break eye contact, so Robin let out a sigh. "Think of the worst thing you would personally do to him for his crimes—what you would do if no one was watching you do it and you could get away with it." After a few moments, Jeffries nodded. Robin's face slowly morphed into a feral, wicked grin. "That's just our interrogation level."

Something about the way Robin had said it made the hair on the back of my neck stand up—almost as if he were speaking from personal experience. I shivered and hunched forward, resting my elbows on the table. "Robin, are ye sure the Chancery will be up for it? After, ye know..." I left the rest hanging. If Robin didn't want to fill in the FBI on the Chancery's mission statement, I sincerely doubted he wanted them to know about their recent schism.

Robin waved that away. "It's been dealt with. They found out who was responsible for letting Mordred out, and are planning to deal with the man, personally."

"I hope that doesn't mean one of our citizens will end up receiving one of those cruel and unusual punishments you described," Jeffries said, eyes narrowed.

Robin sucked his teeth. "I can't promise anything. The man has caused a lot of problems for us, not to mention for our kind on the other side. He's killed more Fae than anyone in centuries, and that's got a lot of us scared. Many feel that he must be held accountable for the havoc he's created."

"Sounds impressive. Who is he?" I asked, brow furrowed. You'd think I'd have heard of someone wantonly killing Faelings, especially on the scale Robin described. I mean, the world was a big place, but I'd always assumed Boston was the epicenter of Fae activity in the mortal realm—

and yet lately, it seemed more like the last exit on the information highway.

"Nate Temple," Robin said, eyes darkening. "He calls himself King of St. Louis, now... but we call him The Rider. Wylde. Many other names, but wherever he goes, death follows."

I tried to keep my expression neutral, but only barely managed it. Nate Temple? A mass murderer? It didn't make any sense. This was the same man who'd bailed Callie out in Kansas City more than once. The man Othello worked—and had nothing but praise—for. The man Hemingway—one of the Four Horsemen of the Apocalypse—routinely worried after and aided like a surrogate father. Hell, even I had reason to thank him; he'd even sent his friends to help me save the lives of trafficked women while I was in New York.

Really, the only negative thing I had to say about him up until now was that he was a spoiled, Uber-stealing brat.

"Temple, huh?" Jeffries asked in a very troubled tone. "I'll admit, I could see it. Years ago, while working in St. Louis, I swore never to betray him. But, from what I hear, things have changed. He's changed. Some say he's become tyrannical. On the other hand, St. Louis crime rates have also dropped considerably, as a result." Jeffries shook his head. "Not that you'll take my advice, but I think your kind would be better off leaving him alone. The last time we spoke, his fiancée was on the hook for murder..." Everyone leaned forward at that, the room suddenly silent. "I heard from a reliable source that he personally executed her for her crimes, in front of witnesses and friends. Nothing we could prove, obviously, but then..." he murmured, trailing off. "None of us are what we once were. We're all stained, to some degree." Sensing all eyes on him, Jeffries cleared his throat. "Idle thoughts. The musings of an old man."

I stared at Jeffries, no longer having to hide my horrified expression. "I'm sorry, rewind. He did *what?*"

Robin nodded. "We heard a... similar story," he interjected. "To be honest, I'm not sure what my superiors are planning, but there will be a reckoning, I'm sure. Until then, however, they will want to be involved. In fact, if you need help finding Frost, call this number," Robin said, sliding an embossed business card I recognized across the table.

"Hansel, Hansel, and Gretel," Jeffries read. "Seriously?"

"They keep meticulous records," Robin insisted. "Trust me, if you need a place to start, they'll point you in the right direction. We are always happy to comply with law enforcement," Robin said, one corner of his mouth going up.

Jeffries grunted. "When it suits you, yes, I see."

Christoff rose, impatient to be on his way, with or without help. "Is time to go," he said.

"Aye," I replied, snagging the rest of my deli sandwich to go; I desperately needed something in my stomach besides alcohol, wildflowers, and dirt. "Let's go find your wife," I said, realizing I had more pressing things to do at the moment than worry about Nate Temple; though, at some point, I knew I would have to discover the truth for myself.

Would the real Nate Temple please stand up?

"Alright," Hilde said as she stood, thrusting her chair violently back under the table, her expression flinty, "let's hunt some bear."

"Aye," I said, my mouth half-full. "That, too."

CHAPTER 30

*GW*e were thirty feet from the exit when someone grabbed me by the arm, causing me to lose my grip on what little remained of my sandwich. It fell to the floor, its contents spreading across the tile. "Seriously?" I asked, before whirling around, prepared to lay a beat down, only to find myself staring at a badge dangling around a familiar neck.

"I asked you to find me when you got here," Jimmy said, glancing over my shoulder at my three companions—an FBI agent, a bartender, and his boss—in contempt. I frowned. I mean, they weren't exactly the most illustrious posse I'd ever had, but I'd hung around with worse.

I waved them away. "I'll meet ye outside in a minute," I called.

Christoff frowned. "One minute," he clarified, pointing to his wrist. "Or we leave without you."

I nodded. "They found me first," I said, turning to Jimmy.

He seemed skeptical but shrugged that off. "Whatever. Where are you all going?"

"Unfinished business to take care of," I replied.

"Which means what, exactly?" he asked.

I arced an eyebrow. "Which means it's none of yours, Jimmy Collins."

Jimmy sneered. "You mean it's Freak related. Of course." He exchanged looks with Maria, who stood on the other side of the room talking with a nurse. "When they brought in one of their people and we heard about the shootout, I knew you had something to do with it."

"Me?" I asked. "Why would ye t'ink I had anythin' to do with it?"

"Because that's what you do. You come in and wreck people's lives. You know, Jeffries kept hounding me to find you, but I knew they'd be better off if I didn't. You get people hurt. Killed." His eyes flashed, and I saw real pain lurking there. Hatred, too. I felt my anger brimming, threatening to spill over into a tirade that would get us both kicked out of the hospital.

But then, of course, he wasn't wrong.

I had gotten people hurt, even if I hadn't meant to. The list grew longer and longer every year. Jimmy had nearly died, and then there was Dez, who'd been kidnapped, and now Warren, who might never wake up. Thing is, I wasn't angry because I felt guilty, I was angry because I was sick and tired of being responsible for other people. Dez was family; she hadn't asked to get taken. But Warren was an FBI agent doing his job—he'd known the risks. And Jimmy? I'd done everything in my power to keep him away from my world once I realized what was at stake. Jimmy had to know that. Which meant what Jimmy hated wasn't me so much as it was his own weakness, his own fragility.

Which was sad.

But not my problem.

"Goodbye, Jimmy," I said, turning away. I had more important places to be, and I didn't think for a minute that Christoff wouldn't follow through on his promise to leave me behind. His wife was in danger; time was something he couldn't afford to waste.

"Quinn," Jimmy barked. "Quinn!"

I left the detective yelling my name in the hospital lobby.

And never looked back.

I frowned, studying the mechanic's garage in Brookline that Robin's directions had led us to. "Are ye sure this is the right place?" I asked, dubiously.

The garage in question was a large one, but privately owned— definitely not one of the chains I was used to seeing around town. Bizarrely, however, there wasn't a car in sight. The bay doors were closed, the lights off. I couldn't see any movement inside from where we were; Hilde had pulled us over a quarter-mile down the road. Unfortunately, getting closer wasn't really an option, especially if the werebears we were after were in there. We couldn't risk them smelling us until we were right on top of them.

"This is right place," Christoff replied, before Robin could answer me. He pointed to a bit of graffiti sprayed above one of the windows. "That sign is from home, it means is safe place for Russian operatives. This area is known for such things. Every major city in the United States has one or two of these buildings, just in case."

"Really?" I asked. "And here I thought the Cold War ended when the wall fell."

Christoff grunted. "War is way of world. It does not end because you give it different name. Now, how will we go in?"

"I'll take point," Hilde said. "Lead with the badge. I doubt they'll try to mow us down in broad daylight."

"Do not be so sure," Christoff advised. "If they see an opportunity, they will take shot. Bodies can always be taken care of, afterwards. And, in this neighborhood, no one will ask questions."

Hilde frowned. "Then what do you suggest?"

Christoff studied the garage, then glanced over at me. "I have idea. But you will not like."

*C*hristoff was right. I didn't like his idea. In fact, I hated it. But, after he'd explained it to me, I could at least see the logic of it. Eventually, pressed for time and with no other alternatives, I'd agreed. Which was how I found myself behind the wheel of Hilde's giant pedophile van, staring at the bay door Christoff had insisted I approach. I honked, pressing the heel of my palm into the steering wheel for a solid ten seconds before finally releasing it.

A man, hands cupped over his face to block out the glare, looked my way, then disappeared. By now, I figured they should have recognized either me, or the van, or both. Of course, it was also possible that—if their noses were as sharp as Christoff claimed— they'd already smelled the older Russian man, who was trussed up and gagged at the rear of the van. Either way, I was betting their curiosity would overwhelm their caution. After all, what threat did the two of us represent to a group of armed, werebear soldiers?

The bay door raised as if in answer to my question. Six men poured out of the opening, each toting a rifle identical to the one I'd left at Callie's. A seventh, dressed in a polo and jeans, ran outside with a sign that read "Closed for Filming."

Well, weren't they just clever as all hell? Any passersby would think they were witnessing a film production, not an armed assault.

A rap on my window drew my attention away from the seventh man. I turned to find the barrel of a rifle aimed at my face. The man holding it made a lowering motion with the muzzle, which I took to mean he wanted me to lower the window.

I did as he asked, cranking it down.

"Turn off engine," the man said, his accent at least as heavy as Christoff's, if not more.

I did that, as well.

"Step out with hands on head," he said.

I opened the door, put my hands on my head, and propped it open with my foot long enough to slide out of the driver's seat. As the man with the gun patted me down, I watched as the seventh man wheeled out a massive, Hollywood-style camera and set it beside the sign. The man with the gun nodded to his companions, who each assumed a pose of relative ease.

One even lit a cigarette.

"Is easy to carry guns in your country," the man said, catching my expression. "Pretend to be actor and is easier still. Now, what have you brought us and why?"

"I brought the man you're lookin' for," I replied.

"Yes, we can smell him. But this is not answer." He leaned up against the van and pressed his ear to the metal. "I can hear his heartbeat. He is worried. This is good."

"We didn't realize who, or what, he was," I said, my lie prepared in advance.

"Who is we?" the man asked.

"The Chancery."

The man cocked an eyebrow and motioned one of his men over, speaking in Russian. His companion nodded. "*Da, Kapitán,*" he said, then hopped into the driver seat.

"One of your people killed two of my men. Are you prepared to pay off his debt?" the Russian Captain asked.

"That's why we brought the bear to ye. To make amends. The Chancery doesn't want a fight but is happy to remind ye that ye can't go around causin' trouble in Boston without expectin' to pay a price. We're even."

The man scowled but seemed to accept the warning for what it was. "And what about children? I do not hear their heartbeats."

I frowned. "Why would ye want the wee ones?"

"Consider it international property rights issue," the man said, smirking. "The bear, as you say, took with him Russian property. It is possible his children will have inherited this also. This cannot be."

The van shook a little as Christoff rolled, clearly enraged to hear they planned to come after his children, as well. The Captain banged on the side of the van. "This was choice you made, Alexei!" He turned back to me. "So, will you give them to us?"

I pretended to think about it while I planned my next move. Much of Christoff's plan had depended on us getting inside the garage, but so far, the Captain and his men had no reason to take our conversation somewhere else; unless an unusually suspicious cop cruised by, I doubted anyone would do much more than snap a few photos, given the sign and the camera.

So, I decided to improvise.

"Aye, but I'll have to make a call. Not out here in the open, though. I don't want me picture taken and tied to this t'ing," I said, only partially lying.

The man glanced out at the quiet street, shrugged, and gestured to his subordinate. "Very well, we will wait inside," the Captain said. His subordinate turned the engine over and pulled the van into the garage. The rest of the men filed back inside, including the soldier masquerading as a film crew member. The Russians spread out without a word, covering the entrances and exits, patrolling the windows and sighting through the bay doors. I realized Christoff had been right; even with Hilde at the helm, we'd never have made it anywhere near the garage.

Not that their vigilance would do them any good, now that most of us were inside.

I pulled out my phone and pretended to put in a few numbers, keeping my ears peeled for any disturbance. According to the plan, the second anything went sideways, I was supposed to find cover, stay there, and let Christoff, Hilde, and Robin handle the rest. Bullets weren't really a problem for them, after all. I, on the other hand, very much preferred all my blood to remain *inside* my body.

I heard a clang, then a grunt, and made for the back of the van.

Only to be stopped short by the Captain, who had a firm grip on my hair. My head whipped back, and I screamed in surprise. "Oh, I'm goin' to kill ye!" I hissed, scrabbling at his hand to get him to let go.

"We found this one below," the driver of the truck called. He had his pistol out and pressed up against Robin's temple. "As you say, he dropped down from undercarriage."

I cringed. That had been part of Christoff's plan; sneak Robin in and let him fall below into the pit operation area that sat below the car. From there, he could work his way around and surprise them from behind. Had something we'd done tipped them off? Or had they simply guessed our plan? At this point it didn't matter, I realized; we'd simply have to depend on Hilde to come and save the day.

The Captain I'd spoken to yanked on my hair again, drawing me close, and released his rifle, trading it for a pistol. He pressed it up under my chin. "You may be beautiful woman, but bad liar," he said. "Now, come out, shield-maiden! You think we did not smell you also? If you do not come and play, I will shoot this woman. Or maybe I will shoot the *fei*," he said, whipping the pistol around. "Is not so hard, finding iron bullets. Is not so good for gun, but," he shrugged, "less good for him, I think."

I struggled, trying to break free from the bastard's grip, but all I ended up with was his gun in my face once more. "Enough, woman," he said, then scanned the garage as if he might find Hilde hiding somewhere. For all I knew, he would; she'd claimed she had a different way of getting in, and none of us had doubted her enough to pry. "Very well," he said. He swiveled his arm around and put two rounds in Robin's chest.

The redcap fell to his knees. He coughed, once, blood spilling from his mouth into his beard, and fell over. I was so shocked, I didn't even scream. I waited, breathlessly, for the redcap to rise and strike back. But if the man wasn't lying, and he really had shot Robin with iron bullets...

The soldier who caught Robin leaned down and tested the redcap's pulse. "Gone," he said.

The van shook again, and Christoff's primal roar tore through the garage. The tires sunk as the weight of a small, muscular man became that of an enormous bear. The man who had hold of my hair grunted and barked out a command in Russian. Three of his soldiers turned and began firing into the van while the rest angled away from the trajectory of the incoming bullets. I tried to cover my ears and watched in horror as dozens of holes began peppering the side of the van, Christoff's agonized roars almost inaudible beneath the sound of machine gun fire.

Blood dribbled along the van's seams, pooling over the fender. Nothing moved inside. Two of the shooters broke off, preparing to open the doors, while the third lined up a kill shot, just in case. They threw the doors open, and I held my breath, prepared to see Christoff take their heads off. But he didn't. The three men lowered their guns, not at all threatened by whatever they saw inside the van.

I dropped to my knees. The man released my hair and put his gun against the back of my skull. "Silver bullets, much better. Easier to buy, and better for rifle," the man admitted. "Tell us, do you think she ran away, your friend?" he asked, sniffing the air, but then his eyes brightened. His eyes shot to the ceiling an instant before Hilde, in full armor, came crashing through the windows above. Shards of glass large enough to impale someone rained down to the floor as she soared above us, wings outstretched. For one, shining moment, I knew we could come out of this in one piece—if I could get to Robin and Christoff in time to pull the metal from their bodies, they might stand a chance. A slim one, but still.

But then I saw Hilde's head snap back as a round from a sniper rifle took her in the temple, where her armor was lightest. The rest of the men took advantage of her distraction, turning as one to fire dozens of rounds at her wings, shredding them to pieces in the process. The Valkyrie screamed, crashing to the ground, but managed to roll and slice off one of the were-bear soldier's legs with her blade as she did so. She shield-bashed another, sending them flying into the van to land in a heap on the floor. Bullets flew, careening off her armor, but also clipping her flesh, which steamed wherever the silver bullets struck. The sniper, an eighth soldier nested in the corner of the room beneath a tarp, loosed another round that took Hilde in the throat.

The Valkyrie dropped her sword and pinned a hand over her neck to stop the fount of blood, her shield protecting her upper body from another spray of bullets. She took a step towards me, but slipped in a pool of her own fluids, falling to one knee. Her shield arm drooped, and eventually fell, as she slid sideways and toppled into one of the pits. The soldiers lined the edges and unloaded like a firing squad, their spent cartridges ringing like pennies hitting the pavement as they hit the ground.

I couldn't believe it. We'd...lost. Epically. My eyes hovered on Robin's back, then flicked to the van, and finally to the pit. I fell forward onto all fours, my breath coming in gasps. How? How could we have let this happen? I clenched my hands into fists, burrowing into my own skin with my nails. I had to get up. To do something. If I didn't move soon, I knew I was going to die, too.

"Now," the man said, crouching down next to me, "you are only one alive. Tell us, where can we find the children?"

I felt something inside me break, then. A part of me I'd felt shatter before—I could still feel my hands on Jimmy's lifeless chest, pressing over and over again as if CPR could save a man without a throat. It was the part of me that refused to lose. The part that didn't want to share, especially with death. I turned, leveling my gaze at the man in charge, prepared to free the power I always knew was hiding, deep inside me.

The power that had been locked away.

But, in an instant, time stopped.

CHAPTER 31

*T*hen, time spun *backwards*.

I could feel it whipping about me, somehow, pulling at me through my belly button the way that woman's voice had when she'd commanded me to leave. The instant I thought about her, I realized my wrist burned; the bracelet I'd been given had become scorching hot. I clutched at my singed flesh, gritting my teeth, but the pain fled before I could cry out, and a single drop of liquid silver hit the ground, sizzling. I stared at it, watching as it cooled, its shape warping and twisting. Slowly at first, then faster, until suddenly a chrome-covered crow no bigger than a pinball leapt off the floor and soared away, squawking.

And left me standing next to the Captain, who waited for me to follow him into the garage as the van—no longer bullet-riddled—pulled forward into the bay, for the second time. I took a half-step forward, then shuffled back. What had just happened? I reached up and brushed the top of my head, which no longer stung from having my hair so viciously pulled. And there, visible in the corner of the room, was the sniper I hadn't noticed before, sighting through his scope at the windows above.

I glanced down at my wrist, which ached, and saw that the bracelet looked exactly as it had before. Except for one thing: it was missing a crow. I only counted two, now. Wait a goddamned minute...

My bracelet...had turned back *time*?

I struggled to remember what the woman from my vision quest had said about the crows, about anything really, but I'd been too busy trying to figure out who she was to really listen to her advice.

"Is there problem?" the Captain asked.

I flinched, eyes wide as I stared at him, still trying to come to grips with what I was seeing and hearing—the past, but not. The Captain brought the gun to his shoulder, instinctively, reacting to whatever it was he saw on my face. I took a deep breath, then shook my head. "No," I said, "no problem. I ate somethin' that didn't agree with me, earlier, that's all." I patted my stomach. "D'ye have a bathroom in there I could use, by chance?"

The man pursed his lips but lowered his weapon. "No. Is for employees, only."

"Well, that's rude," I said, brushing past him to enter the bay right as the man driving the van pulled in. I slid up against the vehicle, fetched my phone out of my pocket, and let it slip out of my fingers right as he stepped out. The driver bent down on reflex and snatched the phone up off the ground, prepared to hand it back to me. Because that's the funny thing about social graces; we all have them—even trained killers.

Which was what I was counting on.

The instant he bent over, I reached out, plucked the pin on the hand grenade I'd seen dangling from his belt when he'd held Robin at gunpoint, and shoved him into the pit where Hilde had been killed.

After that, everything got a little crazy.

The Captain finally seemed prepared to shoot me, raising his rifle right before the explosion went off. The shockwave sent him flying out onto the street. I, on the other hand, had already leapt into the cab of the vehicle—no sense playing the hero only to get blown up.

Fortunately, the van took the brunt of the blast; the wheels on the left side rose, and for a moment the whole damn thing threatened to tip over—which would have sent me flying face first into the passenger side window—but then, miraculously, it careened the other direction, slamming us down hard enough to pop both tires on that side. I could make out shouting and the sound of gunfire after that, causing me to duck down.

But they weren't shooting at the van, I realized, they were shooting at Robin.

With *silver* bullets.

Robin hardly slowed as the bullets collided with his body, tearing gaping holes in his clothes, but little else. In fact, the silver slugs seemed to careen off him, ricocheting everywhere. Two men went down from friendly fire before the rest realized their bullets were having no effect. Before they could reach for their handguns with the iron bullets, however, I felt the van list even further, the hubcaps grinding into the cement with an audible shriek the moment before Christoff burst out of the back in his werebear form, carving his way through the first soldier he encountered.

Unfortunately, I didn't have time to watch what happened next; there was a sniper to take out, after all. If Hilde chose to fly in the way she had before, I needed to make sure she could land, unopposed. So, I crept forward towards the passenger side, the side where the sniper waited. I could see he'd spun, training his rifle on Christoff—easily the biggest target. I swore to myself. If he got off a clean shot, I knew I'd end up scooping Christoff's brains off the floor, so I did the only logical thing I could think of considering my bright orange coat ruined all chances of me sneaking up on the guy: I leapt out of the van and ran straight for him.

Sniper rifles are nasty things. They're engines of war that scare the living shit out of any soldier who's ever been on a battleground—invisible death from above. But they have their drawbacks. They are meticulously tuned and calibrated for the slightest modifications in temperature, wind-speed, elevation, and even humidity. But they're also fucking heavy—so bulky, in fact, that no one in their right mind would use one in close quarters combat. Especially since the slightest impact would fuck up all their precise calibrations. Snipers were trained to fight *strategically*. Which meant that the likelihood the sniper would abandon his rifle the instant he saw me coming was very high—and I had banked everything on it. Unfortunately, that was about as far as I'd gotten, in terms of planning, which is probably why—the instant I got close—I was suddenly fighting for my life.

Because this Russian sniper was multi-talented. The prick.

I stopped mid-run and swung a kick out at the sniper's hand before he could raise it completely, sending the pistol he'd been drawing flying across the garage. Sadly, that didn't slow him at all; he came up with a knife in the other hand, thrusting at my sternum, which I barely managed to avoid by throwing myself to the side, crashing into a cart full of tools.

The sniper rushed me, leaving me almost no time to react. I managed to reach back and grab hold of something lying on the edge of the cart in time to parry. The tire iron I'd snatched off the cart clipped his forearm as he lunged at me, sending his thrust wide enough that it only clipped my shoulder, tearing a jagged hole in Callie's ghastly jacket. Whoops.

I countered, lashing out with one foot, then followed that up by chucking the tire iron at his head as hard as I could. He swatted it away with a gargantuan paw.

Another fucking legendary partial shifter?! Who *were* these guys?

I realized I had to get closer if I wanted to keep him from using his werebear form against me. That, or put him in a checkmate situation. I snatched the edges of the tool cart and whirled it around with all my might, sending the tools scattering across the floor as I flung the whole damn thing at him. He hopped to his left, letting it fall harmlessly to the side, and grinned at me.

I was out of weapons.

But, then, I didn't need any.

Hilde burst through the glass above our heads, right on time. The sniper looked up just as a pane of shattered glass fell and impaled his leg, cutting through tendon and bone. He roared in pain as blood gushed from his wound.

Sadly, that wouldn't be enough to stop him, and I knew it; wereanimals could heal faster than any other creature I'd seen when hit with anything other than silver ammunition, which I was sure included giant shards of glass. Luckily, I had another option, and it was sitting in the corner of the room.

I dove for his sniper rifle, whirling back around as fast as possible.

Sniper rifles *are* heavy. They're cumbersome and impractical at spitting distance. But, if your target is a trained killer who's too busy trying to get a massive piece of glass out of his leg to pay attention to you, they can also be really, really effective.

Especially when you let the muzzle practically rest against his forehead for support before pulling the trigger.

His head exploded like a watermelon, spraying chunks of brain and shards of bone all over the wall. I lay next to the rifle itself, breathing heavily after having held my breath to take the shot, my heart pounding fiercely in my chest.

Once my hearing came back, I realized the sounds of fighting had all but ceased. I turned to look and saw Hilde standing at the bay door, which remained open, staring out at something going on outside. Probably the cops, I figured, given all the noise we'd generated between the explosions and rifle fire. I rose on shaky legs and made my way down to her, fully prepared to go to prison, while keeping an eye out for survivors.

There weren't any.

I counted seven soldiers in total, some of them partially shifted, locked somewhere between man and bear. Of course, there were also parts of each scattered about—a dismembered paw here, a man's leg there. Hilde's handiwork, judging by the clean cuts.

Once I made it to her side, I realized Christoff was also there. Naked. Fortunately, the older Russian man spotted a pair of coveralls on a rack nearby. He snagged them and tugged them on quickly. They were stained with oil and grease but covered everything. I was moments from looking away when I caught the nametag plastered across the breast pocket.

Which read, I shit you not...

Yogi.

Despite everything, I burst out laughing.

Christoff didn't so much as bat an eye at me; his attention was devoted to what was happening outside. I tracked their eyes and felt my own widen. Not the cops, after all. The Captain, the last surviving member of the Fighting Bears, had apparently survived the explosion—which would have made him a lucky son of a bitch, if it weren't for the fact that now he was facing one very pissed off Robin Redcap.

The Captain, having shifted into his werebear form, was almost as big as Christoff, though not quite. What impressed me, however, was his speed; he shuffled and swiped with such ferocity that he reminded me more of a bobcat than a bear. But if I was impressed by the Captain, I had to admit I was astounded by Robin.

Our little redcap was all grown up.

Having completely torn through his Red Sox jacket—rest in peace—Robin's back had become a roadmap of striated muscle, as broad and thick as a Mr. Universe contender. But he didn't move like a weightlifter; bodybuilders were all about form over function, their muscles to be admired, not used. Robin moved like a man who'd spent his entire life laboring—pulling, pushing, lifting, and dropping. Like a Greco-Roman wrestler, his hips were parallel to the ground, prepared for anything.

When the werebear finally reared up to swipe a tree-trunk-sized paw, Robin struck, grabbing the creature by one furry arm and twisting, tearing the arm right out of its socket. When he lunged in to snap at Robin's throat in retaliation, he let him. The bear's jaws sunk maybe an inch into Robin's flesh, but no further. Robin grunted, clasped both hands around the bear's neck, and began to squeeze.

I'd never seen a werebear's eyes about to literally pop out of its head, but I'll admit I found it fascinating. In the end, however, I was denied that joy as Christoff raised a pistol he'd taken off one of the dead and fired, clipping Robin's shoulder. Before I could ask what the hell Christoff was doing, Robin whirled.

I inadvertently took a step back, realizing that the mass the redcap had put on had come at a price; his eyes danced with malice and anger, like an animal in so much pain it couldn't even recognize the outside world except to lash out at it. Blood dripped from his ballcap, running down his face and into his beard, which had grown and hung between his nipples. He huffed, fingers grasping at nothing, as if aching to crush the skulls of his enemies. He snarled and took a step forward.

"I need him alive," Christoff called out in a soft voice.

"He's beyond reasoning with," Hilde said. "The bloodlust has him, now."

Christoff sighed regretfully and raised the pistol once more.

"Wait," I said. "I have another idea, before ye go puttin' him down."

"I was going to aim for leg, first," Christoff replied, as if offended.

I rolled my eyes but stepped forward. What I was about to do could get me killed, I knew, but I had to try something; even if it meant burning for all eternity under the watchful eye of a vengeful God I refused to cater to. Still…maybe, just this once, the Lord would let it slide. I took another cautious step forward and did the only thing I could think of to stop a rampaging redcap.

I prayed.

CHAPTER 32

*I*t's funny what you can recall from your childhood—fragments and snippets of conversations, the way your house smelled around the holidays, the bedtime story you were read every night before bed. Staring at Robin, his face in anguish, kneeling as I prayed, I realized I never knew how valuable those childhood memories could be—the lessons they could impart. The "Our Father" prayer that had been drilled into me day-in and day-out during my Catholic school tenure until it became so rote that I forgot the meaning behind the words, for example. Or the bedtime stories Dez used to tell me featuring pixies, knights, and boggarts, which included a particularly gruesome tale about a redcap that only briefly mentioned how to frighten the thing away.

Don't judge her too harshly, she parented largely through trial and error —same as most.

Basically, what I'm getting at is that I'd never been more thankful for being raised Irish *and* Catholic.

I continued reciting the Lord's Prayer until I could see recognition in Robin's eyes. He'd shrunk considerably, but was still much broader and denser than when I'd first seen him—back when he was built big, but chubby, like an athlete whose glory days were behind him and beer was all he had to look forward to. I finally stopped speaking, mouth dry, and edged closer, snapping my fingers to get his attention. "Oy! Robin, ye in there?"

Robin rolled his eyes. "I was always in here. I'm not the Hulk."

I arched an eyebrow. "Are ye sure? Because other than the turnin' green bit..."

"You have it in reverse," Robin said. "I don't *become* bloodthirsty, I *am* bloodthirsty. What you just saw is what I really am, deep down. But either way...thank you. It becomes harder to come back, the more blood I soak up." He adjusted his hat—which had mercifully stopped bleeding all down his face—and rose, teetering. He shook his whole body, like a dog kicking off water. Christoff, sparing no time now that he wasn't facing off against Robin's animosity, marched past us, headed for the last of the werebears.

"I'll see if he needs help," Hilde said, trailing him.

I gave Robin a once over. "Ye need new clothes," I said, finally.

Robin grunted, inspecting the tattered remains of his jacket with a sigh. "You're right. If only I had clothes that magically healed themselves..." he trailed off in response to my murderous expression. "How is *that* a touchy subject?" he asked, baffled.

"Too soon," I muttered. "Too soon."

Before I could say anymore, Hilde screamed.

Robin and I wheeled around and found the Valkyrie clutching Christoff's arm, holding on with everything she had to prevent him from flying away into what looked like a Gateway of some kind—a bear-sized portal ten feet in the air that seemed to be sucking up everything below it, including Christoff. Cool air spewed from its edges, sending Hilde's blonde locks whipping back and forth and making the skin on my arms pebble. Finally coming to terms with what I was seeing, I ran, Robin hot on my heels, trying to get to her.

She looked back at me and screamed something, the sound of her voice lost in the wind. Then, in an instant, she and Christoff were simply gone—sucked into a vortex which closed immediately, leaving behind only a chill in the air that didn't mesh with the early morning sunshine. I took a few halting steps forward, my arm still held out as if I could snatch Hilde and draw them away.

I fell to the pavement, my adrenaline finally spent, body aching, my brain fried. After all that...after turning back *time*, I still hadn't been able to save them. What had I missed?

Robin knelt down beside me and grabbed my shoulders. "Quinn, we have to go. Now. Regulars are coming to take a look, now that all the shoot-

181

ing's stopped, which means the cops will be here any minute. Come on." He tried to raise me to my feet, but I refused to stand. After everything, all I wanted was to sit here. If the cops came, so be it. Maybe Jimmy was right; maybe everyone would be better off if I stayed away. Frankly, jail seemed like a cozy place, right about now; I doubted anyone I cared about would be there.

God, how was I going to explain this to Jeffries?

To Christoff's kids?

"They aren't dead, Quinn!" Robin hissed. "Didn't you hear her? She told you to find them. You can't do that if you get arrested." He cursed, turned, and ran back towards the garage. I frowned. Is that what Hilde had said? To find them? Easier said than done, I decided.

I glanced up, wondering how many onlookers would be crowded on the street, only to see something shiny a few feet in front of me. A small disk, the size of a foundation case, but thicker—like a hockey puck. I crawled forward and picked it up off the ground, then scanned the sky. This was exactly where the portal had opened, I noted.

I flipped the object over in my hands, checking it over for markings of any kind, but found only serial numbers that meant nothing to me. It looked burnt out, like a bullet casing, little more than a shell of its former self. But it was possible—it could have caused the rift. Technology to create Gateways existed; I'd stolen some, once. From Grimm Tech, the company owned by Nate Temple and operated by my friend, Othello.

Robin was right, I realized.

There was a chance, a slim chance, that we could find them.

I turned to tell him as much just in time to see him throw two fistfuls of grenades through the open bay door and take off towards me, waving his hands in the universal "get down" gesture. I didn't listen—I was too busy staring at the building behind him exploding. Which is probably why I ended up lying flat on my back a moment later, the wind knocked out of me.

Robin lifted me up off the ground, slinging one of my arms over his shoulder as he carried me out towards the street. "Best I could do," he said, his voice dull and low, what with my hearing momentarily impaired. "I doubt they'll know what to make of that."

Smaller explosions began popping off as the bear's armory caught fire, and I nodded, dumbly. Of course. Hiding evidence. I started to walk under my own power, then shoved Robin up into a very narrow alley between two buildings, turning my body to shield his from view as two patrol units came roaring past. Apparently, no matter how hush-hush the neighborhood, even Russian sympathizers had limits to how much noise they could tolerate before calling the cops.

Robin and I stayed there for a moment before I showed him the device I'd found. "I need to get this to a friend of mine," I said. "She'll be able to track 'em down, if anyone can."

"Alright, well then, where to?" Robin asked.

"Well, first we need to find a car," I said. "And then I need to find a phone. I need to tell Jeffries what just happened." My phone, unfortunately, had died an ignoble death alongside the soldier I'd pushed into the pit. Which sucked, since Othello had given me that phone as a gift...at this point, I was going to end up owing her all sorts of favors.

"How about that car?" Robin asked, pointing to a brand-new, freshly washed Audi sitting outside a massage parlor, gleaming in the morning light. Its license plate read DEWME4.

"I t'ink it belongs to someone. And that it's probably locked," I added, cocking an eyebrow.

Robin snorted. "Locks don't work on us."

Oh, right. There was that.

A slow smile crept across my face. "Well, if we're goin' to steal a car... might as well be a nice one," I said, finally. Because sometimes, when you're having some of the worst couple days of your entire life, the universe owes you a little something.

Like a joy ride.

CHAPTER 33

$\mathcal{B}$y the time we were headed back towards the city, storm clouds obscured the sun—the beginnings of one of those freak spring showers that come rushing up on you before you've had time to close the windows. I had my window down, letting the air in, watching the trees sway as we blew past. A peal of thunder echoed as I went back over the last several hours, trying to process what had happened.

"Something on your mind?" Robin asked, glancing at me before returning his attention to the road. I'd let him drive. As much as I enjoyed the idea of driving a luxury vehicle around, I didn't feel like being pulled over in a stolen car. This way, I could at least blame him. I mean, he did say locks didn't work on Fae; I doubted he'd spend very long in handcuffs.

"Hmm," I replied, considering how to respond. Could I tell Robin about what had happened back at the garage? Not with Christoff and Hilde; I still wasn't sure what to make of that, although in hindsight I was fairly certain the soldier Robin had taken down may have used the device I'd found to save himself...or take Christoff with him. But the time lapse? The do-over? Would Robin even believe me? Part of me hoped he wouldn't. Maybe he'd tell me it was all part of my imagination, and I could write off the fact that I'd seen him die...

Yeah, right. Wishful thinking.

Or maybe telling him about it would break the time-space continuum or something. I'd seen enough movies to know better.

I opened my mouth, prepared to speak anyway, when I saw something shiny on the exit road ahead; Robin had taken us on a route off the highway, headed towards the hospital—the only place I could think of where we might find a way to reach Jeffries or Lakota. I frowned and pointed at the shiny surface of the road, trying to figure out what light it was catching with the sky so overcast. "What's that?" I asked.

Robin squinted, then swore. He slammed on his brakes, hard, the tires squealing as he swung us around, trying to avoid whatever it was. But it was already too late. We hit the patch of black ice at a pretty good clip and slid, spinning in circles before careening into a guardrail. The air bags deployed, slamming us both back into our seats.

*S*ometime later, I groaned. My eye throbbed. My chest and shoulder, too. The storm had broken, and I could hear sirens in the background. Rain poured all around us, some of it splashing through the shattered windshield. I fought to turn my head, looking for Robin, and found him unconscious, blood all over his face. A grinding noise brought me back around, but my movement was too sudden. The world went fuzzy as something the size of a crane reached out to draw me, limp and addled, from the wreckage.

That was the last thing I remembered.

CHAPTER 34

$\mathcal{I}$ woke up in chains.

And in a fucking dress.

I opened my eyes, groggily, and immediately wished with every fiber of my being that I could simply pass out again. My body hurt all over, from the accident, which came back to me in pieces. Swerving. The collision. Being carried somewhere.

Outside, the rain beat so hard it sounded like chips of stone striking pavement over and over again. My wrists ached, and my shoulders burned so badly I had to bite my lip to keep from crying out; they were hiked up and held by a thick set of manacles, the chain of which went up higher than I could see. My feet, mercifully, were on the ground, or else I'd be in even more pain than I already was; hanging from one's arms is a torture all on its own.

I glanced around, trying to figure out where I was. A factory of some kind, maybe? It was definitely an industrial building—too many machines with functions I could only guess at. Despite the fact that it was 70 degrees outside, I could see my breath. I shivered, chills making me writhe—which only made the pain worse; I whimpered, then hissed, trying to chase away the pain by getting pissed off.

One day that would work, I was sure.

"Oh, you're awake. Excellent. I hope you don't mind the dress. That jacket was appalling," Jack Frost said as he stepped into my line of sight from behind one of the bigger machines, hands behind his back like some sort of British aristocrat, dressed in a pale blue dress shirt and dark blue slacks. "I'll admit I was surprised to find you'd survived the car crash. I suppose you can thank Throm for bringing you here."

I frowned at the memory of being carried by inhumanly large hands. Inhumanly large and...blue? I shook my head to clear it, but all that did was remind me how much the rest of me hurt. I winced, then glared at Frost. At least the black ice on the road in the middle of spring made sense now. But how had he found us?

A groan to my left gave me my answer; Jeffries, his suit splattered with blood, hung there, visible only in my peripherals when I turned my head as far as it would go. His eyelids fluttered, but otherwise there was little sign of life. How long had he been here? How long had I been here?

"Ah, it seems your companion is also awake."

"What's he doin' here?" I asked, mostly to myself.

"Same as you. Hanging around," Jack said, smirking.

Oh, great. A punny psychopath. My favorite.

"He's a fascinating Manling," Jack continued. "A sensor of lies. Quite the skill. He and the Seer did an excellent job, tracking me down. Of course, they should never have involved the Chancery. Too many prying eyes and ears."

"What d'ye want?" I asked, cutting to the chase. As much as I enjoyed a good monologue, I wasn't all that interested in how I'd gotten here so much as how I could get out of here; the longer he left me hanging like this, the less I'd be able to do when I finally got free.

If I got free.

"Who, me?" Frost asked, surprised. He seemed to consider that for a moment. "What a mortal question to ask..."

"What d'ye want with me?" I clarified, grinding my teeth. Sure, I'd put the FBI on his scent, but abducting me couldn't have been terribly convenient. Had I pissed him off so badly when I shook his hand that he'd come after me to settle the score? Or was it something else?

"Oh, self-interest," he said. "Much better. The truth is I want nothing from you. I'm pretty sure Throm liked the color of your hair and decided to bring you to me as a gift. Like a cat leaving a dead mouse in your shoe. Well, a soon-to-be dead mouse, anyway."

"Throm?" I asked, choosing to ignore his threat.

Frost pointed across the room. I frowned, following his finger. On the far side of the building, something moved. My eyes widened. What I'd originally mistaken for heavy machinery was, in fact, an impossibly large man-like creature. A hand, so big it took me a moment to process it even was a hand, rose and waved. From this distance, at a guess, I'd say he was at least thirty feet tall. Built like a prison inmate—his upper body heavyset, his legs thin and knobby—Throm looked as if he could tear apart houses with his bare, blue hands. Stubble littered his cheeks, each hair on his face as thick as an icicle, with the same consistency.

"One of the smaller Jotnar," Frost explained. "The Ice Giants from Jotunheim."

"Where the fuck d'ye get an Ice Giant?" I asked, my jaw still hanging. Jotunheim was one of the nine realms described in Norse mythology, separate from our own realm, which they called Midgard. Frankly, aside from Hilde, I'd never met—nor expected to meet—any of the Norse races; they were notoriously isolated. I'd taken a professional interest in the Norse pantheon years before, trying to get my hands on some of the epically cool shit their dwarves had reportedly forged.

Frost cocked his head. "You didn't think we took only human offspring to raise in Fae, did you?" He shook his head. "Throm's mother left him to die, thinking him too frail, and so I stole him away to be raised among my kind. Among his own people, he would be considered frail. But the Fae don't discriminate. Size is not strength. Power is strength."

I had a flash of insight. "Is that why you've been murderin' people, *Ripper*?" I asked. "To gain power?"

"Oh yes, the clever FBI Agent brought that up. Impressive. To be honest, I'd almost forgotten. You lose track of such things when you return home. But yes, killing those mortals had seemed the most expedient option."

"Expedient?" I spat. "Ye murdered people. Innocent people. Ye took away mothers from their children! D'ye know what it's like to grow up without a mother, ye Fae piece of shit?"

He waved that off. "You wouldn't understand. None of your kind could. You lot live *here*, after all." His electric blue eyes stared off at nothing for a moment. "I don't know what it is about your realm, but it makes you care so much about abstracts. Justice. Morality. People you've never met. Life. Death. The Chancery," Frost said, scoffing.

"What an absurd thing they've created. They've forgotten what it means to be Fae. But they must be reminded, if they hope to survive what's coming."

Jeffries groaned, again, then coughed. "What's coming?" he asked, his voice hoarse.

"The Fomorians," Frost answered, as if we should know exactly what that meant. "Something has called them here. I sensed it, too, the moment I was sent back to the mortal realm. It's in this city. Like a beacon, drawing them close."

I could still see the writing on the wall, written in the blood of that poor, mutilated woman: Beware the Fomorians. Frost must have written that. But why? Who, or what, were they? Before I could ask, Frost roused himself. "Anyway, don't worry," Frost said, "I'll be sure to kill you quickly, I promise, once I've finished with the Seer."

Jeffries struggled, still groaning, but seemed as securely bound as I was. "Why the kid?" I growled. "What happened to the Twelve Days of Christmas? Couldn't find a convenient target for 'seven geese a' layin'?" I asked, trying to bait him.

Frost shook his head. "That may not be necessary. Not now. The Seer's power should be enough to complete the ritual and finish the song. I believe I can use it to ferret out whatever is calling to the Fomorians. With one sacrifice, I will end the threat that looms over this realm and save you all. You're welcome."

"I swear I won't let you touch Lakota," Jeffries whispered.

Frost snapped his fingers, and the air, already chilly, took on a brittle quality. "Let's test that, shall we?" He reached out and flipped a switch. The sound of grinding machinery whirring to life echoed throughout the building until I saw Lakota, strapped to a conveyor belt, slowly nearing us. He was unconscious and naked from the waist up, and...a girl. Definitely a girl.

Huh.

Talk about a plot twist.

I blinked a couple of times, just to be sure I wasn't imagining anything, but I wasn't. Lakota had breasts. I'd never noticed them under...her clothing, so she must have chosen to dress in a way that hid it from others. Or, I just really sucked at noticing things. I leaned to glance back at Jeffries, but the FBI Agent wasn't even looking; he'd delivered his promise and promptly passed out. I wondered if he knew. But then, at the moment, it hardly mattered.

Boy or girl, Lakota was at the mercy of a killer.

And there was nothing Jeffries or I could do about it.

The Faeling rolled up one sleeve and slid an iron blade across his forearm, hissing as he sliced open his own flesh. He flung his arm up, and droplets of his blood—as red as mine—flew into the air. They froze, then extended, lengthening to become slender needles of ice, and began spinning —interlocking at different points to form a sort of rotating language.

I'd never seen anything like it.

It reminded me of ritual magic; a type of sorcery used to draw circles or cast curses. Elaborate, complex, and time-consuming, ritual magic was routinely practiced by witches or summoners, not by Faelings. As far as I knew, the Fae never bothered with anything that fancy; magic came to them as easy as breathing.

This, well, this looked like work, and it was taking up Frost's entire attention.

Which is perhaps why Frost hadn't noticed that—while the rain had stopped—the thunder hadn't.

And it was getting much, much closer.

CHAPTER 35

*a*n ear-splitting crash tore through the building as what I could only guess was a door went soaring past me to collide with some other contraption, the din of metal on metal almost as loud as the bellowing roar that echoed throughout the building a moment later.

A roar I recognized.

I glanced over to see Frost was too focused on his blood-cicle ritual to notice the party crasher.

Paul, the bridge troll, came lumbering through the opening he'd created, his thick, hairy green hide covered in assorted furs, including shoes made from skunks. Unfortunately, Paul's warrior mode—which included tearing doors off their hinges—also came with a need to assert masculine dominance.

Because he immediately hiked one leg up and took a firehose-sized whiz on the floor.

"Really, Troll?" I heard someone grumble. "Now we all have to run through that, you realize?"

"What'd Paul do?" someone else called out from behind her.

"He peed on their floor."

"Nice one, Paul! Way to show them who's boss!"

Paul grunted and fist pumped before coming forward, walking gingerly around Jeffries. He stared up at the man as if debating whether to eat him or not, then saw me and brightened. "Ruby!" he bellowed, calling me by the nickname he had come up with for me. He wrapped one massive hand around the chain holding me and yanked, tearing it loose from the ceiling. I fell and rolled to my right, which turned out to be pretty lucky; the remainder of the chain and part of the ceiling crashed down only a few feet from where I'd been standing, sending debris everywhere.

I got to my knees, I tried to, anyway—with the dress on, the best I could do was slide my legs underneath myself and sit up—cursing as the pain in my arms grew even worse now that they weren't being suspended in midair. Paul eyed the chain in his hand as if debating whether or not to keep it, then dismissively dropped it—which was good, considering I was still technically attached to it by the manacles around my wrists.

"Quinn! Are you okay?" I heard someone—the voice who'd cheered Paul's dominance by urination—ask. I spun, only to find Robin's bushy beard inches from my face.

"Oy!" I leaned back a little. "Personal space, Robin. But aye, I'm alright. Listen, ye have to get Jeffries and Lakota out of here. Especially Lakota. Frost plans to kill her," I said, talking so fast I sounded like I'd had twelve shots of espresso.

"Easy there, we'll get them," Robin said. He jerked his head back towards the door, where a small host of Fae stood, eyeing the big yellow stain in the middle of the floor as if deciding the best option to get around it. There was Cassandra, astride Black Beauty, her spinal cord whip in hand. Barb, dressed in tattered black robes, hood up, floating in the air like a sexy Dementor. Dementress? And, lastly, a third Faeling I didn't recognize. She was draped in furs, her eyes literally on fire, a black bow strung over one shoulder.

"Who's that?" I asked.

"Don't know. Said she was a friend of someone named Othello. Cassandra seemed to trust her, and I wasn't exactly in a position to turn down help. Besides, she said she could hunt you down, so I followed." Robin shrugged, then glanced up over my shoulder. His baby blues went wide. "What the hell is that?"

I turned. "Oh. That's Throm." Throm, finally realizing it was time to earn his keep since Frost was still completely focused on his ritual, had risen to his full height, looming so far above us that I could barely make out the features of his face from this far down. Only Paul, who was about a third of Throm's size, seemed unfazed; of course, he wasn't exactly the brightest member of Team Quinn.

"What's a Throm?" Robin asked, sounding only slightly terrified.

"Ice Giant. Jotnar," I elaborated, "from Jotunheim. Frost raised him."

"He *raised* him? Like a *pet?*" Robin's eyes went even wider. "What would it take to feed that thing?"

Before I could reply, Paul took off at a dead sprint and charged at the Jotnar, ramming his shoulder into the Ice Giant's kneecap. Throm grunted and wobbled a little before swatting Paul away like you might a small dog trying to piss on your leg. The bridge troll rolled to his feet and prepared to strike again, but I could see it would do no good; despite how hulking and strong Paul was, the bridge troll didn't stand a chance of bringing the Ice Giant down with sheer force.

Thankfully, it seemed the three female Faelings had survived the yellow pond of testost-urine and were prepared to offer reinforcement. The Faeling I hadn't recognized approached, gazing down at me. I felt something, a certain kinship, register immediately. Which meant—if Dobby's warning could be believed—that I should be wary around her. "Get her and the other two mortals out of here, redcap," she told Robin without breaking eye contact with me. "We'll handle the giant," she said, jerking her chin at Cassandra and Barb.

"How d'ye know Othello?" I asked her, just as she was taking a step towards her chosen foe.

The woman paused, considering her response as she turned a level gaze back to me. "She's mentioned me to you before, I should think. If you'd have been smarter, you'd have sought me out, first. Then none of this would have happened." She took off before I could refute that assertion, moving with unbridled grace and speed, testing the draw of her bow in one smooth motion—as easy as brushing aside a spider's web—like a sexier, scarier, more powerful Hawkeye with flaming peepers.

Not Hawkeye, I decided.

More like…Hawteye.

As Hawteye joined the fray, Cassandra slung her whip with the sound of cracking joints that would make a chiropractor squeal, the force of her motion winding the bony cord around Throm's ankle, constricting it. Then, before the Ice Giant could react, the Dullahan turned, tied the whip handle to her saddle, and charged forward with Black Beauty. The whip went taut, and Throm was pulled off balance by the weight of the lunging stallion. The ground shook as the Ice Giant fell to one knee.

That's when Hawteye made her move.

She ran right towards the Ice Giant and commanded, "Troll! Down!"

Paul dropped to all fours as if he'd been struck by the hand of God, eyes bugging out of his head. Hawteye leapt up, planted one foot in the middle of Paul's back, and used her bow to pole vault into the air. She hung, suspended for an instant, before landing gracefully, rolling to her feet.

Throm roared, clutching at his eyes, and Robin winced.

"What was that?" I asked, feeling like I'd missed something.

"She shot him in the eyes."

I hadn't seen a damned thing. No one could draw a bow that fast. Especially not twice.

"But, he's so big…" I drifted off, frowning.

"Can you imagine having splinters in your eyeballs?" Robin asked, cocking an eyebrow.

I winced.

"Exactly," Robin said. "Shit. Cover your ears!"

I did as he asked, too surprised to bother asking why. Then I looked up, and realized what he'd seen: high above, Barb floated in mid-air, having snuck up behind Throm while he cradled his face. The Banshee drew a deep breath and screamed directly into Throm's ear canal, the sound beyond cringeworthy even with my ears covered. The Ice Giant—blood running down his face and from one ear—bellowed and swatted at the air, but Barb was already gone.

Robin nudged me. "I think they've got things handled," he said.

I nodded. "Aye, seems that way. Now it's our turn," I said. I scanned the building and saw Frost, still muttering as his blood spun in the air. I watched as one sliver of frozen blood flew at Lakota, piercing her side. There were already several poking out at different points on her body—more than half, I realized—riddled along her skin like acupuncture needles. In the chaos, I hadn't even noticed. I had a feeling the ritual would be complete the moment the last needle struck, which meant we had to hurry.

And pray Frost was clean.

Because that's how you pick up a nasty FTD—a Fae Transmitted Disease.

"Take Jeffries," I insisted. "I've got Lakota."

"That's *Lakota?*" Robin said, frowning. "That's a *girl.*"

"I know. We can sort that out later. Right now, I need to figure out how to get past Frost and get Lakota out of here," I replied. "Whatever he's tryin' to do, I'd rather not wait to find out how it ends."

Robin grunted, then eyed my manacled wrists. He reached out and flicked them. They fell open onto the floor with a clang. I rubbed at my raw skin. "T'anks," I said.

"Don't ever say I never did anything for you. Oh, and here," Robin said, handing over a pistol. "I stole this off one of the guards from the garage. Seemed handy to have a pistol full of iron bullets."

I cradled the gun like an infant and clutched it to my chest. "Oh, I could kiss ye," I said.

"I mean...I won't stop you," Robin said, hopefully.

"Not ye! The pistol, ye idgit!" I hissed.

"Oh, right," he replied, awkwardly fussing with his hat.

I leaned in and planted a quick peck on his cheek. "That's for comin' to save me. Now, go!" I shoved him back towards Jeffries, who remained unconscious, hanging limp from the ceiling. Robin blushed, but did as I asked, taking off towards the Agent. Which left me alone, with a single gun, to take on a legendary creature from folklore. I rose, tore a massive slit down one side of the dress using a sharp piece of metal, and took a deep breath.

Just another day at the office.

CHAPTER 36

Frost took the first bullet without flinching, completely oblivious to the sound of a pistol going off right beside him. I wasn't that surprised; excluding a period much earlier in history when we'd fired musket balls made of iron, I doubted the Faeling had ever had cause to fear modern firearms.

But then the iron bullet went to work, and Frost realized it hadn't been a run-of-the-mill bullet.

The second shot was a different story.

Frost dove away, already tearing at the bullet I'd put in his side. I supposed I could have put the gun against the bastard's head and pulled the trigger, but part of me remembered Robin's warning; if I killed him now, in cold blood, without the Chancery's permission, I could be in real trouble. So, instead, I'd aimed to maim and slow. As I watched, his wounds frosted over, leaving gaping holes that oozed a ruby red, Slurpee-like substance.

I readjusted and fired once more, taking Frost in the calf. He dragged himself away, hissing in pain, giving me time to undo the strap pinning Lakota to the conveyor belt. I considered pulling the needles out but decided against it; I wasn't medically qualified to pull foreign objects out of people. I slid over to Lakota's face and patted her cheek. "Lakota! Wake up, we have to get—"

Frost tackled me before I could finish. I pumped two more shots into him as we fell before losing my grip on the gun. We hit the ground hard and the gun skittered away. Frost scrambled to get on top of me, surprisingly nimble and strong for a Faeling who'd been shot four times with iron bullets. I thrust my hips, bucking the Faeling, and rolled him off me. Frost snarled and flung a hand at me. A wave of ice shards spewed from between his fingers, crashing against my anti-magic field—or my *cage* as the window lady had called it—mere inches from my face.

Seeing that his magic had no effect, the Faeling's expression became malicious. He rose, limping. "Let's see if you can survive this!" Frost beckoned with one arm, and, before I had time to react, I felt a half-dozen needles pierce my back like hot pokers. Frost smiled, his perfect teeth gleaming, his eyes triumphant—lit up and dancing, as though posing for his candid.

Until Lakota put a bullet between them.

Too bad I didn't have a camera.

Talk about a headshot.

Frost's head jerked back, and I knew he was dead by the way his lifeless body toppled over. I turned to Lakota, prepared to get us the fuck out of here—we could deal with the Chancery's repercussions later—when the needles in my back began to ache. And then to burn. I noticed Lakota had already pulled all the frozen shards out of her body—probably out of reflex. She stared down at Frost's corpse in shock. I fell to my knees as the pain spiked, so intense it was practically unbearable.

It pulled me under.

*I*t was dark out.

"Where am I?" I asked myself out loud, feeling like I was floating.

No, not floating. I was lying down in a snowbank, staring up at the night sky. The stars were brighter than I'd ever seen, and yet I could see nothing of the landscape around me—not even my breath, which had to be visible given the cold.

"They worshipped me once, you know," Frost said, lying beside me.

"*Fuck!*" I scrambled away, my heart suddenly hammering in my chest.

"I didn't ask them to," Frost continued, ignoring my outburst. "But they begged me, pleaded with me. Asking me to leave their homes in peace. To take them, but never their loved ones. At first, I was indifferent. I was a creature of the cold, not the source of it. What did I care about their harvests? I arrived as I wished and left as I pleased."

I scanned the sky and my immediate surroundings, trying to figure out how I'd ended up here—wherever *here* was. And what about Frost? I'd seen him die. Except, the icicles he'd formed using his own blood had been inside me...were we connected, somehow? Was he feeding off me, like a battery?

"Oh no," Frost said, chuckling. "I'm dying, don't worry. You're just joining me on this leg of the journey, that's all."

"Where are we?" I asked, thrown by his confession.

"This is my home. Or it was. I merely thought it'd be nice to see it again, and *poof*, here I am. Well, here *we* are, I guess. I didn't expect company. Although I would have liked to say goodbye to Throm," Frost admitted sadly.

I frowned. This creature beside me sounded nothing like the Jack Frost I knew. If anything, he seemed remorseful. Pitiable.

If you were into that sort of thing.

"We all do what we are meant to do," Frost said, as if responding to my thoughts. "That's all I was saying. It's only when we break away from our natures that we end up with regrets. See, I never once felt guilty for what I did to them. And that was the way of things, for a long, long time. But then things changed. They found ways to outsmart me. To hide. They found shelter, and coal, and iron. And I hated them for that, I think. Never before had I hated any creature. In Fae, we do not hate. Hate is too deep an emotion. At worst, we find others distasteful. Unpleasant, maybe. But you can't hate creatures who always act in their own self-interest."

"And Manlings?" I asked, before I could help myself.

"Manlings," Frost said, with a sigh. "Manlings were different. They heeded our lessons too well, I think. Once, they joined together, forged bonds. Out of necessity, mostly. But then we taught them to crave. To take. Many of my kind left after that, returning home with horror stories. I was one of the few who remained. I was angry, and so I became Jack the Ripper, in an attempt to forge a new legend for myself."

I shuddered.

"Yes, I know," Frost said. "It was foolish. And so, I left soon after killing that last Manling woman. I took out all my rage and hatred on her until there was nothing left in me but exhaustion. And then I went home."

"Why d'ye come back, then, if ye knew it was a mistake? Why kill so many more?" I asked, desperately trying to understand how the Faeling I'd met—the Jack Frost who had tortured and murdered all those other people, the Faeling who'd captured and held me in chains—could be so changed.

"She commanded, and I obeyed," Frost replied.

"She?" I asked.

Frost nodded. "The Winter Queen. She knows what's coming. The Fae here have become too human, and the Old Gods have stepped away from the world. Of course, there's one among you who could step forward to challenge the Fomorians, but—if he does—it's likely he will doom my kind. The Manling Born in Fae has no love for us, you see. He would use us as cannon fodder to keep his own people safe."

The Manling Born in Fae... That sounded awfully familiar, but for some reason I couldn't place it. I shook my head, deciding to dwell on it later. "So, the Winter Queen sent you? But why? Why you?"

"To hunt down the source," Frost explained. "The one calling the Fomorians to Boston. I've always been good at finding those who hope to stay hidden. But, once I got here, I realized that there was another way. That the Chancery was weak. Broken. And that all it would take was a nudge here and there to incite a revolution."

I frowned, recalling Robin's words from the day before; the Chancery was a powder keg, waiting to explode. But what would Frost hope to gain from pushing them to the edge?

"Did you know," Frost continued, "the day we met, I whispered in Morgause's ear, telling her that her son had been freed? I was the one who planted the idea in her head that The Green Knight was responsible." Frost sighed, not sounding the least bit proud of himself. The opposite, in fact. "The truth is, I thought if I could take over—if I could rule—we might stand a chance of defeating the Fomorians. But, of course...now I realize I'd simply been in the human realm too long. Your kind and your abstracts. Pride. Ambition. I caught them like a disease. They've been eating away at me for a while now..." Frost drifted off, his voice weak and thready.

"Wait, what about the Fomorians? I still don't know who or what they are," I admitted. "Why are they so dangerous?"

A light emerged far away, as brilliant as a star, but glowing blue. It got closer, weaving back and forth as though scanning the horizon. I frowned, realizing I could make out Frost's face. He was staring at the light, studying it as if recalling a memory from long ago. "We met them on the shore," he said, finally. "I was young, then, and weak. But I remember the wars. How our greatest champions chased them into the sea. But it cost us, even then. And now our champions have all but disappeared. Clíodhna sleeps, Manannan mac Lir sails alone, the forges of the Trí Dée Dána are cold and empty, and Lugh is lost in a maze of his own making."

What the hell was he talking about?

The beam of azure light spread, arcing towards us, as its source shifted back and forth. I felt something emanating from it, a malevolence I could hardly describe. "He has lost one eye, only to gain another," Frost said. "They have returned to take what is theirs, and he is stronger than ever. I was a fool to think I could stop him."

"Stop who?" I asked.

"Balor," Jack whispered. The light swerved at the sound of his voice, locking onto us. I froze, trapped beneath it like an insect under a microscope. I remembered screaming as the world around me burned and turned to dust.

Then, nothing.

Then, more pain.

*M*y wrist was on fire. I shook it loose, swearing, and saw a silver crow rushing towards an opening in the ceiling of the building where I'd been held captive. A wave of ice crashed against my field. I stared down at the chunks of ice at my feet in surprise.

"Let's see if you can survive this!" Jack yelled. Again.

Acting purely on reflex, I flung myself to the side. Jack's needles passed harmlessly by, crashing against the ground and splintering. Jack snarled and spun, but found Lakota—the gun I'd used to shoot Frost held in both hands —aiming for his face.

"Wait!" I called, distracting Lakota just enough that her shot went wild, clipping Jack's shoulder instead. The Faeling spun and landed on his side, groaning.

"What did you do that for?" Lakota growled. She raised the pistol once more.

"Lakota, please," I said, rising as quickly as my dress would allow. "Please, give me the gun. Ye don't want to do this." I edged forward.

"His soul is one of the most depraved I've ever seen," Lakota said. "He kills mortals in the name of practicality. He thinks he's *noble*," she spat.

"I know," I replied, gently. "But you'll never forgive yourself if ye kill him like this. Come on, give me the gun," I urged. Lakota frowned, but I could see the uncertainty in her eyes as she stared down at Frost. I slid my hands along the barrel and pried the gun from her grasp. She released it, and brought her arms up, covering herself, cheeks red.

I squeezed her shoulder, turned, and trained the gun at Frost.

"What are you doing?" Lakota asked, confused. "I thought you didn't want him dead?"

"No," I replied, "I simply didn't want ye to be the one with that on your conscience."

Lakota stared into my soul from inches away as I lined up my shot. "But you don't even hate him. You…oh, God, you actually admire him. Why?"

"Would ye kill a tiger for bein' a tiger?" I asked, ignoring her question.

"No, but what does that have to do with anything?"

"I would. I wouldn't blame the tiger, or anythin'. But ye can't leave a man-eater alive, even if it's only doin' what it was born to do," I replied. I squeezed the trigger as Jack turned back to look at me, his eyes full of hate and pain and fear. He fell over, eyes empty, blood spilling from the bullet wound in the center of his forehead. "Even if it was only doin' it because it was terrified of somethin' worse."

Because we're all afraid of something.

But not all of us rip mothers away from their children.

CHAPTER 37

*T*he gun felt heavy. Heavier than it should have. I stared into the dead, electric blue eyes of a man who'd mutilated and murdered people, and I wasn't sorry. Hell, I wasn't anything. I felt numb, floating—the way I had looking up at the stars next to Jack, stuck somewhere between life and death. That's how it felt to murder someone in cold blood, I realized—like your soul and body could no longer inhabit the same space.

"Thank you," Lakota said, resting a hand on my gun arm, which was still raised and trembling. I glanced back at her, surprised, and finally lowered my gun. "You did the right thing," she said emphatically as she gingerly took the gun from me, as if I might do something dumb with it. "Not the *good* thing. But the *right* thing. And that's harder."

Before I could reply, another voice whispered in my ear, full of malice, "Wrong. You've doomed us all." I whirled around, only to find myself in a dark, cavernous room—the speaker nowhere in sight.

"Oh, for fuck's sake, what now?" I cursed. I was disoriented, exhausted, my body in so much pain it hardly even registered anymore, and I was fucking sick and tired of being pulled into dreamscapes and different dimensions without warning.

"You should be used to it by now, child," a voice said, slithering across the cavern. I traced the sound back to a recess smothered in shadow. I approached, inching forward, my bare feet sliding across stone.

"Who's there?" I asked.

"Come see for yourself," the voice replied. A faint blue light shone, little more than a glow, and I realized I was looking at—not a recess—but a room. A throne room carved into the rock. The throne itself, formed from massive sheets of ice, stood in the center, illuminated by tiny, glowing fish that swam within the ice.

The speaker—a woman, older, her eyes tired and her face lined, wearing a dark shawl that hid the rest of her body—stood beside the throne. There was something familiar about her face, I realized. The bend of her nose, perhaps, or the slight tilt of her eyes. Something I couldn't quite place.

She held out her hand, revealing a block of ice. Inside it, something dark and amorphous lay, pulsing. I frowned and went a little closer, warily checking my surroundings—but no one else was there. "It is only the two of us," she said, appeasingly. "The Winter Queen and the mortal who killed my son." She reached over and slid her finger across the block of ice. It came up wet and dripping. The block was melting.

I stopped edging forward. The Winter Queen, one of the three powers who ruled over Fae alongside the Summer Queen and Oberon. And...Jack Frost's mother. Suddenly, the resemblance was obvious. So, what was this, revenge? I glanced around the room, hoping to find some sort of weapon to defend myself, but all I saw were bare stone walls. I considered running, but I had no idea where I was, so there was little sense in that.

"I do not plan to kill you," she said, catching my expression. "Once, perhaps, I would have done so. As punishment. But times have changed. I gambled, sending my son to your realm. And I lost." She frowned. "We have lost much, of late. My sister and I are not what we once were."

"Why are ye tellin' me this?" I asked, suspiciously. It wasn't like I was complaining, but in my experience the only time anyone went out of their way to talk to me about their problems, it was because they wanted something.

And I had a feeling the Fae Queen wasn't looking for sympathy.

"What do you know about your mother?" The Winter Queen asked.

"Me ma?" I asked. "Why would ye want to know about her?"

The Winter Queen pointed at my wrist, where a single silver crow still dangled. "She tried to protect you, you know. From killing my son. From dooming us all. That was meant to be a second chance, a chance to work with us, to prevent what's coming."

"That wasn't me ma," I said. "Me ma is dead." It hurt to say, but it felt good to shut down the Queen before she could spout any more nonsense.

The Winter Queen snorted. "Have it your way. But that doesn't change things. She would have wanted you to join us."

"Join ye?" I asked, my jaw hanging open. "Ye mean join up with the ones killin' innocent people?" I accused. "No t'anks."

She arched an eyebrow. "Would you deny us the right to defend ourselves?" She approached, practically gliding across the floor, the block of ice in her hand dribbling water onto the ground as she held it out to me. "Balor is coming. We took his eye, long ago, as a prize. The eye that slayed Nuada." The Winter Queen spun the block, and the dark mass took on a new shape. A floating orb. An eye, with tendrils trailing behind it like the limbs of a squid.

"That's disgustin'," I said, cringing.

"He is coming for it. For us. He and his kind will wipe out your world. They will take it by storm, searching for a way in. A way to come here and subjugate our people once again."

"Here?" I asked, cocking an eyebrow.

"Fae," she said, waving her hand at the throne room as though that were obvious.

"*This* is Fae?" I asked, floored. The Winter Queen snorted and snapped her fingers. Suddenly, the gloomy throne room became something else entirely. I twirled in a slow circle, studying the walls, the floors, the ceiling. She was telling the truth; we weren't in my world. Not anymore. In my world, stone didn't curl in on itself, like smoke, roiling beneath your feet so slowly you couldn't even tell it was happening until you looked down at it. In my world, you might find bats hanging from the ceiling of a cave, but never fish—the same fish swarming in the throne—swimming high above your head, their scales strobing to light the room.

This *was* Fae.

"You have sought us out your whole life," the Queen said, sliding up behind me, no longer old and tired, but young and stunning, "whether you knew it or not. You wanted answers. Answers we can give you. Release the last of your mother's magic, and you can become who you were meant to be."

I frowned and glanced back at the Winter Queen. She looked eager, anticipatory, her eyes locked on the bracelet around my wrist. I held it up to the light, studying the dainty charm hanging from it. Such a tiny, insignificant thing.

Would it be so bad? To be free? To find out what I was truly capable of? I felt something stir inside me. Something fierce and proud and…angry. Why not take her offer? It was true, I wanted answers. I *deserved* answers. I'd been through so much—and why? Why suffer and struggle when I had the power to stop it? And it was there. I knew it was. I could feel it, pressing against the bars of the cage, aching to get out and stretch.

"All that power…" the Queen whispered. "Yours…"

She was right. But it wasn't just about the power; I wanted to belong. To have a family I could call my own. To know my place in the world. Uncaged, I could carve out that place for myself. No more pining after a father I'd never known. No more mourning a mother who'd left too soon.

I could forge my own family.

All I had to do was say *yes*.

Before I could speak, I felt a weight settle in the center of my closed fist. I unfurled my fingers, holding it out. A stone sat in the center of my palm.

A white stone.

"What's that?" The Queen hissed.

"A gift," I said, although even remembering that much was a struggle. Why couldn't I remember? I shook my head in an attempt to clear my thoughts. "A gift," I repeated, "from a man who knows how hard it is to find your way home."

The Winter Queen scoffed. "Cast it aside. You *are* home."

That didn't sound right. This wasn't home…was it? I concentrated on the question, on what home actually meant, my brow furrowed. I closed my eyes, blocking out the wondrous sights of Fae, and pictured Dez, younger, plopping me down on the couch beside her to watch our first of many movies. Christoff, behind the bar, counting the drawers and humming a Russian tune. Othello with her tongue sticking out as she typed, her fingers flying across the keyboard. Paul passed out under a table, snoring. More images flashed. More memories.

I smiled and opened my eyes. The throne room was dark again. The Winter Queen, her skin hanging on her frame, mouth turned down in a wrinkled face, glared up at me. I cocked my head. "Ye planned to use me like ye did your son from the start, didn't ye?" I asked.

Her face, filled with hate and malice, gave me my answer.

I clutched the white stone to my breast and whispered the only word—the only thing—that mattered more to me than my long-awaited trip to Fae.

Home.

CHAPTER 38

*S*adly, it seemed the stone had different ideas.

Apparently, home was a loose concept. Turns out the stone hadn't been attuned to *my* home, but its owners. Which is how I ended up in Hansel's lap, his poor desk chair groaning from the strain of holding up our combined weight. He coughed, clearing his throat.

"Ms. MacKenna, not to inconvenience you, but could you get off me?"

I narrowed my eyes and rose, working my way around the edge of his desk. "Was this your plan all along, ye nasty old man? Have ye just been sittin' here, waitin' for me to use this t'ing?" I tossed him the stone, which had darkened considerably.

Hansel arced an eyebrow as he snatched the stone from the air. "I'll admit, I hadn't expected you to need it so soon." He looked me up and down, frowning at what he saw—a frazzled, battered mess, I imagined. "Busy day?" he asked.

"Just got the recruitment pitch from the Winter Queen," I said, adjusting the strap of my dress and brushing off the grime, ignoring the copious bruises. I didn't even bother fussing with my hair. "Christ, I hate dresses," I said, eyeing the racy amount of leg I'd exposed to move around freely while fighting Jack.

"Oh, that reminds me," Hansel said, snatching a parcel off the side of his desk. "I believe you left these. I'd planned on sending them, but recalled you don't care for our method of delivery." He passed me the parcel.

I hefted it, gauging, then tore it open. "Me clothes!" I squealed.

"I thought you might appreciate having them back," Hansel said, leaning back in his chair.

I briefly considered changing right then and there but decided—no matter how much I despised the idea of wearing the dress Jack had picked out for me—I needed a shower before I bothered. A very hot shower. Followed by a hot bath. And a long nap.

Hansel pointed to a chair opposite him. "Please, have a seat. You mentioned the Winter Queen?"

"Aye," I replied, settling in. Now that I was back in the mortal realm, I felt the residual effects of my brief stay in Fae wearing off; my mind clearing, like a hangover in reverse. "She gave me an offer I couldn't refuse."

"And yet..." Hansel waved a hand, indicating our surroundings.

"Aye, but I t'ink ye had a role in that," I ventured.

Hansel snorted. "I gave you the stone *yesterday*. Surely you don't think I knew you'd need it so soon."

We studied each other.

"I t'ink you've been more involved in t'ings than ye let on," I said, finally.

"I'm afraid," Hansel began, "I don't make it a habit of discussing private conversations I've had with clients. Confidentiality is part of my—"

"Frost is dead," I said.

Hansel's jaw snapped shut. He scowled. "How?"

"I shot him in the face. Other places, too," I admitted. "But the head-shot... that, yeah, I'd bet that was the final snowflake that brought the mountain down."

Hansel's eyes widened.

"So, I may need a lawyer," I continued. "Know any?"

Hansel cursed in German, then steepled his fingers. "I was hoping it wouldn't come to that."

"When ye sent Hawteye to find me, ye mean?" I asked.

"Hawteye?" Hansel asked.

"The Fae with the bow. Flamin' eyes."

"The Huntress. Yes, I reached out to her," he replied, confirming my suspicion. "She's been advocating for you for some time, you know."

I frowned, wondering how that was possible. I'd never even met the

Faeling before today, and I'd only met Othello a couple months back. "Why would she do that?" I asked.

Hansel shrugged. "That, you'd have to ask her. But around here, her word carries weight. She could assume the role and responsibilities of an Adjudicator, if she so chose. I've tried to get her to accept the position, if only to solve disputes between Morgause and Sir Bred...but she refused."

So, Hawteye was actually a Faeling named the Huntress—and a badass to boot. A badass who'd vouched for me, for some reason...I'd have to follow up on that, at some point.

"So, when did ye suspect Jack was the one murderin' Regulars? Or did he tell ye outright?" I asked, switching gears so quickly I caught Hansel by surprise; his face told me everything I needed to know. I wasn't sure when it had hit me—probably the moment my mental fog had lifted, once I'd realized the stone had been purposefully programmed to bring me here, to Hansel's office, and not to my own apartment—but it hadn't taken me long after that to see Hansel's hand in everything that had happened, lately. The stone. Him tipping off the Huntress. Sending Robin to Christoff's house to intercept me.

Which meant there was someone else I needed to talk to.

"Dobby!" I yelled. "Come out, ye wee mongrel."

"I'm right here, my lady," Dobby said, slipping off his ring. He stood behind Hansel, resting against a bookshelf. "I hope you'll forgive me," he said.

"No, the blame is mine," Hansel interjected. "When I discovered you were acquainted with this unregistered Brownie, I took the liberty of asking for his help in exchange for clemency."

I frowned at Dobby. A Brownie? The spriggan held a finger to his lips and winked, which was probably the most off-putting thing I'd seen today— and I'd seen some messed up shit in the last twenty-four hours. But at least I knew now why Dobby had sought me out and sent me after Christoff. I considered outing him to Hansel, out of spite, but the older German man spoke before I could decide one way or the other.

"Robin works for me, as I'm sure you've already surmised," Hansel explained. "I'll admit, the Huntress was quite...upset with me, for involving you. But it seemed the best option at the time. I needed answers and hoped the bar owner would be more forthright with you than he had been with us."

"Why didn't ye simply tell me where he was, then?" I asked.

"I had intended to, once you'd gotten a taste of how things work here. But when you confessed you were looking for a killer, things...changed. I realized you might be able to solve two of our problems."

"That's why ye gave me the stone," I said, hazarding another guess. "Ye knew I'd get meself in trouble."

Hansel smirked. "I suspected. Although, to be fair, I never imagined you'd have to use it to skip out on an audience with the Winter Queen. She isn't one to be trifled with."

"She isn't the only one," I growled, glaring at the man. He'd used me. Granted, he'd tried to help me, too, by sending the Huntress to save me and giving me the stone...but that didn't change the fact that he'd been manipulating me from behind the scenes for days now. "So," I said, glancing up at the books above Hansel's head, "what now? D'ye put me on trial? Or is it lawyer's choice?"

"Jack's death, you mean?" Hansel asked.

I nodded. "I knew when I pulled the trigger I'd be comin' to see ye, one way or the other."

"Yes, well, this is typically more my sister's area of expertise. But, seeing as how you were working as an agent of the Chancery at the time, I don't see why you'd be liable for his death." Hansel eyed me, meaningfully.

I cocked an eyebrow. "Ye sure ye want to do that?" I asked.

Hansel spread his hands out as if laying his cards on the table. "You were an unwitting participant, but you managed to chase away outsiders who were a threat to this city, *and* you put an end to one of our number who would have exposed us to the outside world. The Chancery owes you a favor. And if there's one thing the Fae do—"

"It's return the favor, aye," I finished, for him.

"Which leaves me with this," Hansel said, opening a drawer. He rummaged for a moment and pulled out a squat metal disc, the size of a hockey puck. "Robin recovered it from the wreckage of the car, which we subsequently made disappear. He said it would be important to you."

I took the Gateway grenade—which is all I could think to call it—and cradled it in my hands. "D'ye know what it is?" I asked.

Hansel shook his head. "No, although I'm sorry for your loss. I heard the bar owner and one of the FBI were caught in the crossfire."

"They aren't dead," I said.

Hansel looked dubious but said nothing.

"Will ye do me another favor?" I asked, not considering his definition of the word *favor* until I'd already spoken.

"That depends," Hansel replied, sliding the drawer shut.

"If ye hear anythin' about Christoff or the FBI Agent, call me. Hell, send me one of your letters, I don't care. Just make sure ye get word to me as soon as possible. I intend to find 'em."

"Christoff is still a citizen of this city, and under our protection. If he's still alive," Hansel held up a hand before I could insist he was, "we'll be sure to notify you. No favor necessary."

"T'anks. One other t'ing, then," I said. I leaned forward and planted both my hands on the lip of his desk. "And keep in mind this isn't me askin', it's me tellin'. From now on, ye and yours stay the fuck away from me. I don't want to so much as smell a Chancery member. Until ye find Christoff, I want nothin' to do with ye manipulative bastards."

Hansel's eyes had widened momentarily, but by the time I was finished, he seemed to understand exactly what I was saying. We were square. Even. But that didn't make us friends. It didn't make us anything. I didn't trust him or his organization; Robin, who I'd come to rely on, had lied to me from the very start. Even Dobby had betrayed me to save his own skin.

I'd been right all along.

None of the Fae could be trusted—especially not their lawyers.

"Understood," Hansel replied, tersely.

"Good," I said, before getting up to leave.

"My lady?" Dobby said, propping himself up off the bookcase.

"Be careful out there, Dobby," I said, refusing to meet the spriggan's eyes. "The world can be a tough place, when ye are on your own."

And, with that, I strode out the door.

It was time to go home, for real this time.

CHAPTER 39

I found the spare key to my place in its usual hiding spot and opened the door, still clutching the Gateway grenade and my spare clothes. On the way home, I'd come up with a tenuous plan for the next few hours—and maybe the next morning if I could get hold of Othello.

I had an idea that might save someone's life.

First, I needed a shower. I knew I needed to check on Jeffries and Lakota as soon as possible, but—since I didn't have a phone—that could wait until I was decent enough to go buy a replacement. I considered reaching out to Robin, who would be able to fill me in on what had happened with Throm and the two Agents after I'd been pulled away by the Winter Queen, but the idea of talking to him—to any Faeling—filled me with outrage.

As far as I was concerned, the Fae could go rot in a deep, dark hole.

"Fuckin' Faelin' bastards," I muttered as I flipped on the lights and kicked my door closed.

"I know how you feel," a man said from my living room.

"Jesus fuckin' Christ!" I yelled, ducking into the bathroom, my heart hammering in my chest so hard I felt like I was going to pass out. Or stroke out. At this point, neither would surprise me.

"Sorry," the man called. "I couldn't find the light switch."

I poked my head out once I realized I recognized the voice. The man sat casually in my recliner, ankles crossed, hands clasped in his lap. He had unkempt, ashy-brown hair, and moody green eyes, with a five o'clock shadow that had slept in way past its alarm. I thought I caught a glimpse of gold in those green eyes, like a flicker of lightning on the horizon, but it was gone just as fast.

Nate Temple. The Fae-killer.

Well, I suppose I couldn't hold *that* against him.

Glass houses and all that.

"And just how long have ye been sittin' in me apartment in the dark, ye fuckin' loon?" I asked, dispensing with the niceties entirely; burglars didn't deserve them, after all.

"Not long. Maybe a couple of hours. It's a nice place," Nate said, taking in the decor. "A good place to collect my thoughts. The last few days have been murder." He swung his eyes to me, and I felt the weight of them settle on me, threatening to pull me to the floor with their intensity.

And there it was. Now I had Nate Temple complaining to me about his problems...was he about to try to recruit me, too?

I so didn't have time for this.

"Get out," I said.

Nate arched an eyebrow. "Listen, I just wanted to offer you a job, that's—"

"I don't t'ink ye heard me, so I'll say it again. Get. Out." I stepped out of the bathroom and tossed my spare clothes on the kitchen counter, then set the Gateway grenade on top of them. Nate eyed the grenade for a moment, but then his focus fell entirely on me.

"What the hell happened to you?" he asked, eyes widening.

I grunted, reached under the sink, and pulled out the sawed-off I kept stored there, for emergencies. I swung it around, leveling it at the wizard. "Get the fuck out."

Nate's eyes narrowed. "You don't want to—"

"Now!" I barked.

Suddenly, my door busted open. I swung around, but, before I could react, Jimmy Collins came charging in, headed directly for Nate as if planning to tackle him to the ground. To his credit, Jimmy almost made it; he was a foot away when he slammed into an invisible wall of air. Nate flicked his wrist and the detective slid across the floor, dazed, but unhurt. "He one of yours?" Nate asked, coolly. "If not, I can take him off your hands..."

"You heard what she said, you prick," Jimmy said, rising to one knee. "Get out."

"Jimmy!" I chastised. "I've got this under control. I don't need your help."

"It didn't sound like it from out there," Jimmy said, jerking his head towards my gaping doorway.

"And so ye decided to kick down the damn door? It was unlocked, ye big idgit!"

Jimmy began to hang his head, realizing he'd overreacted, when Nate spoke up again, "Not very bright, this one. I recommend sending the defective ones back." Jimmy's head popped back up. He sneered and lunged at the wizard, only to be knocked back a second time.

Nate sighed and picked a piece of lint off his shirt. "Batteries definitely not included."

"I swear, if ye don't get the fuck out of me place right now," I said, "I'll—"

But I never got to finish. Because this time, when Jimmy lunged at Nate, he wasn't knocked back. In fact, he connected, tearing jagged holes in Nate's shirt from where his claws—yes, Jimmy's fucking *claws*—caught the wizard. Nate danced back in time to avoid a second swipe, ducked, and struck a blow of his own, sending Jimmy flying backwards riding a small fireball. The detective collided against my wall and fell to one knee.

Except he didn't look anything like the Jimmy I knew.

The creature that clambered back to its feet was covered in silver and black fur, with chestnut brown eyes, a full head taller than Jimmy, clearing seven feet; his pointed ears threatened to brush the ceiling. And yet he was thinner than Jimmy, too, his limbs longer. I'd only seen something like this thing once before, months ago, in a different dimension—but she'd been all white, with nine tails.

Nate stared up at the creature Jimmy had become with undisguised glee. "Oh, good," he said, his grin predatory. "I was starting to feel bad for beating up on a Regular. Let's see if that bite can keep up with that annoying bark." Nate threw his arms wide, and, in an instant, whips—one of crackling ice and the other of liquid flame—appeared in either hand, their loose curls popping as the two diametrically opposite elements rubbed against each other.

Oh, and tore holes in my Goddamned furniture.

"Oy! Take it outside!" I yelled.

Jimmy yipped, hunkered down to all fours, and prepared to leap at the wizard. Nate flicked his wrists, his whips snaking incrementally to crack against my floors as he waited for his opponent to attack. I braced myself, wondering how I was going to explain the damage to the Homeowner's Association, cursing.

But then, before either could strike, a golden light burst through the room, blinding us all.

And a voice rang out.

"Did you know that someone is home in three out of every ten burglary cases?" Eve asked.

I groaned, massaging my eyes.

"What the fuck was that?" Nate snarled.

"Nate Temple. Master Temple. Would-be King of St. Louis." Eve's voice was matter-of-fact, as if reading from a database. Nate whirled towards the voice, spotting the potted plant, blinking rapidly, but she simply went on. "The Rider of Hope. The Fifth Horseman."

"Allegedly," Nate growled.

"Catalyst. Murderer. Friend. Son. Father...no..." Eve drifted off, her usual robotic tone gave way to something soft and uncertain that sent the hairs on the back of my neck standing straight up. "No. Not father. Tell me, Master Temple...when did you last see the boy?"

Nate blanched, and his whips winked out as if he had been tased in the groin, the anger in his face replaced by sudden fear. Before I could so much as call after him, he flung out a hand and bolted through the Gateway that abruptly flared into existence with a roar of white flame, screaming someone's name.

The Gateway snapped shut.

Jimmy, meanwhile, had fallen onto all fours. He'd shifted back to his usual self, and sweat poured from him, soaking through his clothes—most of which hadn't suffered from his transformation, though his shirt was singed from Nate's pyrotechnics. I swung to face him, keeping the shotgun out just in case.

But it seemed Eve wasn't done.

"James Collins. Detective James Collins. Jimmy. Former marine. Navy Cross recipient," her voice got quiet again. "Infected."

"Infected with *what*?" I asked, though I suspected I already knew the answer.

"I'm becoming like her," Jimmy said, through clenched teeth. "Like that bitch who tore out my throat. I can feel it. I can feel her…trying to get out, to go through me."

"Detective James Collins," Eve said, sorrowfully. "The Silver Fox."

Everything fell into place all at once. This was what Jimmy had been hiding from me. Why he blamed me.

Jimmy rose, shakily, and met my eyes, his own dancing with rage. "Do you understand now?" he asked. "This is what you've done to me. This is why I hate you. Not only did you not let me die. You made me a monster."

I took a hesitant step back, raising the shotgun barrel a few inches, in case he decided to strike; his body language said it was definitely a possibility. Jimmy glanced down at the gun, snarled, and walked out—leaving me in an empty, trashed apartment.

Well, fuck.

He could have at least helped pick up.

CHAPTER 40

*T*he hospital room was bright, but not particularly cheery. I slid in and gently shut the door behind me. Jeffries sat beside Warren, asleep, one arm in a sling, his head supported by a neck brace. He had bags under his eyes to go with the bruises on his face. Lakota looked better, at least. She'd gone back to wearing her androgynous suit and tie, hair pulled back into a braid. She didn't notice me until I was practically on top of them.

"Quinn!" Lakota rushed over to me, startling Jeffries. "You're alright!"

"Aye, of course," I replied.

"I didn't know what to think," Lakota admitted. "One second you were there, then gone the next."

"She has a knack for walking away from the fights without letting us know," Jeffries interjected. "That makes two, now."

I rubbed the back of my neck. "Aye, and I wanted to say I'm sorry. I came as soon as I found out ye were here." That wasn't strictly true; first I'd called our maintenance guy to come see about fixing my poor door, then showered, called Othello, and slept.

But my lie sounded better.

"Didn't have anywhere else to be," Jeffries said, sounding as bad off as he looked. "The Agency has us on review. One Agent down, and another missing. Doesn't exactly look great."

"So, Robin filled ye in on what happened to Hilde, then?" I asked. I had wondered whether the redcap would be brave enough to break the news about their partner. I certainly wouldn't have wanted to be the bearer of that bad news.

"He did," Lakota said. "He also said you found something we might be able to use to track her down?"

"Aye, I've got me people workin' on that," I said. "Well, me person, anyway."

I didn't really have *people*.

I had *a* people.

But Othello was ten times the investigator I was, so I figured I could rely on her to find answers I couldn't. She hadn't been happy to hear about Nate popping up in my apartment, or to find out she'd missed out on my showdown with Jack Frost and a small contingent of armed werebears. But, once I explained what I needed, she'd been more than happy to help. She'd even managed to pull off a freaking miracle.

"Your person?" Jeffries asked.

"She's especially good at findin' t'ings. People included. Speakin' of which," I said, checking the time on the burner phone I'd purchased until Othello could send me a new one—now *that* had been a dicey conversation, "ye lot should keep an eye out."

"For—" Lakota began, but was cut off by the sound of a Gateway appearing. A tall, blonde woman in a white lab coat strode through the opening, studying a clipboard through trendy spectacles. She pursed her lips and snapped her fingers; the Gateway disappeared. Jeffries and Lakota stared at the woman, eyes comically wide, mouths hanging slack.

"Special Agent in Charge Jeffries and Agent Lakota," I said, "this is Lizzie. She works for the Academy. The Wizard Academy," I added, for clarification.

"Lisandra, please. No one calls me Lizzie," she said, still eyeing the contents on her clipboard.

"I do," I said, winking at the two agents.

Jeffries scowled, and Lakota looked uncertain. "And what is she doing here?" Jeffries asked, finally.

"I'm here to wake up this young man," Lisandra replied. "Sorry, give me a moment. I'm trying to examine his charts, in case I missed anything." She flipped a few pages and tossed the clipboard on the room's only other bed, which was mercifully empty; I had no idea how he'd explain this to a Regular without blaming their medication. She marched to Warren's bedside, opposite Jeffries, and held out her hand. Tendrils of green smoke billowed out from her palm, and then, with a crackle of electricity, a slender scalpel rested in her hand.

"What are you going to do with that?" Jeffries asked, alarmed.

Lisandra grunted. "I'm going to stimulate his brain using magic while I cut away any damage I find. Ms. MacKenna tells me he's psychic, which means the coma is probably more metaphysical than physical. His way of coping with his own pain."

"Oh," Jeffries said, settling back into his chair with an anxious sigh.

Lisandra arched an eyebrow. "No arguments?"

"No, I can sense you're telling the truth," Jeffries replied.

"Is that right?" Lisandra glanced over at me pensively. "Ms. MacKenna, you really do keep the most interesting company."

I frowned. "No pokin' around inside his or any of the other Agents' heads, Lizzie. We had a deal."

Lisandra sighed. "Oh, very well."

"A deal?" Lakota whispered, sidling up beside me as we watched Lisandra work.

"Aye," I replied. "I had to offer her somethin' in return for her help, after all."

"What did you offer?"

"My corpse."

"Your what?" Lakota asked, staring up at me in shock.

"I figure it's like donatin' me body to science...sort of. Besides, this way at least I know somebody's goin' to care when I die," I quipped, winking.

Lakota frowned, studying me. "You actually half-believe that."

Damn. Well, then, no more confessions in front of the Seer.

"And how about you?" I asked, changing the subject entirely. "When were ye goin' to tell me ye weren't a boy, after all?"

Lakota blushed, then shrugged. "It's not like I have an identity crisis going on or anything. It's just, when you work with as many men as I do, and you can see into their souls...let's just say it's for my peace of mind."

I scowled. "Surely, they don't all t'ink like that, do they? What about when they look at Hilde? What d'ye see, then?"

"Hilde's different. She could take any of them, and deep down, most of them know it. The only men who are attracted to her are either true alpha males, or guys looking for someone who'll kick the shit out of them. The ones who are attracted to me, though…different story."

I rested my hand on Lakota's shoulder. "Well, don't worry, your secret's safe with me." Lakota nodded, but I could tell something was still bothering her. It didn't take a genius to figure out what it was, however. I squeezed. "I promise you, I'll find Hilde and bring her home. I don't care how, I'll do it."

Lakota glanced at me in surprise. "You really mean that."

I nodded. I really, really did. There was no way I was going to abandon Christoff or Hilde. The instant Othello tracked down a lead, I would be there. I wasn't about to let Christoff's kids be raised without their parents, and I sure as hell wasn't going to let Lakota down; Hilde meant a lot to her, I could tell.

"There," Lisandra said, "it's done."

Warren's eyes fluttered open.

Jeffries tore his own gaze from the bedridden psychic and met mine but said nothing. A single tear fell down his battered cheek.

Because sometimes you don't even need to say it out loud.

"You're welcome," I said, nodding.

CHAPTER 41

Summer had hit Boston early, the temperatures spiking in late May. Weathermen had predicted record highs, and the possibility of an overly active hurricane season had been the main topic of conversation among my aunt's horde of gossiping churchgoers; I'd been staying over at Dez's for the last several days while they fixed my door, and—if I heard another word about climate change—I swore I was going to wade out into the ocean with cement blocks attached to my feet.

Dez hadn't been happy to hear I'd had a break-in, but even less happy to find out Jimmy and I were on the outs. She'd always liked him, ever since he and I were kids, and hoped I'd find someone nice and stable to settle down with. If only she'd known how truly unstable Jimmy was, now. That didn't mean I didn't feel for the detective, of course. He had been right to blame me for what had happened to him. But, seeing as how I wasn't prepared to apologize for bringing him back to life, there wasn't much else for us to discuss.

Looking at it objectively, I'd have to say radio silence was most definitely in effect across the board. So far Hansel had kept his promise and largely kept the Chancery away from me. Robin had tried to stop by, once, but I'd been out. He left a note, apologizing, claiming he'd ignored Hansel's wishes in order to come see me. Sadly, while I wanted it to be true, I couldn't take his word for it; for all I knew Hansel had sent him to gauge how serious I was about my privacy. Under the circumstances, he'd been pretty lucky I was out; I had *two* shotguns under my sink, now.

One loaded with iron buckshot.

The other with silver.

Because it never hurts to be prepared.

Speaking of which, I had a bag ready to go at a moment's notice, provided Othello figured out where Hilde and Christoff had gone. So far, she hadn't turned up much. We were both leaning towards Russia, since that would be the most obvious place, but—in case you didn't know—that country is fucking massive; searching for a Valkyrie and a werebear within Russia's borders was like trying to find a needle in a needlestack.

Painful, I mean.

It had been Othello's suggestion that I reach out to the headmistress of a school in St. Louis on behalf of Christoff's kids. She'd been extra pissed at me for stealing the "galvanizer," which she'd been busy looking for all week. But, when I filled her in on how it worked, she'd immediately switched gears—grilling me on how it had functioned and how much damage it had done. Apparently, it wasn't a weapon, but a battery; I simply hadn't plugged it in correctly.

Funny, because I thought it'd worked just fine.

The school she'd recommended, a haven for wereanimals, was named Shift. Callie, after speaking with Armor and Starlight, had agreed to oversee the handoff; she knew the headmistress and had nothing but praise. At this point, I wasn't sure what else I could do for them, at least until I had more news about their mom and dad.

Othello did, fortunately, have some news regarding Nate Temple's break-in, but said she couldn't share the details with me until she'd learned everything; she promised to tell me more about how he'd executed his former fiancée, but swore it wasn't as bad as it sounded. As if. On the subject of the Huntress, she'd been a little more forthright, although not particularly helpful. Apparently, the Huntress—or Hawteye, as I preferred to call her—had reached out to Othello after I'd been taken by the Academy Justices. Which meant she'd been watching me a lot longer than I'd thought.

Of course, that was all Othello could tell me. The Huntress was a mystery, supposedly, to even her closest friends. Powerful, but enigmatic, she showed up when she chose and cared only for two people that Othello was aware of: Tory, the very same headmistress of Shift, and a boy named Alex. Which left me with a whole lot of questions.

Of course, nothing new there.

But at least I wasn't dreaming; lately, I'd slept like a baby. In fact, even my waking hours had become relatively uneventful. Eve—after her brief hiatus saying interesting, albeit creepy, things—had gone back to spouting out random trivia as the mood arose. I'd even had time to hire someone to come by and put up a few nifty wards to go along with the state of the art security system I planned to have installed.

Turns out Dobby was right, after all.

If I wanted to be safe, it was time I started shutting others out.

Turn the page to read a brief excerpt from **DARK AND STORMY**, the fourth installment of the Phantom Queen Diaries.

Or get the full book online HERE! http://www.shaynesilvers.com/l/207071

SAMPLE: DARK AND STORMY
(PHANTOM QUEEN #4)

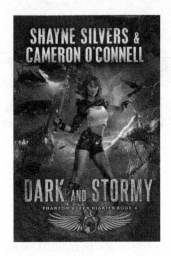

I'd always wanted an office.

You know, a nice, quiet place with my name and profession splashed across the door—Quinn MacKenna: Black Magic Arms Dealer. Maybe a sweet logo, to boot. On the walls, I'd hang pictures of me shaking hands with sheiks and shamans and tribal chieftains. My desk would be sturdy enough to survive a shipwreck, my carpet thick enough to crash on. Naturally, I'd keep a decanter of whiskey within reach at all times—for emergencies.

Of course, all that was little more than a dream, a fantasy. My life wasn't some glamorous, noir thriller; I wasn't some hard-boiled Private Investigator who could be found in the yellow pages, and Boston sure as hell wasn't Chinatown.

Here, doing business in an office meant your enemies wouldn't even have to *inconvenience* themselves to kill you. Hell, you might as well put a sign around your neck that said, "I'll be free to die between the hours of nine to noon, Monday through Thursday, at the corner of Kill and Me Street, apartment 2B."

Or not 2B...

Fortunately, I'd given up on my office pipe dream years ago. Unfortunately, that meant I usually had to make shady deals in shady places—places other people avoided on principle. Like an abandoned warehouse along Boston's Harbor, for example. Or a seedy motel room in Dorchester. Or a cozy little strip club like the *Seven Deadly Inn*, a swanky nudie bar located on the outskirts of Bay Village.

"Can I get you a drink, Miss MacKenna?" the waitress asked, sliding onto the arm of my chair, the bedazzled dragon on her ribcage—a combination of tattoos and dermal piercings that frankly hurt to look at—flashing beneath the strobe of the club's neon lights. I remember she'd given the dragon a name once, but I couldn't recall what it was. Yohan? Sven? Brad? I shook the thought away and slid an inch to my left, worried I might accidentally inhale one of those faux gemstones.

"No, that's alright, Cadence," I replied, my Irish brogue giving the girl's name—Cadence, short for Decadence—a whole new layer of irony. She, like the rest of the girls here at the *Seven Deadly Inn*, had been given a stage name based on humanity's vices. Ava, Jelly, and Luna—or Avarice, Jealousy, and Lunacy if you preferred—were on separate stages, grinding the day away. I knew most of the girls, by now; I'd become a frequent flyer ever since my local watering hole, a pop-up bar run by my friend Christoff, had shut down following his mysterious disappearance several weeks back. Naturally, no strip club—no matter how exceptionally enthusiastic their staff, how excellent their song selection, or how inventive their cocktails—could fill the void my friend's absence had created.

But boy had they tried.

Sadly, I knew I wouldn't be able to enjoy much of the establishment's hospitality on this particular Tuesday afternoon—despite how delicious it sounded. I couldn't afford to get sloppy on their Sinfully Yours chocolate vodka martini. Today's visit was about business, not pleasure.

It wasn't every day I exchanged goods with royalty, after all.

"My prince, I believe we have made a mistake in coming here," Arjun— the non-royal sitting across from me—said, his Indian accent nearly as sibilant as mine. The ultra-conservative Indian man wrung his hands, refusing to look up, which is undoubtedly why he failed to notice my shit-eating grin.

Obviously, I didn't routinely go out of my way to make my clients uncomfortable. No professional in her right mind would. But then no professional in her right mind would have been able to put up with Arjun for a week, either. As payback for his steady stream of passive-aggressive critiques of all things feminine, I'd decided to shove his chauvinistic, thou-shalt-not rhetoric up his ass by insisting we do business in a titty bar.

Because, one, I didn't tolerate that shit.

And because, two, I liked to support local businesses, not to mention working moms; Cadence, like most of the girls, had at least one rugrat at home, tearing up shoes and pissing on the furniture...or whatever it was children did when unsupervised.

"Perhaps you are right, Arjun," the prince replied, his attention drawn to Luna, who had contorted herself into a position that Picasso would have been proud to paint. "But then, such things must be done for the greater good." Luna caught the prince staring from across the room and waved with her toes, curling them invitingly.

The prince waved back with one slender, effeminate hand.

"I'd watch out for that one, if I were ye," I said, studying the prince's soft, delicate features. He was a very pretty young man, with smooth, dark skin. He was also short and slight—a man trapped in a boy's body.

"You will address the prince by his title," Arjun warned.

"Now, now, Arjun. That is not necessary. I am not *her* prince, after all," the young royal replied, good-naturedly. He shook himself, refocusing on the task at hand, though I could see Luna giving the dainty Indian man a solid once-over—which was impressive, considering she was hanging upside down. "So," the prince continued, "Arjun tells me you have found the herb we sought. I will admit, I did not think it possible that such a plant existed. Otherwise we would have cultivated it, long ago."

I shrugged, deciding it best not to get into how I'd managed to find the *sanjeevani*, a magical herb engineered to heal practically any disease or ailment—including death. Firstly, I preferred my hard-earned reputation as the woman who could find any magical artifact, no matter how rare or well-guarded, no questions asked, to remain intact. Explaining *how* I'd done so always felt like I was a magician describing the trick; it ruined the mystery, the magic, and made what I'd accomplished seem prosaic by comparison. And secondly, there was no way they'd ever believe me, anyway.

"It wasn't exactly easy to find," I replied, recalling how the Monkey God I'd contacted had lifted an entire mountain to pluck the *sanjeevani* from the earth like a man lifting one corner of the couch up to snatch a quarter off the ground. "Or get to," I added.

I set the small box I'd brought with me on top of the table between us. Arjun stared at the gift-wrapped box in undisguised horror; the Christmas wrapping paper I'd used featured reindeer performing acts from the *Kama Sutra*. I'd had to express ship it from the online retailer. Totally worth it. "All I could find," I said, ducking my head to hide my smirk.

Which was technically true.

The prince snorted. "I am sure," he replied, snickering. He snapped his fingers. Arjun flashed me a hateful look, but hurriedly produced a thick scroll, tied with a silk ribbon. "As promised," the prince said, urging Arjun to place the scroll on the table. "Though I cannot see what you hope to do with it. It is undoubtedly a hoax, despite its age."

I nodded, fighting the urge to snatch the scroll up and make a break for it right then and there. "That's alright," I replied. "I'm just lookin' to decorate me apartment." I fetched the scroll off the table and untied the ribbon. The parchment was old and cracked, made from the skin of a gazelle—if it was authentic. I handled it carefully, scanned it, then folded it back up, masking my emotions.

I'd gotten my hands on it, finally.

The lost map of Piri Reis—the given name of a famed Ottoman admiral and cartographer who died in the middle of the 16th century for refusing to sanction a war against the Portuguese, leaving behind quite the reputation as both sailor and mapmaker.

"Well hey there, Miss MacKenna," Luna said, sauntering up to us in nothing but a lacey thong. I frowned, sensing trouble. Unlike most of the girls—many of whom were lovely, albeit jaded, women—Luna exemplified her vice. She was blonde, beautiful, and batshit crazy; I saw her stab a guy once for touching her without permission, only to find her making out with him in the parking lot several hours later, prodding his wound every so often to make him moan harder.

"Is that for me?" Luna asked brightly, snatching up the prince's box.

"Put that down!" Arjun commanded.

Luna pouted, slid one leg between the blustering Indian man's thighs, and wiggled her hips. Then, with a flourish, she spun away and settled down onto the prince's lap, one arm draped over his shoulders; he could see right down the line of her body. She held the box up to the light. "So, you didn't get this for me?" Luna asked.

The prince, eyes unfocused, didn't so much as flick his gaze away from the stripper's exposed breasts and taut tummy. "No, no. It is for my father. He is not well. I want to see him healthy again. I am not ready to take on his duties as Maharaja."

"My prince!" Arjun hissed, then covered his own mouth.

"Oh, a prince, huh?" Luna said. She grinned at me. "You always bring me the nicest things, Miss MacKenna."

"Don't say I never did anythin' for ye," I replied, with a sigh.

Luna giggled and began playing with the prince's hair. "So, you want to use this to save your daddy? Wait...if you're a prince, does that make him a king?"

"My father is a maharaja," the prince said. "It is different."

"But," Luna said, grinding against the prince to the tune of "Sex and Candy" by Marcy Playground, "if he dies, then you become the Machu Pichu thing, right?"

Arjun's face purpled with outrage.

"The Maharaja," the prince corrected, saying it painfully slowly, his eyes practically rolling back in his head. "But yes," the prince said, eyelids fluttering, clearly too distracted to follow her Machiavellian train of thought.

Arjun, on the other hand, seemed to catch on remarkably quickly—apparently being a misogynist didn't make him an idiot. He snatched the box from the industrious stripper and held it in front of the prince's face. "My prince," he said, "we should leave. Now. We must return with this and aid your father."

"Oh, do you have to go so soon?" Luna asked, tilting the prince's chin to get him to look up at her. "I get off in twenty minutes," she purred, locking her smoldering gaze on him. "Perhaps you could, too," she murmured suggestively.

I rolled my eyes.

"Twenty minutes," the prince said, breathily. "I can wait twenty minutes, I think."

"My prince!"

But the prince wasn't listening.

"I did warn ye," I said, rising, clutching the scroll.

Arjun's eyes widened. "You did this! You brought him here to tempt him! I bet the herb will not even work, and this was your plan all along."

I laughed. I couldn't help it. "Believe what ye want to believe," I said, finally. "But your prince is a big boy, I'm sure he'll do the right t'ing." I sidled around the table, waved goodbye to Cadence, and headed home with my prize—happy as a saint on a cross on Judgment Day.

That's the thing about being an arms dealer: having a conscience is a liability. Granted, a small part of me felt bad for inadvertently exposing the prince to Luna's attentions, but I wasn't the hand-holding, hand-wringing type; if the prince let his father die to please his new stripper girlfriend, I sure as hell wasn't going to stop him.

Not my throne, not my problem, that's what I say.

Get the full book online! http://www.shaynesilvers.com/l/207071

*Turn the page to read a sample of **OBSIDIAN SON** - Nate Temple Book 1 - or **BUY ONLINE (FREE with Kindle Unlimited subscription)**. Nate Temple is a billionaire wizard from St. Louis. He rides a bloodthirsty unicorn and drinks with the Four Horsemen. He even cow-tipped the Minotaur. Once...*

TRY: OBSIDIAN SON (NATE TEMPLE #1)

*T*here was no room for emotion in a hate crime. I had to be cold. Heartless. This was just another victim. Nothing more. No face, no name.

Frosted blades of grass crunched under my feet, sounding to my ears like the symbolic glass that one would shatter under a napkin at a Jewish wedding. The noise would have threatened to give away my stealthy advance as I stalked through the moonlit field, but I was no novice and had planned accordingly. Being a wizard, I was able to muffle all sensory evidence with a fine cloud of magic—no sounds, and no smells. Nifty. But if I made the spell much stronger, the anomaly would be too obvious to my prey.

I knew the consequences for my dark deed tonight. If caught, jail time or possibly even a gruesome, painful death. But if I succeeded, the look of fear and surprise in my victim's eyes before his world collapsed around him, it was well worth the risk. I simply couldn't help myself; I had to take him down.

I knew the cops had been keeping tabs on my car, but I was confident that they hadn't followed me. I hadn't seen a tail on my way here but seeing as how they frowned on this kind of thing, I had taken a circuitous route just in case. I was safe. I hoped.

Then my phone chirped at me as I received a text.

I practically jumped out of my skin, hissing instinctively. "Motherf—" I cut off abruptly, remembering the whole stealth aspect of my mission. I was off to a stellar start. I had forgotten to silence the damned phone. *Stupid, stupid, stupid!*

My heart felt like it was on the verge of exploding inside my chest with such thunderous violence that I briefly envisioned a mystifying Rorschach blood-blot that would have made coroners and psychologists drool.

My body remained tense as I swept my gaze over the field, fearing that I had been made. Precious seconds ticked by without any change in my surroundings, and my breathing finally began to slow as my pulse returned to normal. Hopefully, my magic had muted the phone and my resulting outburst. I glanced down at the phone to scan the text and then typed back a quick and angry response before I switched the cursed device to vibrate.

Now, where were we?

I continued on, the lining of my coat constricting my breathing. Or maybe it was because I was leaning forward in anticipation. *Breathe,* I chided myself. *He doesn't know you're here.* All this risk for a book. It had better be worth it.

I'm taller than most, and not abnormally handsome, but I knew how to play the genetic cards I had been dealt. I had shaggy, dirty blonde hair—leaning more towards brown with each passing year—and my frame was thick with well-earned muscle, yet I was still lean. I had once been told that my eyes were like twin emeralds pitted against the golden-brown tufts of my hair—a face like a jewelry box. Of course, that was two bottles of wine into a date, so I could have been a little foggy on her quote. Still, I liked to imagine that was how everyone saw me.

But tonight, all that was masked by magic.

I grinned broadly as the outline of the hairy hulk finally came into view. He was blessedly alone—no nearby sentries to give me away. That was always a risk when performing this ancient rite-of-passage. I tried to keep the grin on my face from dissolving into a maniacal cackle.

My skin danced with energy, both natural and unnatural, as I manipulated the threads of magic floating all around me. My victim stood just ahead, oblivious to the world of hurt that I was about to unleash. Even with his millennia of experience, he didn't stand a chance. I had done this so many times that the routine of it was my only enemy. I lost count of how many times I had been told not to do it again; those who knew declared it *cruel, evil, and sadistic.* But what fun wasn't? Regardless, that wasn't enough to stop me from doing it again. And again. And again.

It was an addiction.

The pungent smell of manure filled the air, latching onto my nostril hairs. I took another step, trying to calm my racing pulse. A glint of gold reflected in the silver moonlight, but my victim remained motionless, hopefully unaware or all was lost. I wouldn't make it out alive if he knew I was here. Timing was everything.

I carefully took the last two steps, a lifetime between each, watching the legendary monster's ears, anxious and terrified that I would catch even so much as a twitch in my direction. Seeing nothing, a fierce grin split my unshaven cheeks. My spell had worked! I raised my palms an inch away from their target, firmly planted my feet, and squared my shoulders. I took one silent, calming breath, and then heaved forward with every ounce of physical strength I could muster. As well as a teensy-weensy boost of magic. Enough to goose him good.

"*MOOO!!!*" The sound tore through the cool October night like an unstoppable freight train. *Thud-splat!* The beast collapsed sideways onto the frosted grass; straight into a steaming patty of cow shit, cow dung, or, if you really wanted to church it up, a Meadow Muffin. But to me, shit is, and always will be, shit.

Cow tipping. It doesn't get any better than that in Missouri.

Especially when you're tipping the *Minotaur.* Capital M. I'd tipped plenty of ordinary cows before, but never the legendary variety.

Razor-blade hooves tore at the frozen earth as the beast struggled to stand, his grunts of rage vibrating the air. I raised my arms triumphantly. "Boo-yah! Temple 1, Minotaur 0!" I crowed. Then I very bravely prepared to protect myself. Some people just couldn't take a joke. *Cruel, evil,* and *sadistic* cow tipping may be, but by hell, it was a *rush.* The legendary beast turned his gaze on me after gaining his feet, eyes ablaze as his body...*shifted* from his bull disguise into his notorious, well-known bipedal form. He unfolded to his full height on two tree trunk-thick legs, his hooves having magically transformed into heavily booted feet. The thick, gold ring dangling from his snotty snout quivered as the Minotaur panted, and his dense, corded muscles contracted over his now human-like chest. As I stared up into those brown eyes, I actually felt sorry...for, well, myself.

"I have killed greater men than you for lesser offense," he growled.

His voice sounded like an angry James Earl Jones—like Mufasa talking to Scar.

"You have shit on your shoulder, Asterion." I ignited a roiling ball of fire in my palm in order to see his eyes more clearly. By no means was it a defensive gesture on my part. It was just dark. Under the weight of his glare, I somehow managed to keep my face composed, even though my fraudulent, self-denial had curled up into the fetal position and started whimpering. I hoped using a form of his ancient name would give me brownie points. Or maybe just not-worthy-of-killing points.

The beast grunted, eyes tightening, and I sensed the barest hesitation. "Nate Temple...your name would look splendid on my already long list of slain idiots." Asterion took a threatening step forward, and I thrust out my palm in warning, my roiling flame blue now.

"You lost fair and square, Asterion. Yield or perish." The beast's shoulders sagged slightly. Then he finally nodded to himself in resignation, appraising me with the scrutiny of a worthy adversary. "Your time comes, Temple, but I will grant you this. You've got a pair of stones on you to rival Hercules."

I reflexively glanced in the direction of the myth's own crown jewels before jerking my gaze away. Some things you simply couldn't un-see. "Well, I won't be needing a wheelbarrow any time soon, but overcompensating today keeps future lower-back pain away."

The Minotaur blinked once, and then he bellowed out a deep, contagious, snorting laughter. Realizing I wasn't about to become a murder statistic, I couldn't help but join in. It felt good. It had been a while since I had allowed myself to experience genuine laughter.

In the harsh moonlight, his bulk was even more intimidating as he towered head and shoulders above me. This was the beast that had fed upon human sacrifices for countless years while imprisoned in Daedalus' Labyrinth in Greece. And all that protein had not gone to waste, forming a heavily woven musculature over the beast's body that made even Mr. Olympia look puny.

From the neck up, he was now entirely bull, but the rest of his body more closely resembled a thickly furred man. But, as shown moments ago, he could adapt his form to his environment, never appearing fully human, but able to make his entire form appear as a bull when necessary. For instance, how he had looked just before I tipped him. Maybe he had been scouting the field for heifers before I had so efficiently killed the mood.

His bull face was also covered in thick, coarse hair—he even sported a long, wavy beard of sorts, and his eyes were the deepest brown I had ever seen. Cow-shit brown. His snout jutted out, emphasizing the golden ring dangling from his glistening nostrils, and both glinted in the luminous glow of the moon. The metal was at least an inch thick and etched with runes of a language long forgotten. Wide, aged ivory horns sprouted from each temple, long enough to skewer a wizard with little effort. He was nude except for a massive beaded necklace and a pair of worn leather boots that were big enough to stomp a size twenty-five imprint in my face if he felt so inclined.

I hoped our blossoming friendship wouldn't end that way. I really did.

Because friends didn't let friends wear boots naked...

Get your copy of OBSIDIAN SON online today!
http://www.shaynesilvers.com/l/38474

Shayne has written a few other books without Cameron helping him. Some of them are marginally decent—easily a 4 out of 10.

Turn the page to read a sample of **UNCHAINED** *- Feathers and Fire Series Book 1, or* **BUY ONLINE (FREE with Kindle Unlimited subscription)**. *Callie Penrose is a wizard in Kansas City, MO who hunts monsters for the Vatican. She meets Nate Temple, and things devolve from there...*

(Note: Callie appears in the TempleVerse after Nate's book 6, TINY GODS...Full chronology of all books in the TempleVerse shown on the 'Books by the authors' page)

TRY: UNCHAINED (FEATHERS AND FIRE #1)

*T*he rain pelted my hair, plastering loose strands of it to my forehead as I panted, eyes darting from tree to tree, terrified of each shifting branch, splash of water, and whistle of wind slipping through the nightscape around us. But... I was somewhat *excited*, too.

Somewhat.

"Easy, girl. All will be well," the big man creeping just ahead of me, murmured.

"You said we were going to get ice cream!" I hissed at him, failing to compose myself, but careful to keep my voice low and my eyes alert. "I'm not ready for this!" I had been trained to fight, with my hands, with weapons, and with my magic. But I had never taken an active role in a hunt before. I'd always been the getaway driver for my mentor.

The man grunted, grey eyes scanning the trees as he slipped through the tall grass. "And did we not get ice cream before coming here? Because I think I see some in your hair."

"You know what I mean, Roland. You tricked me." I checked the tips of my loose hair, saw nothing, and scowled at his back.

"The Lord does not give us a greater burden than we can shoulder."

I muttered dark things under my breath, wiping the water from my eyes. Again. My new shirt was going to be ruined. Silk never fared well in the rain. My choice of shoes wasn't much better. Boots, yes, but distressed, *fashionable* boots. Not work boots designed for the rain and mud. Definitely not monster hunting boots for our evening excursion through one of Kansas City's wooded parks. I realized I was forcibly distracting myself, keeping my mind busy with mundane thoughts to avoid my very real anxiety. Because whenever I grew nervous, an imagined nightmare always—

A church looming before me. Rain pouring down. Night sky and a glowing moon overhead. I was all alone. Crying on the cold, stone steps, an infant in a cardboard box—

I forced the nightmare away, breathing heavily. "You know I hate it when you talk like that," I whispered to him, trying to regain my composure. I wasn't angry with him, but was growing increasingly uncomfortable with our situation after my brief flashback of fear.

"Doesn't mean it shouldn't be said," he said kindly. "I think we're close. Be alert. Remember your training. Banish your fears. I am here. And the Lord is here. He always is."

So, he had noticed my sudden anxiety. "Maybe I should just go back to the car. I know I've trained, but I really don't think—"

A shape of fur, fangs, and claws launched from the shadows towards me, cutting off my words as it snarled, thirsty for my blood.

And my nightmare slipped back into my thoughts like a veiled assassin, a wraith hoping to hold me still for the monster to eat. I froze, unable to move. Twin sticks of power abruptly erupted into being in my clenched fists, but my fear swamped me with that stupid nightmare, the sticks held at my side, useless to save me.

Right before the beast's claws reached me, it grunted as something batted it from the air, sending it flying sideways. It struck a tree with another grunt and an angry whine of pain.

I fell to my knees right into a puddle, arms shaking, breathing fast.

My sticks crackled in the rain like live cattle prods, except their entire length was the electrical section — at least to anyone other than me. I could hold them without pain.

Magic was a part of me, coursing through my veins whether I wanted it or not, and Roland had spent many years teaching me how to master it. But I had never been able to fully master the nightmare inside me, and in moments of fear, it always won, overriding my training.

The fact that I had resorted to weapons — like the ones he had trained me with — rather than a burst of flame, was startling. It was good in the fact that my body's reflexes knew enough to call up a defense even without my direct command, but bad in the fact that it was the worst form of defense for the situation presented. I could have very easily done as Roland did, and hurt it from a distance. But I hadn't. Because of my stupid block.

Roland placed a calloused palm on my shoulder, and I flinched. "Easy, see? I am here." But he did frown at my choice of weapons, the reprimand silent but loud in my mind. I let out a shaky breath, forcing my fear back down. It was all in my head, but still, it wasn't easy. Fear could be like that.

I focused on Roland's implied lesson. Close combat weapons — even magically-powered ones — were for last resorts. I averted my eyes in very real shame. I knew these things. He didn't even need to tell me them. But when that damned nightmare caught hold of me, all my training went out the window. It haunted me like a shadow, waiting for moments just like this, as if trying to kill me. A form of psychological suicide? But it was why I constantly refused to join Roland on his hunts. He knew about it. And although he was trying to help me overcome that fear, he never pressed too hard.

Rain continued to sizzle as it struck my batons. I didn't let them go, using them as a totem to build my confidence back up. I slowly lifted my eyes to nod at him as I climbed back to my feet.

That's when I saw the second set of eyes in the shadows, right before they flew out of the darkness towards Roland's back. I threw one of my batons and missed, but that pretty much let Roland know that an unfriendly was behind him. Either that or I had just failed to murder my mentor at point-blank range. He whirled to confront the monster, expecting another aerial assault as he unleashed a ball of fire that splashed over the tree at chest height, washing the trunk in blue flames. But this monster was tricky. It hadn't planned on tackling Roland, but had merely jumped out of the darkness to get closer, no doubt learning from its fallen comrade, who still lay unmoving against the tree behind me.

His coat shone like midnight clouds with hints of lightning flashing in the depths of thick, wiry fur. The coat of dew dotting his fur reflected the moonlight, giving him a faint sheen as if covered in fresh oil. He was tall, easily hip height at the shoulder, and barrel chested, his rump much leaner than the rest of his body. He — I assumed male from the long, thick mane around his neck — had a very long snout, much longer and wider than any werewolf I had ever seen. Amazingly, and beyond my control, I realized he was beautiful.

But most of the natural world's lethal hunters were beautiful.

He landed in a wet puddle a pace in front of Roland, juked to the right, and then to the left, racing past the big man, biting into his hamstrings on his way by.

A wash of anger rolled over me at seeing my mentor injured, dousing my fear, and I swung my baton down as hard as I could. It struck the beast in the rump as it tried to dart back to cover — a typical wolf tactic. My blow singed his hair and shattered bone. The creature collapsed into a puddle of mud with a yelp, instinctively snapping his jaws over his shoulder to bite whatever had hit him.

I let him. But mostly out of dumb luck as I heard Roland hiss in pain, falling to the ground.

The monster's jaws clamped around my baton, and there was an immediate explosion of teeth and blood that sent him flying several feet away into the tall brush, yipping, screaming, and staggering. Before he slipped out of sight, I noticed that his lower jaw was simply *gone*, from the contact of his saliva on my electrified magical batons. Then he managed to limp into the woods with more pitiful yowls, but I had no mind to chase him. Roland — that titan of a man, my mentor — was hurt. I could smell copper in the air, and knew we had to get out of here. Fast. Because we had anticipated only one of the monsters. But there had been two of them, and they hadn't been the run-of-the-mill werewolves we had been warned about. If there were two, perhaps there were more. And they were evidently the prehistoric cousin of any werewolf I had ever seen or read about.

Roland hissed again as he stared down at his leg, growling with both pain and anger. My eyes darted back to the first monster, wary of another attack. It *almost* looked like a werewolf, but bigger. Much bigger. He didn't move, but I saw he was breathing. He had a notch in his right ear and a jagged scar on his long snout. Part of me wanted to go over to him and torture him. Slowly. Use his pain to finally drown my nightmare, my fear. The fear that had caused Roland's injury. My lack of inner-strength had not only put me in danger, but had hurt my mentor, my friend.

I shivered, forcing the thought away. That was *cold*. Not me. Sure, I was no stranger to fighting, but that had always been in a ring. Practicing. Sparring. Never life or death.

But I suddenly realized something very dark about myself in the chill, rainy night. Although I was terrified, I felt a deep ocean of anger manifest inside me, wanting only to dispense justice as I saw fit. To use that rage to battle my own demons. As if feeding one would starve the other, reminding me of the Cherokee Indian Legend Roland had once told me.

An old Cherokee man was teaching his grandson about life. "A fight is going on inside me," he told the boy. "It is a terrible fight between two wolves. One is evil — he is anger, envy, sorrow, regret, greed, arrogance, self-pity, guilt, resentment, inferiority, lies, false pride, superiority, and ego." After a few moments to make sure he had the boy's undivided attention, he continued.

"The other wolf is good — he is joy, peace, love, hope, serenity, humility, kindness, benevolence, empathy, generosity, truth, compassion, and faith. The same fight is going on inside of you, boy, and inside of every other person, too."

The grandson thought about this for a few minutes before replying. "Which wolf will win?"

The old Cherokee man simply said, "The one you feed, boy. The one you feed..."

And I felt like feeding one of my wolves today, by killing this one...

Get the full book ONLINE! http://www.shaynesilvers.com/l/38952

MAKE A DIFFERENCE

Reviews are the most powerful tools in our arsenal when it comes to getting attention for our books. Much as we'd like to, we don't have the financial muscle of a New York publisher.

But we do have something much more powerful and effective than that, and it's something that those publishers would kill to get their hands on.

A committed and loyal bunch of readers.

Honest reviews of our books help bring them to the attention of other readers.

If you've enjoyed this book, we would be very grateful if you could spend just five minutes leaving a review on our book's Amazon page.

Thank you very much in advance.

ACKNOWLEDGMENTS

From Cameron:

I'd like to thank Shayne, for paving the way in style. Kori, for an introduction that would change my life. My three wonderful sisters, for showing me what a strong, independent woman looks and sounds like. And, above all, my parents, for—literally—everything.

From Shayne:

Team Temple and the Den of Freaks on Facebook have become family to me. I couldn't do it without die-hard readers like them.

I would also like to thank you, the reader. I hope you enjoyed reading OLD FASHIONED as much as we enjoyed writing it. Be sure to check out the two crossover series in the TempleVerse: **The Nate Temple Series** and the **Feathers and Fire Series**.

And last, but definitely not least, I thank my wife, Lexy. Without your support, none of this would have been possible.

ABOUT CAMERON O'CONNELL

Cameron O'Connell is a Jack-of-All-Trades and Master of Some.

He writes The Phantom Queen Diaries, a series in The TempleVerse, about Quinn MacKenna, a mouthy black magic arms dealer trading favors in Boston. All she wants? A round-trip ticket to the Fae realm...and maybe a drink on the house.

A former member of the United States military, a professional model, and English teacher, Cameron finds time to write in the mornings after his first cup of coffee...and in the evenings after his thirty-seventh. Follow him, and the TempleVerse founder, Shayne Silvers, online for all sorts of insider tips, giveaways, and new release updates!

Get Down with Cameron Online

f facebook.com/Cameron-OConnell-788806397985289

a amazon.com/author/cameronoconnell

BB bookbub.com/authors/cameron-o-connell

𝕐 twitter.com/thecamoconnell

Ⓞ instagram.com/camoconnellauthor

g goodreads.com/cameronoconnell

ABOUT SHAYNE SILVERS

Shayne is a man of mystery and power, whose power is exceeded only by his mystery...

He currently writes the Amazon Bestselling **Nate Temple** Series, which features a foul-mouthed wizard from St. Louis. He rides a bloodthirsty unicorn, drinks with Achilles, and is pals with the Four Horsemen.

He also writes the Amazon Bestselling **Feathers and Fire** Series—a second series in the TempleVerse. The story follows a rookie spell-slinger named Callie Penrose who works for the Vatican in Kansas City. Her problem? Hell seems to know more about her past than she does.

He coauthors **The Phantom Queen Diaries**—a third series set in The TempleVerse—with Cameron O'Connell. The story follows Quinn MacKenna, a mouthy black magic arms dealer in Boston. All she wants? A round-trip ticket to the Fae realm...and maybe a drink on the house.

He also writes the **Shade of Devil Series**, which tells the story of Sorin Ambrogio—the world's FIRST vampire. He was put into a magical slumber by a Native American Medicine Man when the Americas were first discovered by Europeans. Sorin wakes up after five-hundred years to learn that his protege, Dracula, stole his reputation and that no one has ever even heard of Sorin Ambrogio. The streets of New York City will run with blood as Sorin reclaims his legend.

Shayne holds two high-ranking black belts, and can be found writing in a coffee shop, cackling madly into his computer screen while pounding shots of espresso. He's hard at work on the newest books in the TempleVerse—You can find updates on new releases or chronological reading order on the next page, his website, or any of his social media accounts. **Follow him online for all sorts of groovy goodies, giveaways, and new release updates:**

Get Down with Shayne Online
www.shaynesilvers.com
info@shaynesilvers.com

f facebook.com/shaynesilversfanpage
a amazon.com/author/shaynesilvers
BB bookbub.com/profile/shayne-silvers
instagram.com/shaynesilversofficial
twitter.com/shaynesilvers
g goodreads.com/ShayneSilvers

BOOKS BY THE AUTHORS

CHRONOLOGY: All stories in the TempleVerse are shown in chronological order on the following page

PHANTOM QUEEN DIARIES

(Set in the TempleVerse)

by Cameron O'Connell & Shayne Silvers

COLLINS (Prequel novella #0 in the 'LAST CALL' anthology)

WHISKEY GINGER

COSMOPOLITAN

OLD FASHIONED

MOTHERLUCKER (Novella #3.5 in the 'LAST CALL' anthology)

DARK AND STORMY

MOSCOW MULE

WITCHES BREW

SALTY DOG

SEA BREEZE

HURRICANE

NATE TEMPLE SERIES

(Main series in the TempleVerse)

by Shayne Silvers

FAIRY TALE - FREE prequel novella #0 for my subscribers

OBSIDIAN SON

BLOOD DEBTS

GRIMM

SILVER TONGUE

BEAST MASTER

BEERLYMPIAN (Novella #5.5 in the 'LAST CALL' anthology)

TINY GODS

DADDY DUTY (Novella #6.5)

WILD SIDE

WAR HAMMER

NINE SOULS

HORSEMAN

LEGEND

KNIGHTMARE

ASCENSION

FEATHERS AND FIRE SERIES

(Also set in the TempleVerse)

by Shayne Silvers

UNCHAINED

RAGE

WHISPERS

ANGEL'S ROAR

MOTHERLUCKER (Novella #4.5 in the 'LAST CALL' anthology)

SINNER

BLACK SHEEP

GODLESS

CHRONOLOGICAL ORDER: TEMPLEVERSE

FAIRY TALE (TEMPLE PREQUEL)

OBSIDIAN SON (TEMPLE 1)

BLOOD DEBTS (TEMPLE 2)

GRIMM (TEMPLE 3)

SILVER TONGUE (TEMPLE 4)

BEAST MASTER (TEMPLE 5)

BEERLYMPIAN (TEMPLE 5.5)

TINY GODS (TEMPLE 6)

SHADE OF DEVIL SERIES

(Not part of the TempleVerse)

by Shayne Silvers

DEVIL'S CRY
DEVIL'S BLOOD

Made in the USA
Coppell, TX
26 July 2020